FOSSIL
WOMAN

a novel

Dig in & explore!
Sharon Lyon

SHARON LYON

ACKNOWLEDGMENTS

In memory of my parents, who taught me that all things are possible.

CHAPTER 1

1961, NAIROBI, KENYA

The Dark Continent. Cradle of Humanity. With college behind me and my future in front of me, Africa loomed large in my imagination. After flying from Washington to London, and overnight to Cairo and Nairobi, I stumbled off the plane in a near-comatose state. Checking off my greatest fear from my list—crashing and burning—I released my guardian angel and thanked Bernoulli for his Principle. Hollow-eyed and with stiff legs, I urged my hiking boot-clad feet down the movable wooden stairs. Ready to proceed with my summer assignment and leave my heartache and worry behind, I surveyed the scene from the asphalt tarmac. The early evening air clung to me with the combined odors of dust, sweat, and manure. A herd of gazelles pranced nervously in the tall grass on the far side of the runway, ears and tails flicking in the breeze.

The newly constructed Nairobi Airport shone with sunlight-reflecting glass and polished metal. Military police, in smart uniforms, with insignias on black berets, herded us under a sign marked "Customs". Men dressed in white coveralls unloaded the bags from our plane, creating a pile of luggage that cascaded across the floor inside. I grabbed my duffle bag, stuffed with everything a geologist would need for weeks of digging fish fossils out of the dirt—field clothes, sun hat, notebook, extra film, hand lens, and of course my rock hammer. Straining under its weight, I dragged it to the customs line.

I tapped my foot and tried to appear as if I had done this before. A photographer from the National Geographic Society would meet me, I had been assured. He would continue with me to the Leakey Camp at Olduvai Gorge, my final destination.

"Next!"

Passport and visa in hand, I approached the customs agent.

"Destination?"

"Olduvai Gorge," I said.

"Olduvai Gorge is in Tanganyika. What is your destination in Kenya?" he asked.

"Here. Nairobi. I'm flying tomorrow to Arusha."

"Very well. Make sure you have your passport and proper visa with you then. You'll need them to enter Tanganyika." With two quick stamps, I proceeded into the main terminal.

The bubbling clamor of the international airport hit me full force. Crowds of people, arriving and departing, seemingly represented all races and creeds. Some lugged suitcases or pushed trunks; others carried their belongings on their heads. Porters dressed incongruently in shorts and white dress shirts scurried to help passengers with their bags. Among the chaos, a tall man with sandy hair held up a sign. It read 'H. Ballantine'. I walked up to him. He continued to look past me.

"Hello. I'm Henrietta Ballantine."

He did a double-take, his eyes moving from my head to my toes and back up again. "I'm here to pick up a Henry Ballantine?" he said, his brow furrowing.

"Are you from the National Geographic Society?"

"Yes…"

"I'm from the U.S. National Museum," I said. I reached out to shake his hand as I mentally checked off number two from my List of Fears—being stranded at the Nairobi Airport.

He gave me an engaging smile. "Well, I guess I was misinformed. Welcome to Kenya, Miss Ballantine. I'm Ray Barts."

"Thank you. And please call me Henrietta. I'm so glad you're here to meet me. I wasn't sure what I was going to do if you didn't show up," I said.

He laughed easily. "How were your flights?"

"All fine. No problem making my connections."

"I'm glad you made it. Although you aren't what I was expecting. Are you hungry? We can stop for something to eat."

"No, they fed us on the plane. I'm exhausted though, and have no idea what time zone I'm in."

"Alright, we'll go directly to the Corydon Museum. Dr. Leakey is the curator there. He's arranged for you to stay in a bungalow on the museum grounds."

Ray took my duffle from my hands and we pushed through a crowd of people and headed for the exit.

"How long have you been in Africa?" I asked.

"About five years. I mostly photograph wildlife, which keeps me on the road."

"Have you been to Olduvai before?"

"Yes. I was there last year photographing the Leakeys after Mary discovered the *Zinjanthropus* skull. You may have seen the spread on it in *National Geographic Magazine*."

"Yes, I did see it. Those photos were amazing! They're one of the reasons that I'm here."

Ray led me to a dust-enshrouded Land Rover and tossed my duffle bag inside. I climbed in and we pulled out of the parking area. He narrated like a tour guide as he drove through the city.

"Nairobi is undergoing modernization. See all of these high-rise buildings? Most of them weren't here five years ago."

"I thought Nairobi would be a sleepy colonial town."

"Oh no. Not anymore. This is the main road through Nairobi, Mombasa Road."

Cars, buses, and trucks crowded the roads. Cranes rose above construction sites. Although it was the beginning of the cooler, dry season, mud puddles lined ditches along both sides of the road. In contrast to the muck, flowering shrubs bloomed with brilliant pink and white blossoms. Throngs of people strolled alongside the busy street. Women burdened with bundles or baskets, swished their brilliantly colored skirts around their ankles as they moved. Some carried babies in their arms, balancing their purchases on their heads. Clusters of young schoolgirls, looking proud in their uniforms, giggled with each other as they rushed home. Produce sellers in white caps hawked their wares behind overflowing baskets on the sidewalks.

"Hold on!" Ray said, as we swerved around a truck to enter a traffic circle. Horns honked. Someone shouted out a window. I clutched the door handle. Ray grinned. "I take it you've never been to Africa before?"

"No, I've never been overseas," I replied.

We pulled up at a busy intersection. A policeman stood on an elevated platform directing traffic. Dressed in his buttoned shirt, black shorts, and knee socks, and wearing a pith helmet, he blew through a whistle while motioning animatedly with his arms.

We turned off the main road and headed north along an avenue lined with palm trees. Outdoor cafes catered to lounging European crowds hungry for dinner. We arrived at the Coryndon Museum, an unimposing, one-story almond brick building with an attached side wing. Two marble steps supported four statuesque columns surrounding the front door. Bypassing the entrance, Ray circled to the back, where several huts of differing construction and vintages dotted the landscape. He pulled in front of the most tumbledown of the bungalows, a tiny wooden hut with a thatched roof.

"These houses are used for visiting dignitaries and scientists. And the Leakeys lived in that large one over there for several years."

Jumping out, Ray grabbed my bag and set it by the front door. I climbed out, wobbly and weary.

"Here's the key. I'll pick you up at eight o'clock tomorrow morning and bring breakfast. We'll catch the flight to Moshi and be driven to Olduvai from there."

"Thank you, Ray," I said, eyeing my accommodations.

"Oh, and Henrietta. That's Eastern Africa time," he said, smiling.

Nodding, I stuck the key in the doorknob. The door creaked open, the bottom edge scraping across a concrete floor. No one would call it fancy. Or particularly clean. The furniture was limited to a metal twin bed with a stack of blankets, and a wooden table with two rickety chairs. In the far corner, a folding screen shielded a commode. A sink with a hand pump served for washing up.

I dragged my bag inside and shut the door. Sleep-deprived, stiff and sweaty, I collapsed fully clothed onto the bed. An unseen varmint rustled in the straw ceiling overhead.

Swell. Although compared to the accommodations where I'm headed, this is probably the Ritz.

I stared out the cracked window as the setting sun refracted against the cloud-streaked Kenyan sky, turning my view into orange agate. My heart quickened in anticipation of the coming days. *What did Olduvai Gorge hold in store for me? Would I make any scientifically significant discoveries?* Images of the path that brought me here filtered through my mind. My goal since childhood to explore, dig and discover lurked in my subconscious like the critter hiding above me in the thatch.

CHAPTER 2

1949, ARLINGTON, VIRGINIA

The American flag in front of Barcroft Elementary School hung limply against the pole. I stared out the classroom window, eyes following the clouds overhead. The rolls of cotton candy, white on the tops, dipped heavily, darkening into leaden lumps at the bases. Stratocumulus. A classification compromise. Neither all fluffy cumulus nor continuously blanket-like stratus. The clouds inched across the sky, moving westward, exposing patches of robin's egg blue.

Why was that? No wind blew the flag. But the clouds drifted by. Were winds different at differing heights? How...?

"Henrietta? Are you with us today?"

My fifth-grade teacher, Miss Beale, a string-bean of a woman, with bangs and the face of a horse, addressed me from across the room. I turned my head and realized that her previous commands had escaped my notice. My classmates stood in a line at the door, staring at me with sheep eyes.

"It's time for recess. Would you care you join us?"

The flock snickered and grinned.

I rose from my desk, dragged my feet to the back of the line, and fell in.

Miss Beale frog-marched us outside for compulsory sport. A game of kickball provided today's torture. Evidently, it was imperative to learn how to kick a sizeable pink ball away from home plate and run around bases while other children tried to pummel me with the ball. I waited in line for my turn, staring at my loafers, scuffing at the dirt. My classmates cheered and clapped while my stomach flipped and flopped.

"Great job! Bases loaded!" someone called.

Queasiness worked its way up my throat. Almost my turn, I left the line and stalked up to my teacher.

"Miss Beale, I have a stomach ache. I need to go to the nurse," I said.

Miss Beale glared down at me and grimaced through her over-bite. "Henrietta, you are just making that up so you don't have to play the game. There is nothing wrong with you! Get back in line."

With her bark of a voice still ringing in my ears, I turned back toward the line. My cheeks burned from the other children's stares. Hyperventilating, I promptly bent over and vomited into the grass.

"Eww," called out several of my classmates, as my vision turned fuzzy and I fainted into the grass.

No school nurse was on duty that day, so I spent the next hours, alone, lying on a cot in the infirmary. A cold washrag placed on my forehead turned tepid, like my feelings for Barcroft Elementary. When the final bell rang, I pulled myself up and joined the horde of students bursting out the front door.

The crossing guard assured my safety across busy Wakefield Street. After that, I meandered home on my own without being manhandled, carpooled, clucked over, or pampered. I poked along, taking in the scents of Spring suburbia—crabgrass and car exhaust, hyacinths and rubbish cans. Clouds obscured the sun and I shivered, although perhaps not from the chill. Suspecting what was in store for me at home, I strode slowly up the porch steps of our humble clapboard two-story. The front porch shielded three upright wooden rocking chairs. A permanent indentation in the seat of one rocker evidenced my mother's obsession with watching, and later commenting on, all the happenings on 6th Street.

Banging through the screen door, I entered our living room, with its brick fireplace, worn sofa, and my grandmother's recliner, still occupying a corner years after her death. Our brass clock bonged four o'clock from the mantle, counting down the days. Continuing through the dining room, I passed the matching maple table and hutch and tossed my books on the sideboard.

My mother called to me from the front bedroom.

"Henrietta, is that you?" she asked.

Who else did she think it might be, entering the house without knocking? I knew better than to ask.

"Yes, Mother," I called down the perpendicular hallway.

Reaching the kitchen in the back of the house, my shoes made a repeating sticky sound as I traversed the compulsively waxed floor. The enormous pantry contained the 'icebox'—a refrigerator, but the terminology had stuck—and I reached inside and grabbed an apple. Munching, I stared out the wide window overlooking our backyard. Chain-link fencing and overgrown azaleas separated us from the side and back neighbors' properties. My wooden porch swing hung from a metal frame, shaded by chokecherry and cigar trees.

"Henrietta, I got a call from the principal today," my mother said as she strode into the kitchen. "It seems she wants to have a conference with me and your dad. Again. Do you know what it is this time?"

My high-strung mother, Mrs. Henry Ballantine, first name Dorothy, 'Dottie' to her friends, was, from an outsider's view, a beautiful decorator, delightful hostess, and spectacular cook. As an insider, my opinion leaned quite differently. On various days, she alternately ignored or terrorized me. On good days, a hands-off sort of mother, on bad days, she displayed her anger at everything, usually placing blame on my father or me.

"I wouldn't play kickball," I said, taking another bite of my apple.

Her eyes bored into me. "Why not?"

"I hate kickball." I pursed my lips.

Steam seemed to rise from my mother's head. Frown lines etched her forehead. "Why can't you just do as you're told?"

I offered no answer. The apple turned sour in my mouth.

"Go upstairs, young lady, to your room, and think about it!"

Tears welled behind my eyes as I tossed the apple core into the can under the sink, turned, and meandered back through the dining room. I opened a door in the adjacent hallway, accessing the steep wooden staircase that led to the second floor, my sanctuary. I clomped up the stairs, holding onto the handrail. My dad used the landing at the top of the stairs as a storage attic, the edges stuffed to the eaves with all matter of debris—trunks, old books, model trains, and boxed Christmas ornaments. Doing a one hundred and eighty-degree turn at the top of the steps, I entered my bedroom on the left. The spare room was located on the right. I opened a dresser drawer, took out a sweater, and shrugged it on. The slight smell of mothballs emanated from my dresser, which had been my great-grandmother's. Everything was recycled one way or another.

My dormer window, located high off the floor, provided only a sky view. My mood darkened like the obscured heavens, the clouds now thickened and menacing.

<hr>

The next afternoon my parents conferred with the principal, a nasty old crone named Miss McMurphy. That evening, I crawled stealthily down my attic stairs to crouch behind the closed door. A perfect site for eavesdropping, I listened to their conversation incognito.

"That frustrated old maid has a lot of nerve, calling us for another conference," my mother said. "This must be at least the tenth one this year."

"She just wants what's best for Henrietta, dear." My dad was a calm man, tall and thin, slightly balding but handsome. His analytical, scientific mind gave him a steady nature. I, as his only progeny, had been named for him.

"No, she wants to wash her hands of her," my mother said.

As my parents argued, my head began to pound and my throat tightened.

My dad replied, "What do you think about her skipping fifth grade and advancing to junior high school? The curriculum would be more challenging for her."

"There's no way she can navigate junior high school. Not with her immaturity. Those older kids would eat her alive."

"Then we need to hire a tutor and home school her. We could afford for someone to come three days a week."

"It's fine and good that you want her tutored at home, Harry. But you won't be here. She'll be at home *every day*."

"She can come to the museum with me one day a week. I'll put a desk for her in the corner of my office. We can call it her 'museum study day.'"

My mother sighed. "But she won't have any interaction with children her age."

"She's way ahead of all of those children in school, Dottie. She's wasting her time there. And wasting her intellect. And, according to her teacher, she doesn't interact with the other kids anyway. She's too shy."

"Shy?" said my mom. "She's an absolute stick!"

Their discussion continued. I crawled back up the stairs on all fours. Treading softly across the creaky wooden floor, I climbed into bed and allowed the tears to come. *Why couldn't I be like everyone else? Then maybe I would have someone to confide in. A friend to talk to.* As my mind softened, a sense of comfort descended over me. My blanket tucked around me like an embrace and I somehow understood that everything would be alright.

Climbing the towering expanse of gleaming marble steps of the Smithsonian Institution U.S. National Museum, taking two strides for each one of my father's, I felt like one of the luckiest girls in the world. We were a study in contrasts. My distinguished father dressed in his suit, tie, and dress hat, and I, gangly and tall for my age, with my mane of dark hair, wrestled into submission in a plait down my back. My mother had made sure I was well turned out, not that girls had much choice in attire. In my modest skirt and jacket, knee socks, and loafers, I looked exactly like a typical school girl, though I felt so grown up, striding past the massive columns, through the heavy glass doors and into the rotunda. The African elephant, permanently planted on an oval pedestal, held his raised trunk in welcome. Although I had visited the museum before, today I would call it home.

"Can we go see the dinosaurs?" I asked my father.

"Of course! This way," he replied.

My father, Dr. Henry Ballantine, Harry, to his friends, worked as a paleontologist at the museum. His official title was Natural Historian, and his interests ran the gamut from ancient pelecypods to extinct flightless birds and everything in between. His expertise, however, and most of his publications concerned discoveries of fossil fish. Technically, he was a paleoichthyologist.

He led me through an arch with an overhead sign declaring 'The Hall of Extinct Monsters.' The cathedral ceiling rose above us. Our steps echoed across the hushed space as the tourists had not yet arrived. I gazed at the enormous *Diplodocus* skeleton, my eyes following its neck vertebrae upward to its head, perched to peer into an upper balcony. I read the plaque and imagined flesh on the articulated bones.

My eyes widened as we passed the huge early whale *Basilosaurus*. "Why is the whale here with the dinosaurs?" I asked.

"When the Hall was designed, all these animals were considered to be 'monsters.' It's outdated thinking now."

I lingered by the *Triceratops* skull, staring at its sharp, piercing horns. My dad smiled down at me. "Let's go on up to my office. You'll have plenty of opportunities to spend time in the halls."

We climbed a set of back stairs to the third floor and unlocked a door to the restricted area. Offices lined a dark, narrow hallway. Behind the third creaky wooden door, my father's office overflowed with wonders. Books, bones, rocks, and fish skeletons littered his shelves. A manual typewriter sat on his desk amid piles of papers, scientific publications, and periodicals. Behind his coatrack, a tiny table and chair had been wedged into the corner.

My dad pointed to the table. "Here's your desk. And your assignment for today. Read this article on the Galapagos tortoises in the *Washington Star*, and let me know what you learn about them."

While my father worked, I read, wrote notes, cut out the article, and pasted it carefully in my new notebook. In my looping handwriting, I constructed my summary. At lunchtime, he escorted me to the staff dining room, a dark, windowless enclave. I read to him from my notebook while we ate our sandwiches.

"That was a good summary of the species, Henrietta. But why do you think the tortoises grow so large?"

I pondered. "Perhaps they have no natural predators in the Galapagos so they can grow huge."

"Is this sound evolutionary theory?" he asked.

"I suppose so, if they came from somewhere else and evolved to be bigger once they got to the islands," I replied.

He smiled and nodded. I grinned back, always eager for his encouragement.

Of course, my father was a staunch evolutionist, a position understandably taken by his colleagues in the scientific community, but rejected by most of the general populace. When we returned to his office after lunch, he reached up and unpinned some stapled papers from his bulletin board. He handed them to me. There was a large red letter "F" written on the top of the first page.

"I wrote this paper when I was in high school. I outlined the evolution of man, as explained by Charles Darwin, for my biology class. The teacher failed me. Look what she wrote on the back page."

I flipped the pages, and on the bottom of the back page was the scrawled message—'There Is No Such Thing as Evolution. This is heresy.'—in bold red pen, underlined twice.

"I keep this paper as a reminder," he said, "Of how some people, no matter how well-intentioned, will try to hinder science. Let it be a reminder to you, Henrietta, that dogmatic thought is often the mark of a closed mind. Science requires an open-minded, analytic approach to data. Do not forget that."

"I won't," I nodded solemnly. Later I would look up the word 'dogmatic' in the dictionary.

Returning home that evening, as I leaned my tired head against the car window, I mulled over his words. Our talk had reminded me of a summer trip we had taken a few years before to the Natural Bridge of Virginia. The tour leader claimed that God eroded the bridge into its arched shape to be pleasing to Himself. My father had thought this preposterous.

"These people would have God, wasting His talents, by eroding each grain of sand to form this arch! Can you imagine? That God himself, in all His duties, worries so much about geomorphology that He erodes sandstone grain by grain? It is Uniformity, my dear, make no mistake about it. In one thousand years, this bridge will have fallen to the ground, crushing anything that happens to be wandering below. Would that be pleasing to God?"

"Good heavens, Harry, you'll get us thrown out of the park!" my mother had exclaimed. "Can't you let it go for once?"

I had not known what was or was not pleasing to God at that time and did not pretend to now. One thing that I did know was that my tutor would arrive the following week. And I certainly hoped that whatever I did would be pleasing to her.

CHAPTER 3

1949, ARLINGTON, VIRGINIA

My tutor, Ana Sekomova, came with an outstanding recommendation from the public schools and having survived an interview with my parents. I waited in the living room and gnawed at my thumbnail in anticipation of her arrival. She would instruct me in writing, literature, foreign language, and social studies. My father would see to my math and science education.

A stout, middle-aged woman strode up our porch steps and rang the bell.

"*Dobray ootra*," she said in Russian as I opened the door. "Henrietta, I presume? I am Madame Sekomova."

I attempted not to stare at her brusque features and unnaturally dyed purple-auburn hair pulled back in a loose bun. My mother called out a greeting from the kitchen and I led Madame upstairs. For a hefty woman, she managed the steep steps with a fair amount of agility. We entered into the spare room, now fitted as a classroom. Two large wooden desks faced each other in the middle. A rolling blackboard rested along one wall.

"This will do quite nicely," she clucked. "Let's get started. We shall begin with some Russian phrases. And then dive into Tolstoy."

My eyes must have widened in shock.

"In English," she assured me, pulling a novel out of her bag.

War and Peace. How apropos. For my family anyway.

At lunchtime, we ate with my mother in the kitchen. Madame Sekomova brought her own repast. Thus, I was introduced to pirozhki, while I chomped on peanut butter and jelly on white bread. Practicing my newly acquired Russian sentences in front of my mother, I tried to imitate the sharp guttural sounds.

"What in the world is that, Henrietta? You sound like you're gargling," she laughed.

After lunch, Madame and I launched ourselves outside for a suburban nature walk. The trees displayed subtle hints of early autumn color, the leaves rustling in a light breeze. Strands of Madame's hair escaped her bun to form a garnet halo around her head, like iridescent clouds around the Moon.

As we walked, she regaled me with the story of her childhood. "You know I am descended from the Russian royal family? *Da?* We escaped to Paris right before the czar was killed. I grew up there." We continued along the sidewalk, dodging falling acorns. "The avenues, the cafes, the Eiffel Tower. All magnificent. Drinking café au lait, watching the crowds of people stroll by, the nouveau rich with their noses in the air, the workers scurrying by, the gape-eyed tourists. You must go to Paris when you are older. Travel. See the world."

I imagined her walking along the Champs-Elysees, eating baguettes, and feeding the pigeons. Maybe she thought it was exciting. But people and crowds? No thank you. I would not be rushing to Paris.

Our destination that day was my Uncle Al and Aunt Esther's house. They lived about a mile away, in a house of similar vintage to ours, surrounded by boxwood hedges. Uncle Al was my dad's much-older brother. He worked odd hours as an assistant manager of a Rexall drug store. He had a forlorn face and was always 'under the weather.' My mother claimed that he 'enjoyed poor health.' A semi-permanent fixture in his Barcalounger, he loved to watch an array of goldfish swimming in his back-lit aquarium, the air pump giving off a constant burble. His wife, my Aunt Esther, was employed as a bookkeeper, quite a good job for a woman. She always dressed to the nines and styled and sprayed her hair into an updo that looked like a helmet.

Uncle Al and Aunt Esther owned a beagle named Miss Tiny. That afternoon, since they were both working day shifts, it was my job to let Miss Tiny outside. True to her name, she was small in stature and a happy-go-lucky dog. I unlocked their back door and she sprang outside like she was freed from prison. Before I knew it, she scampered through an arch in the arbor and raced to the parkland behind their house, disappearing into a field of wildflowers and overgrown blackberry bushes.

"Miss Tiny!" I yelled. "Come back here!"

No chance. I ran into the brambles, calling her name. Bees buzzed around my head. Thorns scraped at my arms. Miss Tiny was my responsibility. *Where had she gone?* I reached the other side of the field, which backed to more homes. No sign of her. Tears came to my eyes. Panting, I leaned over, hands on my knees to catch my breath. I turned around and began another, more circuitous route back through the blackberries. I shouted her name. The thorns pulled at my skirt and blouse and stuck in my legs.

"Henrietta!" Madame Sekomova called. "She's here!"

Returning through the arbor, I spied Miss Tiny, sitting by the back door, a box turtle clutched in her mouth. Her canine teeth smiled up at me.

And that was why, on my first day of tutoring, I learned the Russian word for 'turtle'—*cherypacka*—and a few Russian curse words. To which Miss Tiny paid not one bit of attention.

On Sundays, the suburbs buzzed alive in a hive of conformity as most of the neighborhood families paraded to church. My family was part of this well-oiled machine, so I faced the day with steely resolve. I pulled on a fancy dress with a scratchy Peter Pan collar and struggled with the pearl buttons on my white gloves. Our church was Arlington Presbyterian, a beautiful stone church with a white steeple on the corner of Columbia Pike and South Lincoln Street. We drove the short distance in our boxy tan Chevy.

My parents walked me to my Sunday School class, my black patent leather shoes pinching my feet. I entered the classroom and passed the basket for weekly donations resting strategically next to the door. Biblical scenes decorated a bulletin board trimmed in corrugated cardboard. Uncomfortable wooden chairs rested under two long tables. I parked myself on one of the chairs as my parents abandoned me to disappear toward the sanctuary to do whatever mysteries adults did in church.

I kept to myself, listening to the weekly Bible story, putting my nickel in the collection basket, and coloring. Each week's story came with an activity sheet that we filled in with crayons. Meticulous with my coloring, I inhaled the pungent waxy smell as I picked through the collection of Crayolas, making careful selections of earthy colors for Biblical scenes—raw sienna, sepia, mahogany, desert sand. Perhaps brick red for the Romans' cloaks. Always staying within the lines, I made the activity last the entire hour. The monotony of the task proved strangely relaxing.

At the end of class, my parents collected me and I carried my worksheet home, depositing it as an artifact in the bottom drawer of my desk. It rested on top of previous pages: Adam and Eve, Noah's Ark, the Ten Commandments, David and Goliath, the birth, life, death, and resurrection of Jesus. All stacked neatly, Old and New Testaments, like preserved strata, oldest to youngest, the Principle of Superposition in a drawer.

Secretly I wondered if my father, although accompanying us to church on Sundays, did so only out of a sense of familial obligation. With all of our talk about evolution, did he believe in a creator God? Or was he an agnostic?

My mother, on the other hand, treated the church as her social club. She hosted a Bible Study for Ladies in our home on Fridays.

Although a fair amount of gossip seemed to be exchanged on the telephone in the days afterward. Since I was never actually present, I could only imagine the ladies discussing scripture's intricacies in our living room. It was no coincidence that my 'museum study days' fell on Fridays—my mother wanted me out of the house and out of her hair.

Thus, my education continued in this atypical manner, a combination of Presbyterian doctrine and whatever curricula Madame Sekomova and my father cobbled together, loosely approved by the Commonwealth of Virginia. Yet I longed for more. I yearned for some unknown intrigue. My future seemed as hidden as the bedrock beneath my toes.

CHAPTER 4

1961, NAIROBI, KENYA

The early morning African sun streamed through the cracked window glass, awakening me from my hibernation. Straggling out of bed, I stretched, the stiffness from my flights still cramping my legs. Mud-tinged water spilled out of the hand pump to fill the sink and I sponged my skin to remove the airplane staleness. A black fly buzzed around my head as I changed out of my rumpled clothes. I slipped on my hiking boots and manhandled my duffle out of the hut. A gorgeous morning. *What adventures would today bring?*

Ray pulled up to the front of the Coryndon Museum in his Land Rover. He popped out and grabbed my duffle, handing me a paper sack. I peeked inside. What looked like triangular powdered donuts yielded an enticing yeasty fragrance.

"These are mandazi," he said. "Kenyan donuts. Help yourself. I also brought you a mug of chai."

Famished, I bit into a donut.

"What is chai?" I asked, my mouth half-full.

"Chai is tea with spices, sugar, and milk."

The slight taste of coconut from the mandazi rolled around on my tongue. I wolfed down two in a very unladylike fashion and gulped the chai. Sweet and velvety.

"Thank you. I didn't realize how hungry I was."

We sped back to the Nairobi airport to catch our early flight on East African Airways to Moshi in Tanganyika. A suspect-looking prop plane waited on the runaway, a wobbly set of metal stairs jammed against its fuselage. One would think I had developed some immunity to flying nerves by now, but this plane was ancient.

"This plane looks like it was welded together out of spare parts," I said.

Ray grinned. "Yeah, it's an old World War II transport plane that's been retrofitted. You see them all over Africa. The price was right, I guess."

As we walked up the stairs I examined the plane more closely. I swore I saw holes in the fuselage.

"Are those bullet holes?"

"It's probably better not to think about those things," Ray replied.

We boarded and the captain greeted us. He appeared to be about my age, which I did not find particularly comforting.

"Welcome aboard. It's a great day for flying," he said.

The plane held fifteen passengers, with two seats on one side of the aisle and one seat on the other. Ray and I sandwiched in beside each other. As the plane sprinted down the runway, it shook and rattled like an old tin can. I gripped the armrest, white-knuckled. Just as the plane lifted off the ground, an air vent fell from the ceiling and clattered to the floor. I looked at Ray in terror. He smiled at me. "Welcome to Africa," he joked.

After our takeoff into the clear emerald sky, we cruised toward billowing cumulus congestus clouds. We bumped along, rising and falling with the thermals, riding a meteorological roller coaster. Palms sweaty, my stomach lurched, and I swallowed hard, white-knuckled, and prayed not to see the mandazi again. The view alternated between terrifying and spectacular. Ray, unfazed, smiled reassuringly at me.

"There's Mt. Kilimanjaro. Moshi sits at its base," he said. He reached for his camera under his seat and began clicking away as we cruised toward the mountain.

Leaping out of the ground, the massive volcano with its frosted caldera stood guard over the African plain. Its upper flanks appeared craggy from deep erosion and landslides, anciently majestic. A distant side peak was snow-streaked, barely visible through cloud towers. Below the tree line, stream channels incised forested green escarpments. The streams flowed out onto the surrounding alluvial plain, meandering to provide sustenance to farmlands.

"There are three peaks to Kilimanjaro," Ray explained. "The main peak is Kibo. There are active fumaroles inside its crater, so although Kibo is considered dormant it could erupt again. The farther peak is Mawenzi. And that lower, flatter crater closer to us is called Shira. Mawenzi and Shira are extinct."

Skirting the mountain's western flank, the plane banked to the left to make a southerly approach to the airport in Moshi. The term 'airport' could only be loosely applied to the one-story shack greeting us when we landed. I oozed off the plane, relieved to be back on terra firma. We ambled into the building, and Ray waved to a young man of African descent who approached us.

"Henrietta, let me introduce you to Kimaru Kimu," Ray said.

"Welcome to Tanganyika. I will be looking out for you while you are here," Kimaru said, with what sounded to me like a British accent. Dressed in white shorts and a pink dress shirt, open at the collar, his face was creased, yet friendly.

Two porters unloaded luggage into a mound on the airport floor and Kimaru spoke to them in another language. Ray and I grabbed our bags and Kimaru took mine from my grasp. He led us toward the parking area.

"What language were you speaking to them?" I asked.

"Swahili. I also speak Kikuyu and, of course, English," he said. "And as I'm searching for fossils, I talk to the dead in a different language that only they can understand."

Ray and I exchanged a look behind his back.

"How long have you been working for Dr. Leakey?" I asked.

He replied with a smile. "For about two years. At first, I thought I would be digging graves. But Dr. Leakey explained to me that we would be discovering fossils, so I took the job. I've learned a lot from him so far. And from Mrs. Leakey also, of course. Who is also a 'Dr. Leakey.' It's a bit confusing." He led us across the dirt. "Right over here is our lorry."

Having no idea what a lorry was, I followed along to a canvas-backed truck with large mud-spattered tires. Kimaru tossed our duffels in the back. Ray sat up front, and I squeezed into the narrow second seat.

Kimaru continued, "We are going to drive to the town of Arusha to pick up supplies and eat luncheon. Then we'll drive past Lake Manyara and through the Ngorongoro Highland. For part of the time, we'll be driving overland, and it will be bumpy. We should see a lot of wildlife along the way."

"Is it far to Olduvai?" I asked.

Kimaru nodded, "Yes, it will take us the rest of the day. We should arrive just before dark. If all goes well."

It would prove to be a cramped ride. Rambling over the compacted dirt road to Arusha, we passed a native village with huts made of mud and sticks. The huts surrounded a central area with animal skins mounted on wooden stakes, drying in the sun. Statuesque villagers were dressed in rusty-red fabric that wrapped around their bodies. Women wearing hooped beaded earrings and broad circular necklaces pounded stone mortars with pestles. Ahead of us, men and boys herded donkeys in the road and we stopped the lorry for them to pass. In the distance, tall men tended herds of humped-back white, black, and gray cattle.

"This is a Maasai village," Kimaru explained. "The Maasai wear red robes called Shuka. Red represents blood and acts as protection against lions. It also represents courage. And see the collars the women wear? They are a mark of their clan."

"What are the women grinding?" I asked.

"Maize," he replied. "Maize is a big staple of the African diet. I'm sure you will eat ugali for breakfast tomorrow at Olduvai. We eat it every day."

"Ugali?" I asked.

He smiled, "It's a sort of pudding. Made with maize. You'll see."

"Are the Maasai your people?" I asked.

"No, I'm of the Kamba people," he replied. "Most of the workers at Olduvai are Kamba." He jammed the lorry into gear and we proceeded.

I had a lot of questions about the different tribes but decided not to pry. I was unsure if it was polite to ask.

My stomach rumbled by the time we arrived in Arusha. Even after the bumpy ride, I was ready for lunch. Although a small town, Arusha appeared to have modern amenities, with automobiles driving up and down the streets. The people wore current fashions, men in khaki slacks and collared shirts, women in floral dresses. Groups of young boys in shorts and white short-sleeve shirts hurried along the streets. The volcanic cone of Mt. Meru, not as large as Kilimanjaro, but still impressive, served as a stately backdrop to the town.

Ray pointed out a photograph displayed in many of the shop windows.

"Tanganyika is changing governments. The country is currently a territory of the United Kingdom, but the British will turn it over for self-governance in just a few months. All without bloodshed," Ray said. "These are photographs of Julius Nyerere, who will become the first prime minister. An election was held last year."

Kimaru pulled in front of the Arusha Hotel, a one-story mocha-colored building with lime-green awnings over its two front windows. I peeled myself out of the back seat, my leg muscles protesting.

"I'm going to take the lorry and pick up our supplies while you two have luncheon at the hotel. I should be back in ninety minutes," Kimaru said.

"Do you want us to get you some food?" I asked.

"No, I'll buy something at the market," he replied. "But thank you for the offer."

Entering the hotel lobby, ceiling fans slowly stirred the warm air, and scents of tropical flowers wafted across the space. The black and white class system, also prevalent in the United States, was on full display here. White patrons sat in upholstered chairs in the lobby, reading, chatting, and smoking. The hotel workers were all native Africans. I wondered what would happen to this dichotomy after independence.

Ray led us past the check-in desk to the tea room. We approached the host, a young African man wearing a fez on his head.

"Good afternoon," he said, with a nod. "Will you be joining us for luncheon today?"

"Yes, thank you," Ray replied.

As we were led to our table, I noticed a few glances directed our way from the better-dressed patrons. I felt my face reddening as I clomped across the wooden flooring in my clunky field boots.

"Would you favor a pint?" Ray asked me.

"A what?" I asked.

Ray smiled. "Beer. Would you like a pint of beer?"

"No, thank you." I wrinkled my nose.

"If you don't like beer, you should try the ginger beer. It's nonalcoholic and very good."

Expecting it to taste like ginger ale, the ginger beer's deeper, richer flavor fizzed in my mouth each time I took a sip. It also helped to settle my stomach, which I appreciated. After shoveling down a filling meal of roasted chicken and shepherd's pie, we still had some time before Kimaru's return.

"Let's walk to the market," Ray said. "You'll see some local color."

I nodded. "Okay, my legs could use a stretch."

At home, what we called the 'market' was the grocery store, so I was unprepared for the noisy, open-air extravaganza of stalls, live animals, tea stands, produce, and milling masses of people. The smell of grilling meat filled the air. Maasai traders, wearing white or red Shuka and carrying spears, called out in their language. Boys wore wide-brimmed hats while they wrangled a small herd of goats. Tribal women sat in small groups, pulling their Shuka over their heads for shade. Sunlight reflected off their metallic bracelets, and their necklaces jangled as they weaved baskets. Bunches of sunny bananas hung in a stall. Crates held a colorful array of maize, rice, beans, and potatoes, in addition to other grains and roots, which I did not recognize.

I pointed to some brown tubers in a basket.

"What are those?" I asked.

"That's cassava," Ray said. "It's a major crop here. It's usually boiled and mashed. I'm sure you'll eat some at the camp while you're here."

Turning down an intersecting dirt road, we came upon a man selling tortoises in a pen. Another man paraded a tiny elephant on a leash, its trunk swinging from side to side.

"Oh, look at the baby elephant!" I said. "It's so cute."

"Those traders sell animals to private clients and zoos," Ray said. "The mother elephant was probably killed for her ivory."

I stopped and stared at him. "What?"

"Poaching is an ugly business. Unfortunately, it's also very lucrative. Hunters kill the elephants and cut off their tusks to sell the ivory. They leave the bodies to rot. I've filmed the aftermath."

The luster of the market dimmed for me.

"That's really awful," I said. Ray nodded in agreement.

We meandered silently back to the hotel. Kimaru stood out front, the back of the lorry packed with goods. Our duffels now shared space with bins of grains and roots from the market, boxes of tea, coffee, ginger beer, beer, flour, sugar, and Poultex Kenya Eggs. Loaves of fresh bread stuck out of a basket. Several cans marked "Petrol" wafted the stench of gasoline.

"Ready to continue ahead to Olduvai Gorge?" Kimaru asked me.

I nodded. "You bet," I said, climbing in. I was ready to get my hands dirty and get to work. I had been tasked with preserving some newly discovered fish fossils, using my skills learned at the Smithsonian. The sediments from the Ice Age lake beckoned to me. As well as something unidentified, calling to me from within. And of course, I could not wait to meet my personal hero, the famous Dr. Mary Leakey.

CHAPTER 5

MIDDLE PLEISTOCENE
(1.5 MILLION YEARS AGO), AFRICA

With the forested caldera behind her and the Rift Valley stretching to the horizon, the young girl rested with her tribe. Named Ifa, for the sound of the wind, she leaned against her mother's legs, her intelligent eyes squinting. She turned her broad face highlighted by slight brow ridges, toward the equatorial sun and stretched out her dark arms. The sky overhead, like a brilliant turquoise dome, reflected off a shimmering lake, the tribe's destination.

In her primitive language, a mixture of gestures, facial expressions, mimicry, and tongue clicks, Ifa called out. "Ma! Sun! Morning."

Her mother nodded, patting Ifa's head of woolen curls.

In this wet season of abundance, swollen streams cascaded down the volcano's slopes, expanding the lake and nourishing the savanna. Great herds of Ice Age mammals—giant flat-domed elephants, wildebeest, antlered giraffes—nibbled on the grasses and watered at the lake.

Unknown to the people, their valley, a wide chasm in the earth's crust, continued in its rifting, the result of mother nature's internal turmoil. On a timeline they could neither notice nor comprehend, the earth altered. Climate fluctuations forced changes in flora—the deep, rich African forests transformed into semiarid grasslands. The animals adapted in turn. Grazers galloped across vast savannas, their hooves evolved to pound the ground at high speed. Early hominids long-ago leaving behind their arboreal existence, sprinted across the plain with their bipedal adaptations, and expanding brains. Predators and scavengers—cheetahs, lion-sized hyenas, saber-tooth cats—shadowed their prey, feasting on the young, the slow, and the weak.

The tribal patriarch ended the people's respite. "Come," he indicated with gestures, rising off the ground.

The tribe, a small nomadic band, grabbed their meager belongings. Digging sticks. Hand axes. Hides. The fire-carrier clutched an antelope's stomach containing hot coals from last night's fire, insulated by stones.

Ma gathered her children. "Ifa. Nama. Get up."

Onward they trekked across the plain, munching on captured locusts. The men led the group and the women surrounded the children in relative safety. Walking upright, Ifa and her sister, Nama, similar in appearance, shared the closeness of birth sisters. The people treaded with cautious footsteps, no sound above a whisper. Each step across the savanna evoked danger. A wound could become a festering menace, a snakebite a summons from the gods. Saber-toothed lionesses stalked through the tall grasses, hungry and protective of their cubs. Hooves, fangs, claws, tusks could each be deadly.

As the sun blazed above their heads, the tribe reached a boggy edge of the lake. Sweat ran down their faces and beaded on their bodies. They approached the marshy shore, on alert for crocodiles and hippos. The women and children cautiously knelt to drink as the men kept watch. Ifa's toes squished through the muck, the cool wetness soothing her calloused feet. Her parched throat rejoiced as she leaned to sip the life-giving water. She smiled at Nama, next to her, mud coating their elbows and knees.

Cattails grew in clusters along the shoreline, the brown tubular heads bursting with fluff. Ifa picked a floating fragment and blew it into the air, giggling as it sailed away. She reached up and grabbed a furry spike and wrenched off the top. Fluff poured out, spilling down on Nama's head. Nama squealed and moved out of the way.

"Ifa!" Ma's sharp voice commanded. "Stop!"

Nama elbowed Ifa, always the troublemaker. Ma herded the girls to a cattail with a thick stem. Ifa's stomach rumbled. She stripped off a waxy leaf and stuffed it into her mouth. She grinned with mischief in her smile, the frond sticking out of her mouth.

"No," Ma said with a click. "Spit." She reached into Ifa's mouth and pulled out the leaf, tossing it on the ground. She gave a small sigh. "Tsk, tsk, tsk."

Ma pointed at the root. "Here. Dig."

Ifa and Nama knelt next to Ma and gouged their digging sticks into the earth. Loosening the dirt around the spindly root, they pulled the plant from the ground. Ma snapped off the root and the lower stem, tossing the rest of the plant back into the water. With her teeth, she peeled the outer husk off the shoot, exposing the tender center. Spitting out the chaff, she broke the tender tuber in half and handed it to Ifa and Nama.

"Eat," Ma said with a gesture.

Ifa chewed the edible root, the crunchy tartness filling her mouth. "Sour," she spoke with a click and stuck out her tongue. Nama nibbled on hers without complaint, looking askance at her sister from the corner of her eye.

The other women joined in gathering the rhizomes, peeling and munching as they dug. The men waded along in the shallows, digging for freshwater clams. Handfuls of clam-filled muck piled up on the bank. Along the distant shore, a herd of gazelles dipped their graceful heads to drink from the lake. Weaver birds chirped overhead, diving for bugs, their pouch-like nests hanging from a nearby thorn tree. When the patriarch decided the bounty was sufficient, he called for a halt. The people gathered at the shoreline, languidly resting in a glade of trampled grass. With their oversized molars, they masticated the cattail fibers. Clams, picked from the mud piles and pried open with robust grips, were slurped raw from the shells. Ifa dug her fingernails along a clam's hinge but the bivalve would not yield. She placed the shell on top of a rock, and gripping another, smashed at the shell. Smack! Smack! The valves cracked under her pummeling. Triumphant, she let out a "Whoop!" and dribbled the syrupy clam juice into her mouth.

As the sun moved toward its sleeping place, the tribe sensed a coming storm. Clouds billowed into towers, dark and predatory. Winds began to gust as the skies turned the hue of dusky moss. Ifa's name, now humming on the lips of the gale, sounded piercing to her ears.

"Ifa, Nama!" Ma vocalized with clicks. She grabbed them by their hands.

Together they sprinted to an eroding remnant of a long-forgotten lava flow, rising high above the grass. They hunkered under a ledge, squeezing into a cleft in the weathered rock. A furry hyrax peeked its chubby head out of a crevice. It glared at the intruders with its inquisitive squirrel-like face. Ifa poked at it with her finger and it scampered back into its hole. Nama giggled. Then lightning crackled across the darkened sky. A sudden thunderclap and Nama cried out, planting her hands over her ears. Ifa grabbed her in a hug, their hearts pulsing as one, rumbling with the thunder. Warm rain began to pour down, playing a staccato beat on the ground in front of them. All other sounds faded as the young girls pressed together against the rock, inhaling the fragrance of marl, dung, and ozone.

With the season's rhythms ingrained within them, the people anticipated the end of these replenishing rains. By the next moon cycle, the wet season would end, completing the savanna's revival. Soon the time of hunger would arrive. The people knew to prepare.

CHAPTER 6

1950, ARLINGTON, VIRGINIA

The newly sprouting grass brushed my legs as I reclined in my backyard, leaning on one arm, fresh sun on my face as I studied the ants. Classified as Little Black Ants—according to my *Golden Nature Guide of Insects* ('*225 Species in Full Color*')—the short-lived workers served one fat queen. Fascinating creatures, these hard-working arthropods, lined up, organized, cooperative. None left out, alone. We could learn much from ants, I thought. Staring at their mounded soil nest, my eyelids drooped and I dozed.

In my mind's eye, the nest grew, taller and taller, until it loomed over me, like a brick-colored pinnacle. The ants grew too, larger and red, with swollen heads and biting mandibles. Strangely I felt unafraid, ducking behind the tower, laughing, hiding.

"Come and find me," a voice called out. "I'm somewhere in the reeds." We played a child's game. I peeked from behind the ant hill but did not see anyone. Only dirt and dried grass. "Be careful of the ants! They will bite you! Brush them away."

Her voice seemed so familiar, innate.

A yipping noise carried across a distance.

Rusty hinges moaned. A door slammed. My eyes opened, gritty, slowly refocusing through my slumbering haze. Tiny ants crawled across my hand, tickling. Brushing them off, I heard the call of my neighbor.

"Ignore the weirdo next door. She's so strange." The words were piercing. "Heigh-ho, weirdo."

My nemesis lived next door. Lana Sawyer. Blond pageboy haircut, pink bows, tongue of honeyed acid. Ringleader, class president, May Day princess. She and her nasty group of followers played with dolls and jumped rope in her backyard.

Undertones of giggling reached my ears.

Sitting up, cross-legged on the grass, I began a mantra of Linnean taxonomy in my head. The layered organization from broad to narrow categories calmed my mind. "Kingdom, phylum, class, order, family, genus, species..." I silently recited, over and over, stacking them in vertical lines in my mind.

Nonetheless, a steady thrum of insidious commentary reached my ears.

"Henrietta, dressed in yellow, went upstairs to slurp some jello..." Lana squawked in her sing-song voice, as the jump rope struck rhythmically against her patio.

"What a mistake. She kissed a snake. How many doctors did it take?" chanted another girl.

"One, two, three..." they all counted together, rope smacking the concrete.

What a lot of nonsensical claptrap.

I tried not to let Lana's taunts bother me. But I was only ten years old.

CHAPTER 7

Fridays proved to be my salvation. In the museum, all negative memories and hurtful commentary evaporated from my mind. As long as I accomplished my tasks, my father gave me carte blanche to wander the halls alone. Just me and my shadow, happily invisible. The guards largely ignored my presence. The coat-and hat-check girls gossiped inside their closet. The docents at the Welcome Station busied themselves with answering questions and handing out maps. School children on field trips filed behind their teachers in stiff arrays. The museum was a buzzing ecosystem and I observed it like a fly on the wall. As long as I stayed behind those glass doors, all was copasetic.

What drew me to the Hall of Mammals that day, I could not say. Never my favorite hall, I found the great beasts rather dismal. Shot by game hunters, they posed frozen in glass-eyed perpetuity, their destinies to be stared at as curios. The African mammals seemed to beckon me, however, through the entryway. I shuffled past the North American mammals—foxes, wolves, opossums, raccoons—toward the stylized savanna. Long-stemmed dried grasses glued onto sandy manmade substrates provided the backdrop. Ungulates posed in suspended animation—two stuffed giraffes (genus *Giraffa*), three rhinos (genus *Rhinoceros*) in a family group, a lone zebra (genus *Equus*, like a horse), various species of antelope (a 'wastebasket taxon' for many hoofed ruminants according to the information card). One antelope was posed with a cattail in its mouth.

Odd. Were cattails even edible?

I meandered farther down the hall. A wildebeest, with its sharp horns, black muzzle, and white beard stared at me through vitreous eyes. I could almost see his dowager hump swaying and stringy tail swooshing. My hands grew a bit clammy. I turned to my right and a yawning hippo flared his nostrils and displayed his spiky teeth, his mouth aligned with my head.

What was that smell? Like the scent of wet mud after a rainstorm, along with a whiff of earthy musk.

Rounding a corner, only a thin velvet rope separated me from the bared teeth of a lioness, posed as though springing to attack. Her stony eyes bored into mine, the slitted pupils menacing. Behind her, a pair of spotted hyenas smiled predatory grins. Goosebumps appeared on my skin. I stepped back.

It's just an illusion. These animals are all dead.

Yet I wasted no time scrambling out of the hall, my legs wobbly, my heart beating like wings in flight.

CHAPTER 8

MIDDLE PLEISTOCENE, THE RIFT VALLEY, AFRICA

Late on a still moonless night, the sky as dark as smoke, a saber-tooth stalked. Padding on soundless paws, drawn by hominid scents, the lioness stealthily approached the camp. Nestled around the hearth fire's dying embers, the sleeping people had no warning of her approach. The giant cat struck, quick as a cheetah, with a biting force that could crush an elephant. Grabbing a young boy with its fangs, the cat sped away with the flailing child. The boy's mother screamed into the night. Hearing her, the tribe reacted as one, crying out in terror. Ifa and Nama jolted awake and reached out to clutch at their mother. The men grabbed their hunting clubs and gave chase, carrying a lit branch as a torch fire into the inky blackness. Scrambling to rekindle the embers, the women huddled together and tried to comfort the anguished mother.

As the amber sun peeked over the edge of the rift valley, the men returned. Exhausted, with downcast faces, they were empty-handed. The lioness was too swift, the attack too sudden, the darkness complete. Seeing the men return, the mother began a deafening wail. The women gripped her arms and joined the cacophony, their voices piercing the still air. Ifa joined in, her tear-streaked face an imitation of her mother's, her body shaking as the finality set in.

Just before sundown, the tribe prepared for the blood ceremony. Carrying clods of red ochre to the lakeshore, the people moistened the hard clay. Rubbing the paste with their fingertips, they smeared the earth over their faces and bodies. Ma reached down and painted the girls' faces with the blood symbols. They trudged back to camp, eyes downcast, to surround the burning dung fire. The patriarch led the ritual, beating his chest, beseeching the gods to guide the boy to his beaming spot in the night sky. The people flailed their arms and cried out in lamentation, howling ululations of pain and prayers.

CHAPTER 9

1961, The Rift Valley, Africa

My face pressed against the lorry window during our astonishingly scenic excursion from Arusha. We skirted past the northern edge of Lake Manyara. The shallow lake appeared as a moving entity, hosting a flamboyance of pink flamingoes wading with their knobby knees bending backward, their bills dipping up and down in search of brine shrimp and algae. An even more awe-inspiring sight, a herd of elephants lumbered down to the water's edge to drink. Spouting water from their trunks onto their leathery hides, the ancient behemoths bathed in the alkaline water. Wide-eyed, I took photo after photo from my window. Who knew that a young woman from Virginia would have the opportunity to see these sights?

"Lake Manyara is a National Park now. Hunting is no longer allowed here," Ray explained. I was relieved to hear this, especially after seeing the orphaned baby elephant in the market.

I recognized gazelles and zebras intermingling with other grazers, live versions of the museum's stuffed menagerie.

"I thought we would see wildebeest," I said.

"There are great herds of them, but they have already moved north. They migrate each year to follow the rains," Kimaru said.

Driving farther onto the plain, we spotted a solitary gray rhinoceros. With its tough armor, it reminded me of a two-horned

Triceratops. Scampering around the rhino, a fox panted in the sun, its huge ears sticking up above its black face.

"Do you see the bat-eared fox?" asked Ray. With his camera in his hand, he photographed the animals, one after another, even though he had probably seen them countless times before. "And look carefully over there in the grass. See the lioness?"

Slinking among the reeds, I could just make out her tawny, camouflaged coat. Goosebumps stood up on my arms.

Rumbling farther along, we came upon an entire pride of lions, eight females and one male, reclining as they yawned in the sun. There were at least as many cubs as females, many hidden in the grass. One female nuzzled the male with her head while flicking the black tip of her tail. A knot of fear formed in my throat. I swallowed it down as we moved on.

Stalking through the weeds, a flock of birds with white bodies and black tail feathers picked up bugs with curved yellow bills, their breast feathers blowing in the breeze. They appeared oblivious to the lions.

"Look at those birds—right among the lions!" I said.

"Those are European storks," Ray said. "And over there are crested cranes."

The cranes appeared like noble peacocks, with stork-like legs, white and black bodies, red throats, and crowns of golden plumage sitting on their heads.

As we curved to the west, a watering hole came into sight. Banded zebras nibbled on the grass or drank from the pond. Gazelles, with their V-shaped horns, dark-tipped ears, and masked faces, joined the zebras. Their tawny bodies with racing stripe flanks and legs pranced daintily, swinging their stubby black tails like contented metronomes.

My heart beat with childlike excitement. The animals seemed exotic, yet familiar at the same time. Terrifying, yet beautiful. Granted, I sat encased inside a metal sheath, protected from the claws.

Kimaru pointed to the opposite side of our truck. "Do you see the ostriches?" he asked. "The male ostriches are the black ones, with the white plumage on their wings and tails. The females are gray."

The oversized birds bent their fishhook-shaped necks toward the ground. Once startled by the noise of the lorry, they raced away on backward legs.

Looming in front of us, a massive escarpment, vegetated by acacia and baobab trees, stood like a sky-piercing shrine. Our lorry climbed in elevation, gears straining, scaling the walls up this massive caldera, the Ngorongoro Highland. When we reached the top of the rim road, we leaped from the lorry to take in the view. The magnificent panorama from the top of the escarpment caused me to hold my breath. The teaming savanna extended into the distance, a scene so vast and lush, I found myself trembling. Peering through field glasses from this upper vantage point, I viewed the entire ecosystem. A sudden feeling of connectedness sprang within me, inexplicable. Somehow I knew, even before I viewed them, that two volcanic cones stood in the far distance, their eroded summits soaring skyward to blend with clouds of gray and white stratus.

"This is the Serengeti Plain," Kimaru said. "Olduvai Gorge is within the plain. Fortunately, we are past the long rains so the roads are passable."

"The view is incredible," I said. "It's like a painting. I could stand here all day."

"Yes, it is. But we can't stay here long. We need to continue so we reach the camp before dark."

"Welcome to Olduvai Gorge," Kimaru announced as he down-shifted the lorry to descend along the deeply rutted dirt track over the ravine's edge.

The gorge dissected the rift valley like a deep cut, exposing outcrops of horizontal strata. The change was immediate, from the lush grasslands of the plain into a barren desert. The sparse vegetation included succulents and patchy scrub bushes sprouting from the dry soil. A few lone acacia trees rose incongruently above the valley floor.

"The gorge was named for the wild sisal growing here."

"What's wild sisal?" I asked.

In response, Kimaru slowed the lorry.

"See that plant? The one with the thick leaves? That is sisal. The leaves can be soaked in water and stripped to make rope. And the juice is used on wounds."

"Hopefully I won't need that," I said with a wan smile.

The ravine walls exposed chalky gray, tan, and buff-colored layers of sediments in alternating cliffs and slopes. Fans of alluvium coalesced as piles of talus across the ground. Tall monoliths of eroded rock stood as sentinels in the distance.

We bumped along for two more hours, the heat pounding down in full force. I shifted in the back seat, legs cramped, sweat glistening on my face. With the sun setting and a first quarter moon glowing in the eastern sky, the outlines of huts and tents appeared in the distance.

The Leakey camp.

Voices rang out as the lorry pulled up next to a ramshackle lean-to. I escaped out of the back seat. Kerosene lanterns blazed a luminescent glow over the tents. Mosquitoes buzzed around my head as my eyes adjusted to the sudden brightness. African men converged on the truck, opening the back to unload the cargo. A foreign language, which I assumed was Kikuyu, floated in the air.

A clipped British voice rang out. "Kimaru! Ray! Welcome back!" A woman approached Ray and shook his hand. "Glad to see you wanted to return for more photographs."

"Always a pleasure, Mary," Ray said, shaking her outstretched hand. "Let me introduce you to Henrietta Ballantine from the Smithsonian U.S. National Museum."

She turned toward me. "Hello. I'm Mary Leakey."

I froze, mute. I had read about Mary Leakey's successes in my Physical Anthropology class and seen her photographs in *National Geographic Magazine.* Here was the woman who, digging alongside her husband, the infamous Dr. Louis Leakey, had made exciting new scientific discoveries. She helped trace our ancestry back millions of years. Last year, the National Geographic Society began sponsoring the Leakey's expeditions here in Olduvai. The resulting publicity instantly made them the most acclaimed paleoanthropologists in the world.

And here she was in front of me. I tried to find my voice but I must have left it in the lorry.

CHAPTER 10

MIDDLE PLEISTOCENE, THE RIFT VALLEY, AFRICA

The early morning dawned, cool and breezy. Near camp, Ifa crouched within the reeds, her eyes level with the seeding tassels. Returning once again with the rainy season, grazing herds spread across the savanna in front of her. Her heart quickened as she spied movement in the middle distance. Not prey. Not predators. Men. The figures advanced toward her hiding place. She gripped her hand axe and motioned for Nama, kneeling on the ground next to her.

"Shhh. Quiet," she whispered.

Nama rose and peeked over the grasses. Three men approached, running quickly, sharpened sticks in their hands.

"Others," Nama said.

After twelve yearly cycles, Ifa and Nama had entered adulthood. Ifa, tall for a woman, loomed over her shorter sister. The tribe had changed much during her lifetime. The old patriarch was dead, a new regime established. Ma, now gray and stooped, was recognized as matriarch.

The young women ducked down into the reeds as the men headed toward the smoke from the hearth fire. Muscles taut, long legs pounding, the warriors sprinted past, their faces holding determined looks. One of the men appeared younger and beardless, the others older. Ifa and Nama recognized them as members of the northern people. A tenuous peace existed between the groups. They met when one traveled south and the other north. Occasionally the tribes hunted together to slay larger beasts. Mates were sometimes sought. But the people remained leery of each other. Ifa knew that watches would be kept that night.

Ifa and Nama followed stealthily, threading their way through the reeds. From their hiding place, they waited until the patriarch welcomed the men. Hand and arm clasping gestures were exchanged. As the patriarch called his people, Ifa motioned to Nama and they stepped into camp.

The timing of the men's arrival was fortuitous, as a herd of wild cattle grazed nearby. Following the ancient migratory rhythm of the animals, the adults readied for a hunt. Ifa grabbed her hand axe and joined the group. With a signal from the patriarch, the hunting party advanced, crawling through the grasses toward the multitude of cloven hooves. On hands and knees, the people approached the beasts, men in the front, women fanning out behind them. Ifa strove to remain silent, brushing at red ants that bit her arms and legs.

Oblivious to the hunters, the bovids cropped the seeds in the pasture. The size of buffalo, they shook their heavy heads and shaggy auburn hides. Their giant dagger-like horns arched downward, measuring longer than a human from base to tip. Suddenly, two of the giant bulls vied for dominance, grunting and pawing at the ground. With loud snorts, they rushed toward each other, bashing their heads in an antagonistic display. The females lowed and ushered the calves out of the way.

The hunters kept advancing, stealthily crouching. Vigilant, they remained downwind. Luck was with them, as the cattle were distracted by the fighting males. Carefully placing her hands and feet through the reeds, Ifa felt the scratches against her body as she crawled. She swatted at the pesky buzzing of black flies. Heart beating in anticipation, she glanced over at Nama crawling adjacent and gave her a small smile of encouragement.

When all were in position, forming inner and outer lines of ambush behind the herd, the men exchanged hand signals. As one body, the people leaped to their feet, calling out while clapping their hands. Ifa and Nama shouted and waved their arms over their heads.

"Haaahaaahaaahaaa!"

The cattle, startled at the burst of noise, replied with loud moans. The males lowered their heads and snorted through their noses. They posed to attack, when the largest male, his humped back quivering, turned away with loud bellows and led the herd from the noise. The rest of the startled animals followed him, stampeding away, hooves pounding, mooing in distress. With a practiced maneuver amid the bovine chaos, a group of brave men separated two of the cattle from the rest of the herd. Driving the two beasts, a cow and her calf, the men gave chase, long legs carrying them swiftly across the plain. Ifa, a fast runner, kept pace with the men, her feet striking the ground, her lean body adapted for long-distance running. Sweat glistened on her face, cooling her and keeping her from overheating. The trackers followed the animals, keeping pressure on the pair. The terrified beasts, unable to cool sufficiently, tried to pant and rest but were driven relentlessly forward. Surrounded, they were redirected, driven back toward camp. Eyes wide, nostrils flaring, the calf succumbed first, collapsing from exhaustion with an anguished cry.

The cow stopped and faced the hunters. She lowered her great head and lunged with her horns, treacherous blades. The hunters surrounded her, attacking from all sides with sharpened sticks and stone knives. Ifa approached from the side, lunging at the beast, piercing the tough hide with her hand axe. She dove away as the howling animal swung its great horns. Sweat pouring down her face, heart pounding, Ifa stabbed again and again. Finally, with a final bellow, the cow fell. Ifa and the other hunters called out, their victory cries echoing across the plain.

The hunters collapsed after the punishing drive. Bovine blood caked Ifa's arms and body. Walking to a nearby stream, she knelt and drank her fill, the water cooling her parched throat. She then slid into the gurgling brook. Relief coursed through every pore of her body. The water swirled around her as she sighed, brushing off the blood and grime. She leaned back and allowed the current to float her downstream, where she climbed up the bank to stretch her wobbly legs and rest. Above her, clouds drifted across an azure sky. Vultures circled overhead, drawn by the blood scent advected on the breeze.

After a short rest, Ifa cleared a wide area for a hearth, ripping out grasses in a circle to expose the barren ground. She piled dung patties in the middle. The firekeeper added a precious coal to the dried patties, blowing on the embers. Smoke rose in the air, a signal to the rest of the tribe. Several men gathered quartzite cobbles and chipped them together, creating the stone scrapers needed for butchering. This was a talent few possessed, striking along the rock grain, making the fluted cores. Ifa grabbed one of the scrapers and began to cut through the cowhide. Setting the skin aside to be scraped clean, she sliced large chunks of meat from the carcass. Her arms bloody once again, she breathed in the tang of iron hanging in the air.

The young man from the north approached Ifa and settled next to her. "I am Kho," he said, placing his hand on his chest.

"Ifa." Her heart fluttered as he leaned toward her. Working silently, she tried to concentrate on her task. But her awareness of his closeness, his strength, his arms working beside her, caused her chest to tighten with each breath. She watched his powerful hands cutting into the meat and imagined them on her.

As the sun began its lowering, Ifa heard the shouts of the rest of the women and children arriving, drawn by the smoke. Nama ran up to Ifa, and stared at the size of the kill. A wide smile spread across Nama's face and she trilled, "Ahahahaha!" The women joined her and their ululations rang in the air, celebrating the success of the hunt. Several of the women joined the butchering, cutting chunks of meat, impaling them on sticks to set at the fire's edge for roasting.

Meat strips were set across poles and placed in the smoke. The children gathered more dung patties and fed the now-roaring fire.

While Ifa worked next to Kho, Nama helped set up the new camp. She constructed a small dwelling of sticks covered with an antelope hide. Gathering rocks, she placed them around the edge of the hide in an anchoring circle. Crude huts soon surrounded the new hearth.

A brilliant red moon rose to laud the night, illuminating the way for the people to drag the rest of the carcasses from the camp. A trail of offal, blood, and bones smeared the grass. Away from the protection of the leaping flames, hyenas circled, and lions paced. Black flies descended, biting the exhausted tribe. Ifa, panting from exertion after helping to drag a carcass, slapped angrily at the insects as they drew blood. At the roar of a distant lion, Kho reached out to grab Ifa's hand, pulling her quickly back toward the fire. They settled next to each other around the hearth. Smoke surrounded them and the smell of roasting meat made Ifa's stomach complain.

The patriarch began the feast, thanking the Spirits for the success of the hunt. He grabbed the raw vitamin-rich liver, bit off the end, and passed the rest around the circle. Each man tore off a portion with his teeth, sharing this gift for strength. Kho took a bite and passed the liver to Ifa. She stared down at it. Only men were allowed this reward. She passed it on.

Using his hand axe to crack open the calf's leg bones, the patriarch exposed the creamy, rich inner marrow. He handed these to the children, who giggled and smiled at the rare treat. The women began to pull beef strips from the fire and served the men. Kho watched Ifa as she tugged a chunk of roasted meat off a skewering pole and handed it to him. His eyes seemed to appraise her through the smoke. He took a mouthful, grinning as he chewed, and leaned over to her, holding out the piece. She bit into it, smiling back at him, her heart swift in her chest.

After stomachs were full, hunger abated, the patriarch stood among his people. With threads of language, he recounted the tale of the people's beginnings, how they were given life from the earth but returned to the sky. Ifa, having heard the story many times, sighed and leaned into Kho's shoulder. His warmth seemed to spread through her, his presence a balm to her exhausted state.

With grateful hearts, the women started to thrum a low tune, a celebration to the Spirits. Ifa joined in the rhythmic chant, clapping her hands to the rhythm with tired joy. One by one, the people settled in for the night, dozing by the fire. Nama tapped Ifa on the shoulder and pulled her to stand. Separated from Kho's comforting presence, Ifa sleepily allowed Nama to guide her toward their hut. Once inside, the girls settled on reeds stacked on the ground. Ifa wrapped her arms around her sister and Nama melted into her embrace.

As Ifa sank into sleep, a premonition fell over her. Perhaps Nama felt it also. *Change was coming.* Ifa tamped down the surge of fear and exhilaration threatening to sweep through her. She hugged Nama tighter, realizing as she did that Nama was shedding silent tears. Ifa rocked her back and forth to comfort her. "All alright. Sleep now."

From a distance, the chortles of the hyenas echoed as they reveled over the leftover bones.

Ifa awoke the next morning and climbed out from beneath the hide-hut to stretch her sore muscles. The sun's liquid yolk beamed at the valley rim, glancing off the dew-glistening grass. A herd of crested oryxes honked in the distance, their shaggy heads and striped bodies barely visible. Looking across the camp, Ifa's eyes widened as she noticed the northern men wrapping strips of meat in traveling hides. They were packing to leave. Kho stood with the patriarch, heads together, conferring. The patriarch nodded. They turned to face her. Then she saw Nama's anguished face. Ma's tears. And Ifa realized that the men had not come to hunt.

Kho had come for her.

With long strides, Kho walked across the camp toward Ifa, stopping in front of her, his eyes bright. He reached over and placed his hand on her shoulder.

"Ifa. Come with me. To my home."

Ifa gazed upward, seeing the reflection of the caldera in his eyes. Her kinsmen faded into the background, becoming part of the grassland, the birds, the acacia trees. Heart racing, tears brimming, she nodded. "Yes, I will go."

CHAPTER 11

On my thirteenth birthday, I unwrapped Betty Crocker's Picture Cookbook from my mother. The red and white floral 3-ring binder, complete with recipes and black-and-white photographs of finished concoctions, credited the authors with their husbands' names. *Recipe by Mrs. James Bakker. Recipe by Mrs. Horace Parker.* Their identities usurped by wedding vows.

"I thought we could cook your birthday dinner together using the book," my mother said.

I put on a thankful face.

From my dad, I received a fish fossil with a display stand. Its bones were etched perfectly out of the encasing limestone. The tag read "*Knightia sp.*, Herring, Green River Formation, Eocene, Wyoming."

"Oh, thank you, Dad!" I ran my fingers over the intricate bones chiseled to stand in relief on the surface of the rock. What I loved most in the world were fossils and I prized my collection above all else. I had purchased most of my specimens with my allowance at the museum gift shop. I owned a tiny piece of petrified wood, a trilobite, a brachiopod or 'lamp shell,' a shark tooth, a fern imprint, a sand dollar, and a crinoid—an animal called a 'sea lily.' I kept my fossils in egg cartons, each sitting within an individual cup on cotton balls, like tiny pampered royals. I added the fossil fish to my collection, displaying it on the top of my bookcase, the reigning monarch.

That afternoon I joined my mother in the kitchen, pulling out ingredients, mixing bowls, utensils, pots and pans. My favorite dessert, chocolate meringue pie, was on the menu. We peeled potatoes and snapped string beans. While working together, she threw out motherly advice as one would toss feed to a chicken.

"A lady never drinks alcohol to excess or curses," she instructed while I mashed the potatoes.

Fortunately, she did not speak Russian. Thanks to Madame Sekomova I could both offer a toast and swear like a sailor in Russian.

"A lady does not talk about her personal ills. She does not complain of a headache or cramps. Especially in front of a man. She should take an aspirin, fill a hot water bottle, and go to bed," she admonished me for no reason, while vigorously chopping onions.

"Do not air your dirty laundry in public. Family business is not to be strewn around," came with a demonstration on how to whip meringue.

Gossiping about the neighbors must be permissible though, I thought to myself.

"A lady never chews gum. It makes her look like a cow," she said, as I scorched chocolate pudding on the stove.

"Don't wear white shoes before Memorial Day or after Labor Day," she coached while tenderizing the pot roast.

It all seemed more complicated than Euclidean geometry.

My mother reached for the pudding pan. "Oh, Henrietta, you've burned it. You really need to be more careful. Your future husband will expect you to know how to cook."

Certainly, she knew I harbored no desire to learn how to cook, or to acquire any kind of homemaking skills for that matter. The last thing I wanted to become was a housewife. A lump formed in my throat as my mother pulled the pan out of my hands and scraped the pudding into the trash can. "Try again," she said, handing me another box of pudding mix.

I poured milk into the pan and set it back on the stove. "Maybe my future husband will have to fend for himself. Or maybe he'll know how to cook. Or I just won't ever get married. I'm going to be a paleontologist. Like Dad. Not a housewife."

She stared at me. "Henrietta, women don't become paleontologists. Do you want evidence? I'll show you."

Marching into the living room, she retrieved the *Washington Star*. She strode back in, leafing through the sections. She held the paper in front of my nose and jabbed her finger at the *Jobs for Men* and *Jobs for Women*. "You see, you can work as a nurse, a teacher, or a secretary. Those are your choices."

Tears of frustration built behind my eyes. "Paleontologists don't advertise in the *Star*," I replied.

She harrumphed and shook her head.

At dinnertime, we seated ourselves around the dining room table for my birthday celebration. Uncle Al and Aunt Esther joined us. First, we tasted my attempt at Potato Soup—'the homey, old-fashioned kind' according to Betty Crocker.

Uncle Al slurped a spoonful. "This tastes like something I had to eat during the war," he whispered.

"Al, behave yourself," my aunt said.

The roast beef and gravy that my mom had prepared were of course, delicious. The pudding in the chocolate meringue pie tasted like burnt charcoal, my second attempt as charred as my first.

"Don't worry, Henrietta. You have other talents," my aunt said, kindly.

I sure hoped so. I knew for certain they did not include cooking. Would anyone ever recognize them, or would I ever get to use them?

CHAPTER 12

By the time I was sixteen, my journal articles advanced to ever more complex subjects, and a tradition evolved on Fridays as some of my father's museum colleagues joined us at lunch. Huddling around tables in the dingy staff dining room, naked light bulbs hanging on wires from the ceiling, an informal colloquium sprang up. Questions and opinions flew back and forth like shuttlecocks in between bites of sandwiches and gulps of burnt coffee. Holding my own was a challenge, but I contributed what I could. I believed the gentlemen looked forward to it.

"What are you working on this week, Henrietta?" my father asked.

"I'm reading an article on the hypothesis of 'species senescence' as a cause for the disappearance of the dinosaurs. The idea is that they had become overspecialized. Their gargantuan sizes, bony plates, and armor became a burden on each species. Further evolution could not overcome all of this specialization and they could not adapt to new circumstances," I said, referring to my notes.

"And what do you think of this hypothesis?" he asked.

"I don't think it can explain the extinction of so many species."

A colleague agreed. "Yes, look at turtles. Their shells could be seen as an example of overspecialization. Yet they have remained mostly unchanged since the end of the Cretaceous."

"What about environmental change? The inland seas retreated, ocean currents changed, temperatures began to vary seasonally," another added.

As the discussion swirled around me, I soaked in their opinions like a siliceous sponge, brittle yet absorbent, enjoying the camaraderie of equally passionate people.

After lunch, I headed to one of the storage rooms. The number of fossils on display in the museum's galleries composed the tip of the iceberg of the Smithsonian collection. An exponentially greater quantity resided in closets, drawers, cabinets, boxes, and bins. Scholars often visited with the sole purpose of secluding themselves with the hidden collections, poring over the manna harbored, often forgotten, dusty and crumbling. Rediscovered specimens could transform old interpretations, a claw now recognized as a horn, a chimpanzee finger bone reclassified as human. Taking advantage of my access to this trove, I huddled behind a door, the storage room blissfully empty. The wood floor pressed unforgivingly against my knees as I knelt. Sliding open a low drawer of ammonites, I leaned over to view the coiled shells, ranging from nickel- to dinner plate-size in circumference. Once encompassing squid-like animals, similar to the chambered nautilus, but now extinct, each species exhibited distinct patterns on the shells, where the internal chambers met the exterior. The contacts, known as sutures, varied in shape, from curves to loops to exquisitely repeated meanders. Each pattern was a testament to evolution. As teleost fish evolved stronger biting jaws, their ammonite prey added ballast to their shells by increasing the calcium carbonate along the suture lines. In other words, they become less chewable.

Holding up a pyritized specimen to the light, I twisted it back and forth, mesmerized, as it flashed its metallic luster like a false prophet, the original shell replaced by fool's gold. Bending my head over my notebook, I was absorbed in sketching and labeling its suture pattern frozen in time—*ceratitic*, like a serrated knife.

Despite my concentration, I became aware of two men conversing as they trod down the adjacent corridor.

"Harry's daughter is a smart thing, isn't she?"

"Yes, she is."

I beamed behind the door, a self-satisfied smile spreading across my face.

"But is he doing her any favors? I mean, realistically, how far can she go with her studies? I think he may be setting her up for a big disappointment."

"Maybe, but you never know, someday she may be your boss!"

Bursts of laughter barked out, both of them cackling like wheezing coyotes.

"Yeah, I don't think that will ever happen."

"Nope."

Their footsteps scuffed away, receding as my pride diminished. My heart could have dropped into the open drawer, now a dead, petrified stone. Taking a big gulp of bitter air, I swiped at the corners of my eyes. Returning to my notebook, I buried their comments deeply along a new internal fracture zone.

———

Madame Sekomova now came to the house only twice a week, mostly to provide feedback on graded assignments and collect new ones. I was still smarting over the overheard conversation when she arrived the following Monday. I met her at the door.

"*Dobray ootra*, Henrietta. *Kak dela?*" Madame asked as she breezed into the living room, removing her coat. Her newly colored hair glowed in an especially vivid shade of magenta. *Good morning. How are you?*

I did not answer in Russian, our usual practice.

"What is the point, Madame Sekomova?" I asked.

"I beg your pardon? What do you mean? What is the point of what?"

I collapsed onto the couch, staring at my lap, shoulders hunched. My mother clanked away in the kitchen, cleaning up the breakfast dishes. Glancing toward the back of the house, Madame reached down, pulling me back onto my feet.

"Let us go upstairs," she said.

We trudged our usual path up the attic steps. The radiator clanked unhelpfully in the chilly second-floor rooms, the lack of insulation negating any rising warm air from below. Madame set down her folio of papers as I plopped into my chair, elbows on my desk, chin in my hands.

"Now, what is this? You look like you have swallowed a lemon," she asked.

"Madame, why am I studying? Russian, literature, art, science? If I can't hope to do anything important with the knowledge, why should I bother? Why should you teach me?"

Her eyes pierced into me. She tilted her head.

"I suspect that this is more than the usual resistance?" she said, inclining her head down and back, indicating my mother in the kitchen below.

I nodded, frowning.

"You want to study paleontology, *da*? Why? Explain to me."

I stood up and walked into my bedroom. Grabbing the trilobite from my collection, I walked back and handed it to her. "See this fossil?"

"Yes," she said, turning it over in her hand. "It looks like a pill bug."

I smiled. "It's called a trilobite. It lived in the ocean five hundred million years ago. The preservation of this fossil took a miracle. This trilobite might have been eaten by a sea scorpion or crushed by waves. It could have died and rotted on a beach. Instead, it fell to the seafloor and became rapidly covered in sediment. It stayed buried for millions of years while the surrounding sediment turned to rock. Its carapace became rock too, replaced and in-filled by minerals. But even then, it might have been buried deeper and destroyed by extreme heat and pressure, by metamorphism. Or millennia of weathering and erosion might have broken it up. A fossil is a really rare thing."

She took one of my hands in hers, set the trilobite back into my palm, and squeezed.

"Henrietta, you are very passionate about this subject. I cannot predict what you will do with all of the knowledge you accumulate. Perhaps you will become an important scientist. Perhaps you will have the honor of teaching a brilliant student, as I have." She gave me a wan smile. "Sometimes the search for knowledge has to be a purpose unto itself, no matter the destination. You have the thirst. The quest may have to be reward enough. *Ve poneymyete? Understand?*"

"*Da. Spaceba,*" I said. *Yes. Thank you.*

As comforting as Madame Sekomova's words were, I had left out the most important part from my description. After a fossil miraculously formed, somebody had to discover it. Someone had to recognize that the object was something different, something special, a marvel, a glorious exception. And I wanted to be that person. It had to be someone. *Why not me?*

CHAPTER 13

1956, ARLINGTON, VIRGINIA

In Sunday school, I advanced to the high school class, where we were expected to participate in discussions about the Bible. I took a seat in the back, opened my Bible to the appropriate chapter, and stared down, elbows on the cramped desk. Our teacher, a spindly lady by the name of Mrs. Paterson, paced at the front of the room. Today's challenge was to wring out new meaning from the book of Genesis, specifically the story of Noah's Ark. Which I thought to be total malarky.

As she had every year, that self-aggrandizing snot, Lana Sawyer, held court from the front of the class. She had undergone a metamorphosis, now resembling one of her plastic fashion dolls, painted eyelashes, rouged cheeks, vacuous head.

Lana raised her hand. "How did Noah get all of those animals on the ark? I know God helped, but there were so many of them. What about the ones in Australia? How did he get them?" she asked, wide-eyed.

I could not help it; I laughed, a sort-of snort, then covered my mouth with my hand in mortification. I never called attention to myself in Sunday School.

"Henrietta, do you have something to add?" asked Mrs. Paterson. She had been unsuccessfully trying to pull me into the discussions for weeks.

I took a deep breath, staring at the desk.

"I'm sorry," I began with an apology, "but there is no way on God's green earth that all animals fit on the ark. Even if there were only two of each, it would mean that all animals alive today would have had to evolve from the few that did fit. It is biologically impossible. Not even all of the insects known today would fit in the ark," I said. I was proud of my summary since I was passionate about this topic. I could hear my father's voice echoing in my ears.

There was a long pause. Slowly glancing up, I eyed my teacher. Once I had uttered the word 'evolve', all was lost. It was 1956, and evolution was a verboten topic in church. Mrs. Paterson stared, her mouth agape like a flycatcher. Whatever she had expected, it wasn't that. Lana and her squadron of followers snickered and rolled their eyes. The boys followed their cue like fawning toadies. Too late, my error dawned as their reactions settled around me. My face burned in mortification, and I tried to make myself smaller, no mean feat for a tall girl.

When my parents came to collect me, they were dragged into a stern side conference that did not include me. At sixteen, I found this insulting.

"Come on, Henrietta, let's go home," my mother said, her voice sharp.

My father, however, winked at me.

On the silent ride home, I puzzled over the difference between speaking up in school versus giving my opinions at the museum. One kept getting me into trouble, and the other won me admiration, at least on the surface. I realized I had not considered my audience. In Sunday school, I felt like a zebra in a room of appaloosas. Perhaps at the museum, we were all zebras of a sort. Although even there, a female zebra did not equal a male zebra.

In my mother's mind, this episode was entirely my father's fault. Instead of retreating upstairs, I remained in the kitchen, where she railed at the two of us.

"You both have a complete lack of propriety!" she hollered. "This is church, for heaven's sake. Save your theories about evolution for the museum!"

I considered her with scientific interest, a bit like observing a lab rat. Her rant played like a 45 rpm record on a phonograph set at 33 1/3 rpm speed. When she worked herself into this state, no one could appease her. I had no intention of returning to Sunday School anyway, so to me, it was all a moot point. Eventually, my mother deflated and lost interest in forcing me to attend. I had been confirmed in the church, and anything after that, she decided was gravy.

CHAPTER 14

1961, OLDUVAI GORGE, TANGANYIKA, AFRICA

A heavy canvas tent served as my assigned abode at the Leakey Camp. My tent-mate was a British sparkplug named Maggie St. Jean. Meaning that she sparked hot and cold—enthusiastic and chipper to everyone else, and indifferent to me. The previous evening she told me that she was a student at Cambridge University, 'reading anthropology.' It took me all night to figure out that she meant anthropology was her major. Short in stature with dark hair cut in a bob, she was a veteran of the dig, having spent last year's field season at Olduvai.

"Breakfast will be served in the banda," she told me that first morning in our tent. "Make sure you zip the tent closed or Simon will get into your luggage."

"What's a banda? And who's Simon?" I asked.

"I'll show you. Simon is a very naughty Sykes monkey. Be careful. He likes the ladies."

I climbed out of our tent, stretched my arms up over my head, and breathed in the dry air. The sun barely peeked along the eastern horizon. The scent of fried food drew my eyes to a nearby lean-to hut.

Maggie exited the tent and pointed. "That's the banda."

"I'll meet you there in a minute," I said. "I need to visit the choo."

What I would call an 'outhouse,' here was called a 'choo.' I had used it last night in the dark. In the morning light, I opened the rickety door and observed the wide assortment of arthropods housed inside. All manner of creeping insects and spindly spider-like creatures waved their appendages at me, upon which I had no desire to sit. But I had no choice.

I then ambled over to the ramshackle-looking banda. Supported by wooden poles, the hut was open along the front with a thatched roof and dirt floor. The wooden back and side walls held storage shelves crammed with boxes of supplies, canned food, and wrapped fossils in a jumbled mishmash. A small table and six chairs crowded in the middle, and a kerosene-powered refrigerator squatted in a corner.

"Let me introduce you to Wawira," Maggie said, motioning me over. "Our wonderful cook."

I sat down at the table next to Maggie. An African woman of large girth stepped forward.

"Good morning," she said. "Would you like coffee?"

I nodded numbly as she handed me a cup of the steaming brew.

I took a careful sip. Smooth and creamy, caramel and cacao hit my tongue. The warmth slid down my throat, and with that first swallow of the morning, all tension oozed away.

"Nice to meet you, Wawira. This coffee is delicious!" I said.

"Why yes," she smiled. "Where do you think coffee first came from? Africa, of course. This coffee is from a local farm on the slopes of Mt. Meru. African coffee is the best."

I laughed. "I have a friend from Central America who would disagree with you."

"Would you like to try ugali for breakfast?" She motioned to a plate of cornmeal paste in the middle of the table. "Thanks to our new supplies that you brought, we also have bread and jam and fried eggs."

Imitating Maggie, I took a scoop of ugali with my fingers and plopped it on my plate. Shoving some in my mouth, it had the texture of ground-up rice. The taste resembled bland popcorn.

Mary Leakey joined us, sitting down at the table across from me. She peered out of large dark-framed glasses, perched above her aquiline nose.

"Good morning, ladies! Maggie, what are the plans for today?" she asked.

Maggie gave her a brilliant smile. "Good morning, Mary. I'm going to take Henrietta to the quarry this morning. To teach her the stratigraphy," she replied.

Mary Leakey was quite pretty, I thought. Laugh lines crinkled on the side of her eyes when she smiled. Her brown curly hair was cut short and parted on the side. She was dressed in long tan slacks, a brown shirt, maroon cardigan, and leather walking shoes.

Mary turned to me.

"Henrietta, did you sleep well last night?" she asked.

I swallowed the ugali. Thankfully, I had found my voice the previous evening. "Oh, yes, thank you. I'm very excited to be here."

"We are happy to have you," she said.

Maggie looked less than thrilled and stared at her plate.

"It's important that you learn the stratigraphy. Maggie will also show you our *Deinotherium*. A fossil elephant."

At that moment, Ray strode into the tent. "Wawira, coffee, please. I need coffee," he called. He came over and slipped into a chair.

"Good morning, everyone." He nodded at each of us. "I'll be taking some background shots today of the Gorge. Perhaps tomorrow I can do the shoot at the quarry if that fits your schedule?"

Mary answered. "Yes, that will be fine. We can all work on the elephant after the shoot. I'd like to finish extracting that skull this week."

She turned to me. "I was expecting an expert on fossil fish from the Smithsonian. You aren't exactly what I expected. You are here to work on the fish, correct?"

I replied. "Yes, I've worked on fish fossils for the past two summers. The museum might send another lab technician to help me with making the jackets and with transporting the fossils back to the States."

"Alright. If you can give us a few days working on the elephant, then Maggie and Kimaru will accompany you to the fish site after that."

"Yes, I'd love to work on the elephant skull too," I said. "Also, I was wondering if I can take samples for pollen analysis? I want to study the change in flora in the Gorge throughout the Pleistocene for my graduate work."

"Fascinating!" Mary replied. "That will add an exciting element to our work here. You can take samples at the quarry. The section is continuous there. Will you need help?"

Out of the corner of my eye, I could see Maggie roll her eyes.

"Maybe, if the section is too tall for me to reach."

"No worries," she said. "Kimaru can bring a ladder if you need one. But the way the quarry is terraced, you'll probably be able to reach all of the levels."

"Okay, thank you," I replied.

"The other diggers can also help you at the fish site. And if you have time at the end of your stay, I thought you might like some experience searching for new fossils. Maggie can help you with that as well."

A young boy meandered into the banda. I estimated him to be about twelve years old. He had the gangly gait of a boy growing into his arms and legs.

"This is my son, Philip," Mary said. He nodded shyly at us and grabbed a plate. "My other two sons will arrive later with Louis. If they both decide to come. They're away at school."

Louis was, of course, the famed Dr. Louis Leakey.

Two dalmatians trotted up to the table behind Philip. They settled down next to Mary.

"What are the dogs' names?" I asked.

"This is Sally and this is Victoria," she said.

I reached over and patted Victoria on the head. She stuck her nose on the table, looking for leftovers.

As soon as Mary, Philip and Ray meandered off, Maggie turned to me.

"Alright. Let's go," she said. "Be sure to fill your canteen from the cistern."

Wawira brought over two bagged lunches and handed them to us.

I thanked her. "I'll grab my hat and rock hammer too," I said.

As we walked back to our tent, the morning sun rose over the caldera to the east, coloring the sky a softened aquamarine. Our tent flap was unzipped.

"Oh no," Maggie said. "Did you zip the tent?"

"I thought I did. Maybe I didn't zip it all the way?" I said.

She frowned at me. "Wait here."

She pulled back the flap, ducked and entered the tent.

"Simon, get out of here!" she admonished.

A fuzzy gray monkey flew out of the tent. He tilted his simian face at me, called out an "Eep!" in surprise, and scampered toward the banda.

I slipped inside. All of our belongings were strewn around the tent.

"Be sure to fold up my clothes when you pick up yours. And next time, make sure the zipper is tucked into the top loop," Maggie said, sharply.

At least the monkey was welcoming.

CHAPTER 15

"Henrietta, I was working on a fossil fish, and it just came to me out of the blue!" My father, having worked all morning in the prep lab, entered his office wearing his dust-covered lab coat.

I looked up from my *Life Magazine* article on Ontogeny Recapitulates Phylogeny—the idea that an organism goes through its entire evolutionary sequence while an embryo—and squinted my eyes in puzzlement.

"What did, Dad?"

"Dr. Miller! You need to meet Dr. Miller! Next month he is coming here to give a lecture on an extinct shark—I believe it's called a '*Megalodon*'—fascinating, a huge specimen evidently—anyway—you need to meet with him. He is a professor at the College of William and Mary.

"That sounds fascinating. I'd love to go," I said. I chanted the taxonomy in my head since I knew a lot about fossil fish—Kingdom Animalia, Phylum Chordata, Class Chondrichthyes (sharks), Order....?

His next statement startled me from my concentration.

"I'll write to him and ask if we can talk to him afterward about their degrees, get a feel for their programs, that kind of thing. William and Mary is co-educational—they accept women. Would you want to speak with him?"

A hardball formed in the pit of my stomach. *Change.* Change was not something I embraced. In my heart, I knew I could not stay in my attic forever, but I had tried to ignore the inevitable.

Pasting on a smile, I said, "Excellent idea. What does that have to do with fossil fish?"

He looked at me with his brows knitted together, "What? Oh, my train of thought? Fish…fish are sharks…lecture…Dr. Miller… viola!" as if it were apparent.

Waiting with trepidation for the eminent lecturer from Williamsburg, I tried to decide what kind of audience he represented. A teacher who wouldn't want to hear my opinions? Or a colleague who would? How did one distinguish in this case?

The event was publicized throughout the Smithsonian, at nearby universities, and professional societies. Tickets, although without charge, were required to attend. My father was able to obtain two tickets, which was fortunate because I would never have gotten one on my own.

The day of the lecture arrived, having been billed as 'Taxonomy and Paleobiology of the Miocene *Carcharocles megalodon* of Virginia,' with a subheading stating, 'A lecture on the ferocious colossal brute unparalleled in these modern times.'

"Do you think he is anthropomorphizing a bit?" I smirked, whispering to my father and pointing to the subtitle as we passed the entrance poster. He smiled in response. The room was set up with chairs in a U-shape fronting a podium and screen. A slide projector sat in the middle. We trailed in behind several museum colleagues and took seats toward the back of the room. The primarily homogenous audience of men in suits and ties included few students and even fewer women. I was a subset inside a subset. The Geological Society of Washington was the only local society with liberal enough views to allow women entry.

Dr. Alexander Westmoreland, Secretary of the Smithsonian Institution, and my father's supervisor introduced the speaker. Dr. Westmoreland was tall and well-dressed, with a prominent nose and white hair held in place by a fair amount of hair tonic. "Ladies and gentlemen," he said. "I have the pleasure of introducing our esteemed speaker for today. I have been anticipating this lecture for weeks. As an ornithologist, I do not often hear about scientific research concerning sharks. And this shark seems to be one for the record books!"

He paused, and I noticed he had managed to mention his specialty in the introduction as well as the speaker's, a bit of self-promotion, I thought.

"Dr. Gerald Miller is today's speaker. He has been studying the *Carcharocles megalodon* for over ten years. Dr. Miller received his undergraduate and graduate degrees from Yale University. He is currently a Professor of Natural Sciences at the College of William and Mary, with collaborations with the Virginia Institute of Marine Science, where he studies both ancient and living sharks. Without further ado, please welcome Dr. Miller." Applause echoed across the room.

Dr. Miller took the stage. He was young and relatively short, with an elfin beard, no mustache, and a twinkle in his eye. Though he was dressed in a suit, he looked like he belonged on an Amish farm. "Good morning!" he boomed, like a minister in his home parish. "Welcome to the Miocene—20 million years ago, the lovely campus of the College of William and Mary was underwater. The carapaces of millions of scallop shells—*Pecten jeffersonius*—in all of the creek beds on campus attest to this fact."

On the screen behind him, he focused a slide of strata embedded with stacks of fossil scallop shells. "This is the Yorktown Formation; current research indicates it is Miocene in age, and within these beds are fossils of a carnivorous creature so large, so heinous, it would make even the whales swim away in terror." He paused for a second and stared right at me. "Of course, maybe I am guilty of anthropomorphizing." And he smiled.

My throat went dry, and I felt a blush forming across my face. Dr. Miller must have been behind me and heard my comment to my father about the lecture's advertisement. No one else glanced my way, and the lecture continued. The projector hummed and clacked as the slides advanced. Photographs of students digging in creeks and quarries, some holding fossils for the camera, augmented his story. Schematics of *megalodon* and photographs of modern sharks flashed on the screen. Samples of gigantic fossil teeth were passed around the audience.

Without Dr. Miller knowing, what I received from his lecture was complete confirmation. I was meant to achieve my goal. The time had arrived for me to explore, to dig, to discover. I felt it down to my bones, like a well-spring, shutting out my mother's mantra of 'paleontology is not for ladies.' My father's tutelage had given me the start I needed. I sensed Dr. Miller's enthusiasm propelling me forward. I needed to be brave enough to leave my home and my tutor, pack up my notebooks with my evaluations of other people's work and say goodbye to the safety of my museum corner.

After the lecture ended, my father and I approached Dr. Miller. "Dr. Miller, I'm Henry Ballantine. I wrote to you…" he said, reaching out his hand.

"Dr. Ballantine, of course. I've read your papers. It's a pleasure," Dr. Miller said, shaking hands.

"This is my daughter, Henrietta. She is interested in learning about William and Mary."

Dr. Miller turned to me. "Hello, Henrietta. I hear you are interested in natural history and geology. I hope you'll come down and see the college. We have a beautiful campus and a lot of opportunity for fieldwork," he said.

"What is the order?" I asked.

"I beg your pardon?" he seemed perplexed.

"The order. The taxonomic order. Of *megalodon*," I said.

He stared at me. *Was it really such an odd question? He was the expert, wasn't he?* I added helpfully, "I know the kingdom and phylum, obviously, and the class must be Chondrichthyes for a shark."

"Oh, right, the taxonomy. Order and family are Lamniformes and *Lamnidae*, the same as the great white shark."

I tried out the words. "Lamniformes and *Lamnidae*." I gave him a big smile. "Thank you, Professor."

My father looked a bit pained for some reason.

Dr. Miller gave me an appraising look.

"You know, Henrietta," he said, after a moment, "I think you should definitely apply to our program. You would fit right in."

I doubted that. I did not fit in anywhere. But it was kind of him to say so.

CHAPTER 16

MIDDLE PLEISTOCENE, THE RIFT VALLEY, AFRICA

The wind whooshed her name. "Ifa, Ifa". Trekking with the three men, Ifa scoured the horizon for danger. Her hunting stick grasped in her hand, a pelt filled with smoked meat and stone tools burdened her back. She kept pace with the men, refusing to show weakness, her brow furrowed, heart racing. The memories of her sister's forlorn face, her mother's choked voice, her own farewell tears played in her head. She pushed them into the recesses of her mind. She had made her decision. Sunlight glanced off the endless stalks of swaying grain, the seeded heads bowing heavily. Herds of wildebeest and giant crested elephants intermingled nearby, snorting and trumpeting. Spiral horned antelope leaped daintily among the blood lilies.

In the afternoon, cool breezes increased, and darkening clouds scuttled across the sky. The heavens opened and rains pelted down. Soon drenched, droplets ran off Ifa's nose and trickled from her hair. Shivering, she pushed forward in the torrent.

After several sundowns, the band approached the base of the massive caldera. Legs sore, lungs exhausted, they halted at dusk. The steep forested slope towered over them. Jagged rockfalls of ancient lava blocks nestled at the foot of this dormant volcano. Making camp among the boulders, the trekkers chewed on smoked meat and settled in for the night. Without the means to create a fire, Ifa huddled next to Kho, wary of hungry predators both beyond and within the group. She shirked away when she saw the men's hungry gazes. Kho crouched in front of her, grimacing and baring his teeth at the signs of aggression from his kinsman. Ifa was unsure if the taunts were real or in jest.

After daybreak, the group skirted along the mountain's base. In the distance, two volcanic cones pierced the clouds, dwarfed in size by the adjacent caldera. Kho motioned toward the farthest one.

"Home," he said.

Ifa's heart plummeted. *So far away.*

With the morning sunshine, numerous creatures appeared from their hideaways in the craggy rocks. Ifa pointed to a den and called out, her mimicry so precise a bat-eared fox appeared at the entrance. Upon spotting her, it yipped and ducked back inside. Crossing a pile of dismembered birds' feet, the trekkers gazed upward to discover a steppe eagle's burrow high above their heads. They avoided snake holes and circumvented honey badger lairs. Ifa, spying a thicket of low bushes along the slope, climbed up to retrieve two handfuls of red berries. She carried them back down and handed them to the men. They tucked the berries into their cheeks, savoring the sweet taste, then spit out the inner bean and tough fibers as they trekked along. The fruit invigorated them and they picked up their pace.

Leaving the caldera behind, the two volcanoes still ahead, the group again hiked across open savanna. In some places, the grasses were trampled, easily navigated. In others, the reeds topped their shoulders. Progressing single file, Uka, the eldest, led, followed by younger Yanso on his sturdy legs. Ifa and Kho followed. Uka parted the tall grass and spotted a herd of giant ratite ostriches ahead. As tall as two men, the birds guarded an elliptical egg-filled pit. Two females incubated the nest, while others poked through the grass, swallowing grasshoppers. The males raised their elongated necks, beady eyes on alert for predators. The largest male perceived human scents. His neck bulged and his wing plumage swelled as he flapped his wings and boomed an avian warning. All ostrich eyes turned at once. The humans, approaching too closely, fell back. Too late. The large male rushed at Uka.

"Run!"Uka cried.

Kho grabbed Ifa's hand, and they streaked away in tandem, just as the ostrich burst through the reeds. Yanso followed at their heels.

Aiming for Uka, the giant ostrich raised his talons and slashed. More ostriches joined in the tumult. Uka fell to the ground, his anguished cries echoing in Ifa's ears. She turned her head, eyes brimming.

"Don't look," Kho said, pulling her along.

Panting, sweating, the three ran on until Uka's voice no longer reached them. They huddled together, squatting on the ground, with sticks raised. Kho grabbed his hand axe. But the ostriches did not follow.

Waiting until dusk, they crawled back toward the nest. Kho signaled for Ifa to stay back as he and Yanso crept to Uka's body. Gashed and pecked, Uka laid on the ground. Dead. They shooed off the vultures. Ants had arrived, devouring the corpse. The scent of blood and birds intermingled, a certain draw for hyenas. The band retreated before the predators arrived.

After many weary nightfalls, Yanso, Ifa, and Kho approached the flank of the farthest mountain and began to climb. The acacia and wild olive trees thickened. The air chilled and silenced except for birdsong. The herds' noises were dampened by the forest. Branches scraped against their arms as they navigated around a thicket of thorn bushes, but the band continued upward, calf muscles stretching until Kho called out.

"Oooo!" A shout of joy.

Ifa glimpsed a hazy mirage of mounded structures through the leaves. Her new home. Yanso picked up the pace. With a pounding heart, Ifa forced her feet forward.

The huts were larger and more permanent than those of Ifa's tribe. Frameworks of sticks, bent and woven, covered in hides, were built into the lava blocks. Human jackal dens. As the trekkers drew closer, women appeared, waving and shouting. Children shrieked and babies startled and wailed. Rushing forward, a woman embraced Yanso, welcoming him home. He reached down and lifted a young boy into the air. An older woman approached Kho, arms open.

The tribe looked past Ifa, as if she were mist, searching.

"Uka?" a woman asked.

Kho shook his head, regret across his face. "Ratite attack," he said, pantomiming.

The women watched his proclamation, and joy turned to shock. A woman began to moan, and the others joined her, pulling on their braided hair. A dissonance of mourning.

Ifa stood back. The women appeared strangely ornamented. Chalky white mud slathered their bodies, bone shards pierced their ears. Their faces were painted with yellow ochre, the color now streaked with tears. Pieces of vine and flowers stuck from braids in their hair.

Amid the sorrow, Kho pulled Ifa forward toward the older woman. "Kalama." Kho introduced his mother.

Short and broad, with a flat nose and jutting brow ridges, Kalama tilted her head to study Ifa. Ifa tried to smile. She arrived unadorned. Naked. And brought sadness with her. A harbinger of bad luck.

A bellow sounded as a wizened old man emerged from his hut, summoned by the women's cries. The patriarch. Bent in stature with bulging swollen knees, he nonetheless exuded an air of authority. He limped toward Yanso and Kho, clasping them on the shoulders. Each dipped his head in respect.

"Uka?"

Kho shook his head. "With the Spirits."

The old man sighed and nodded.

Kho grabbed Ifa's arm and pushed her in front of the patriarch. "Ifa," he said.

Ifa dipped her head as the men had, looking at her feet. The patriarch stared for a long moment, grabbed her chin, raised her face, and turned it from side to side. His breath on her neck, his gnarled hands ran down her arms. He grasped her at the hips and bumped against her with his body, grunting a remark she did not understand. Kho smiled slightly. Ifa's heart pounded and bile rose in her throat. The women, now silent, stared at her with suspicious eyes, deep frowns etching their faces. With a nod to Kho, the patriarch offered his approval.

But that would not mean acceptance.

CHAPTER 17

The next Fall I was bound for the College of William and Mary. As my father packed my belongings into the Chevy, my mother hugged me and managed to squeeze out a few tears.

"Please write, Henrietta, and let us know how you're doing."

I promised I would, and we were off, my father and I, two rolling stones, tumbling down Interstate 95. Of course, much of the drive contained a geology lesson.

"We're driving right on top of the Fall Line here, Henrietta. It's the zone where the edge of crystalline rock from the Piedmont dives below and is buried by Coastal Plain sediments. We'll pass by Fredericksburg and Richmond, which both sit on the line. In colonial times, ships couldn't navigate any farther up the rivers because of the waterfalls, so the cities were built right on the Fall Line," he said. "When you get to Williamsburg, you won't see any rocks. The only hills will be ancient scarps that were once shorelines. All you'll find are unconsolidated sediments. And young fossils, Tertiary age."

The trip seemed interminable, yet my heart pounded upon arrival. Turning in front of Barrett Hall, where I would take up residence for the year, my dad parallel parked along the side street. My eyes were drawn to the imposing brick women's dormitory which faced Jamestown Road, with its elegant portico, white columns, and stately cupola. My hall was Barrett 3rd West—lucky us having to lug all of my possessions up three long flights of stairs. As exhausting as I found the physical moving, the emotional tug felt much worse.

After depositing my suitcase and belongings in my new, barren room, I walked with my father down the steps and out the front door to say goodbye. We passed another freshman girl moving in, she and her parents crushed under a load of boxes. Outside, two squirrels chased each other across the lawn, springing up a live oak tree, as we traversed the driveway toward the brick sidewalk. I glimpsed more girls down the road, arriving for orientation, car trunks open, doors slamming, nervous laughter. My dad and I crossed the street to reach our car. He turned and hugged me.

"Henrietta, I know you'll do great things here. Just remember you're as smart as everyone else. Probably smarter." He climbed into the car and gave a brief wave. The car pulled away, becoming smaller and smaller as he left me. Alone on the edge of the street, looking down, chin to my chest, I fought back tears. A single pebble caught in a whirlpool while the other pebble meandered back to the ocean.

Without glancing up, I stepped into the road to cross back toward the dorm. A speeding engine roared, close and sudden. Startled, I raised my head. An unseen hand yanked me backward, knocking the breath from my lungs as a car raced by, inches from where I stood. Eyes wide, my hand clutched at my chest as I gasped for air. The car turned onto Richmond Road without slowing.

Heart racing, I turned to thank the person who had pulled me from the street.

No one was there. The athletic field stretched behind me, empty.

If I had a guardian angel, this had been her. Did I believe in such things? I didn't think so. Did I?

Home of a nation, capital of a Commonwealth, at least for a time, Williamsburg was a quaint, restored colonial village, with the college on one end of Duke of Gloucester Street and the Capitol on the other end. To the students, it was DOG street, one mile in length, and a stout walk on a beautiful day if one avoided the manure piles from the horses and didn't mind the cobblestones. From the inside of the cupola on the roof of Barrett, one could look across the road to the Bookstore and the Campus Center, where we ate our meals, east to the historic Brafferton and Wren Buildings, and north to Ewell Hall, where all students were required to take at least one music class.

My new roommate, Miss Delilah Tompkins, had sailed the seven seas due to her father's employment in the State Department. Well, not quite. But compared to me, raised in my suburban home, she was well-traveled and lived in Central America, so seemed worldly and sophisticated. She smoked unfiltered cigarettes and drank tequila, neither of which had been available to me, which made her more exotic. She was a short girl with scads of curly auburn hair, which she tried to tame under hats, bandanas, or headbands, to no avail.

In the mornings, she brewed coffee in a little pot on her desk, the beans sent to her by her parents currently stationed in Guatemala. I smashed my head under my pillow as she would loudly hand-grind the beans each morning. Although I loved the smell, I had yet to acquire a taste for coffee, with my previous exposure being only watered-down Maxwell House—'*Good to the last drop*'—with lots of sugar and creamer. I'm sure I seemed a total bore to Delilah, but she never said so. A natural leader among the girls in our hall, perhaps she saw me as malleable. She was a magpie, and I was a little wren nesting in her shade.

Our dorm room was part of a suite, meaning it connected to another dorm room by the bathroom we all shared—four girls with one shower, one sink, and one commode. Our suitemates were as different from each other as Delilah and me. Debbie McAlister was a sweet-faced, tiny sprite with a quick mind and a beau at the

University of Virginia. We quickly nicknamed her 'Little Debbie,' as if she were a snack cake. After Delilah, she was the most sophisticated of the four of us, having an eclectic taste in modern jazz. Her roommate was a Bible-thumping lumpy brick named Carolyn Kloister, who was dating an older man from her home church in Richmond—older being a relative term. I never knew Johnny's age, but he was both balding and a huge stick-in-the-mud. He would visit Carolyn on Sunday afternoons, and they would sit in the first-floor lounge and read from the Bible together. Not that I had anything against Bible reading—*to each his own.*

It was still the 1950s, so rules and chaperones kept us out of trouble. There was a house mother, a stodgy older woman who lurked in the halls, a ten p.m. curfew, and resident assistants who took turns sitting at the front door checking girls in and out after dinner. The resident assistant for our hall was an uptight twig with blonde pincurls named Sarah. Sarah wallpapered our hall with hand-drawn signs espousing the dorm rules, the most notorious of which was a sketch of two students clasping hands with a big X through it and the caption 'No PDA on Campus.' PDA stood for 'public displays of affection.' Delilah called her 'the nun' behind her back.

After my isolating childhood, living in a dormitory made me feel like a Vienna sausage in a can. Girls congregated in the sitting rooms, in the hallways, in the laundry room. They hung around the payphone, which was, thankfully, at the other end of our hall. With Delilah being a social butterfly, it seemed there were always girls cluttering up our room. When the mob became overwhelming, I headed to the library. The library's murmured quiet soothed me like a lullaby, and I spent many afternoons in my corner carrel, paying homage to my books.

I took to my self-imposed daily routine like a fish to water, which seemed appropriate since fish had gotten me there in the first place. After enduring the morning coffee grinding ritual, I dressed and headed to the Campus Center for breakfast, attended my classes, then returned for lunch. I did not mind eating alone—I always had a book. Sometimes groups of girls from Barrett would invite me to eat with them. I forced myself to join these informal bands, listening to the ebb and flow of the conversation, rarely contributing, but eventually settling into the companionship. After the tray-clattering, chatter-filled cacophony of lunch, I headed back to class or the library, depending on the day.

The disciplines of geology and biology were lumped together in the Natural Sciences department. I hoped Dr. Miller would be my official advisor, but I was assigned to Dr. Zaharias, an older professor who was a small mammal specialist. A short, husky man with a booming voice and a bulbous nose, his office was full of skeletons and taxidermic critters. Fist-sized skulls with protruding rodent incisors collected dust on high shelves. Perched on his desk, a stuffed chipmunk quizzically studied me with creepy fixed eyes. At our first meeting, Dr. Zaharias appeared too busy to deal with me, looked me briefly up and down, and barked, "So you want to be a paleontologist, I hear?"

"Yes, sir," I said. "My father is a paleontologist, and I've been studying with him..."

"Yes, yes, I know of your father," he said. "Frankly, most students who graduate with a geology emphasis either head out west to work in mining, or to Texas to the oil patch. Neither of those industries will hire a woman."

He leaned back and folded his arms. Even the chipmunk seemed to mock me.

"I plan to go on to graduate school," I said.

He continued as if he had not heard me. "Not many women decide to major in natural sciences. It's a difficult course of study. Why don't we see how you do in your classes before you declare a major? That's probably the best plan of action for you."

Signing my form, he waved me out. I loitered in the hallway, my head hanging down, staring at the paper. Another obstacle to surmount, but I was determined to earn the grades to prove him wrong.

After my epiphany of 'I want to explore, to dig, to discover,' I ascertained that life as a lowly freshman resembled my years of museum study. There were readings, memorizations, and papers. I studied geology, calculus, English, beginning music theory—knowing nothing but how to read the treble clef—and, God help me, Russian. While placed in third-year Russian classes, I found that while I spoke adequate Russian, my reading and writing abilities were lacking. Cyrillic became my torturer and catching up required much of my time.

"Henrietta, enough with all these Russian scribbles all over the room," Delilah whined at me, pointing to the index cards with Russian vocabulary words that I had stuck all over our walls. "We need to do something fun this weekend!"

"Delilah, do you know how many nouns I have to learn to spell this week in Cyrillic?" I groaned. "I've got to study this weekend."

"Can you spell 'fun' in Russian?" she asked, tilting her head and giving me a mocking grin.

I looked at her and burst out laughing. It was impossible not to love her irreverent sarcasm.

As late summer turned to Fall, it began to rain. And it rained. And rained. Delilah joked we could build an ark, and launch it from our third-floor window. My bobby socks, along with my loafers, and often the bottom half of my skirts, clung to my legs, perpetually soaked. Williamsburg's topography resembled a pancake and all of that rain did not run off but formed semi-permanent stagnant puddles. Walking to class was like skirting land mines. The monsoons made any cloudless days feel precious. Students could wander around Colonial Williamsburg—we called it 'CW' being insiders—and enter any of the buildings or gardens for which the tourists needed a ticket. The Governor's Palace's gardens, with its boxwood maze, was one of my favorite escapes on these dry days. I perched on the grassy knoll overlooking the pond. In between reading my textbook and taking notes, I watched the turtles sunning peacefully on lily pads and kept an eye out for the huffing, aggressive swans. For some reason, they reminded me of home.

———◆———

By January, I developed a taste for Delilah's coffee, the smooth creaminess of the Guatemalan beans outshining the pabulum found in the Campus Center. But on this first day of Spring classes, the earlier warmth from the brew was forgotten as I rushed across the campus, late, to Bryan Hall. A balmy morning, the scuttling clouds overhead portended the imminent arrival of a cold front. A northwest wind wafted the pungent fumes from the West Point paper mill over the campus in a choking fug.

Hurrying down a corridor on the second floor, jitters of anticipation unsettled my stomach. This semester's geology course, Historical Geology, would be my first class offered only to science majors. I peered into the classroom, hoping to slide unobtrusively into a desk near the door.

"Hello, Henrietta," boomed a voice from the front of the room. Dr. Miller would be our professor for the course. "Come on in!"

I stood frozen at the door frame. Heads turned simultaneously to stare at me. *All men.*

Nodding at Dr. Miller, I slipped into an empty desk. The chilly room felt airless, confining. Muttered comments reached my ears from a few seats away.

"I didn't know this was going to be hysterical geology."

"Or hysterectomy geology." The comment brought forth a cluster of snickers.

Dr. Miller looked over at them. "What was that, gentlemen?" he asked.

No one answered. Several of the young men hung their heads, smirking into their desks and giving sideways glances to their buddies. As time went on, I would ascertain that freshmen males, collectively, had the maturity of a troop of chimpanzees, and were best ignored. But that day, as the new class began, I felt a slow burn of humiliation behind my eyes. With a lump in my throat, I straightened my spine, opened my notebook, and stared straight ahead.

"Here is your syllabus for the course," Dr. Miller said. "Please pass them around. You can see my office hours on the top. If I'm not in my office during those times, look for me in the lab. The textbook is listed. There will be a mid-term, final exam, and a research project. Note that there will be fieldwork required on Saturday mornings, starting in March, so plan your weekends accordingly."

"Will it be every weekend, sir?" someone asked.

"As many Saturdays as you will need to complete your research project," he replied. "Now, who can read the course description aloud for us? Henrietta, will you do that, please?"

I froze. My jaw clamped shut. *Concentrate*, I told myself. *Open your mouth.*

I cleared my throat.

"Historical Geology is the study of the history of the earth and its inhabitants," I read, my voice scratchy. "Geologic features such as rocks and fossils are used to interpret and date past events. The evolution of life will be studied through the geologic time periods."

"Excellent. So let's begin."

With a book in one hand, he grabbed a stool from the corner of the classroom and set it in front of us. Perching himself on it, he opened the book.

"Reading from the Revised Standard Version of the Holy Bible, starting with Genesis, Chapter 1, verse 1," he said.

"In the beginning, God created the heaven and the earth. And the earth was without form and void, and darkness was upon the face of the deep. And the Spirit of God moved upon the face of the waters. And God said, 'Let there be light' and there was light...."

My mind flashed to my elementary Sunday School classroom, to that week's accompanying worksheet. I visualized the image, clear as day, of the Biblical creation depicted as a globe surrounded by a monstrous sunrise. My logical mind had colored the sunrise as if refracted and reflected through droplets of water, using the colors of the rainbow—red, orange, yellow, green, blue, indigo, violet. I remembered my teacher's incredulous face as I explained the electromagnetic spectrum to her. God as a sunrise resonated with me at that time. I wondered if perhaps I was more akin to ancient sun-worshippers than to my fellow Presbyterians.

I snapped back as Dr. Miller continued reading, through Genesis, Chapter 1, the Lord creating the waters, the land, the seas, the grass, herbs, fruit trees, seeds. On to the separation of days from nights, the stars placed in the firmament, the creation of the great whales and every living creature in the waters and every winged fowl. Then cattle and creeping things and beasts of the earth. Finally man and woman.

He finished with verse 31: "And God saw everything that He had made, and behold, it was very good. And the evening and the morning were the sixth day."

Pausing, Dr. Miller raised his face to the class, closing the book. "Any questions?" he asked.

We all stared at him.

What was that?

No one moved. I became aware of the ticking of the wall clock. "No?" he asked, waiting for a response.

Silence reigned.

"Well, it's going to be a long semester then," he said. "I expect you all to think about what I just read. Look it up and read it again. Then read chapter one in your textbook. And come back next time ready to be students and not just recipients. Class dismissed."

The next day, after an evening of perplexity, I waited outside Dr. Miller's office. He strolled in a few minutes before his office hours began.

"Henrietta, nice to see you. Come on in," he said, unlocking this door.

Dr. Miller's office resembled the aftermath of a tornadic storm. Cardboard boxes of *Pecten* shells littered the floor. Heaping stacks of papers and publications tilted on his desk, threatening to spill over. Books crammed willy-nilly on shelves with no apparent organization. Overlapping geologic maps and cross-sections papered the walls in push-pinned mosaics.

Grabbing a stack of periodicals from an office chair, he set them on the floor and indicated that I should take a seat.

"How are you doing, Henrietta? Are you ready for the Spring semester?" he asked.

"Dr. Miller, I'm confused about yesterday's class. We aren't going to be studying religion, are we? I wasn't sure what you wanted from us when you asked for questions. I want to be prepared for next time. Are we debating the truth of the Bible?"

He studied me from behind his desk.

"Directly to the point as usual, huh?" he said with a smile. "No, our class will not be a religion class. You read the course description, after all."

"Then why start with the Bible?"

"I could have started with another ancient text. The Egyptian Book of the Dead perhaps? Hinduism's Rig Veda?"

I stared down at my fingernails, momentarily stumped.

"Why start with a religious text at all?" I asked. "Isn't this science? I just don't understand."

"Why indeed?" he said. "You know, there are no wrong answers here, Henrietta. My job is not to lecture to you, hand-feeding facts like crumbs to pigeons. Of course, I'll be doing some lecturing in class. But my job is to make you think. What did ancient people believe about the formation of the earth and its creatures? How does this compare to what the fossil record tells us? Does that help you?"

Why did he not tell us that in the first place? I guess that was supposed to be the thinking part.

The next day, the cold front had arrived, a sleeting rain pelting down. After sliding across campus on a layer of icy slush, my useless umbrella pushing into the wind, I arrived at the classroom. My soaked shoes and knee socks clung to my legs, and my coat drooped like a soggy bog. Shrugging it off my shoulders, I draped the coat over the back of my desk chair. The men in the classroom looked equally cold and bedraggled.

Dr. Miller swung in the door, grabbed the stool, and positioned himself in the front once again.

"Good morning! I realize it is a terrible morning outside," he said. "Let's try to shake off the weather and put our minds to work. Now that you have read chapter one in your textbook, an overview of earth's formation, what parallels can we see with the Genesis account that I read last time?"

I hesitated. No one else jumped in, so I began.

"It says in the Bible that in the beginning, the earth was without form and void," I said. "Astronomers think the earth was made of bits of matter that accumulated due to the gravitational force. That could be one parallel."

"Excellent. What else?" Dr. Miller replied.

Silence.

I waited.

"What about life?" he asked.

I replied, "The Bible states that vegetation came first. And paleontologists think that photosynthesizers evolved first and formed the atmosphere."

Several of the male students turned to stare at me. Their bulging eyes reminded me of the carp in Uncle Al's fish tank.

"Yes! We'll be discussing the earth's early atmosphere next week. What else?"

An awkward quiet pervaded. Sleet tapped on the windows. The dampness of my coat collar seeped into the back of my sweater. I leaned forward.

"The living creatures are first mentioned as arriving in the waters, and that is where life first evolved," I said.

The stares now appeared a bit hostile.

"Very good, Henrietta. Anyone else care to join today's discussion? he asked.

"Maybe the Big Bang was on Day One?" someone replied.

He nodded. "Yes, many religions' creation stories explain the universe with a sudden appearance. What about discrepancies?"

"There are a lot of…" I began.

One of the men interrupted. "The sun and the moon are created after vegetation. That's a pretty big discrepancy."

"Yes, there is light before the sun appears," another chirped in.

"And the stars appear…" I said.

Another student interrupted me. "All of earth's animals are created at the same time. There's no mention of evolution."

And so it went. Every utterance I tried was truncated. I leaned back and folded my arms.

Finally, Dr. Miller stood up. "Our time is up for today. Excellent discussion."

For whom?

"Next week we'll start chapter two, the Precambrian," he said. "Come prepared to discuss the various hypotheses about how life began."

The men flowed around me, out the door, like sand grains in a stream avoiding an unwelcome obstacle. One bumped my shoulder as he left, with nary an apology. Pulling on my sodden coat, I heard their none-too-subtle comments in the hallway.

"What a show-off."

"Good thing we put a stop to that."

"Yeah, it was almost a hen show. Get it? *Hen*-show?"

I guess I should be thrilled that they bothered to learn my name.

CHAPTER 18

Decorum dictated that women wear skirts or dresses to classes, meals, the library, church, and on dates. The college dress code reinforced this, allowing women to wear slacks, outside of the dorm, only on weekends. Fieldwork began in mid-March as the weather warmed and on that first Saturday, I pulled on dungarees, rolled up at the ankles, a pair of mud-stained women's tennis shoes, and a wide-brimmed straw hat I had purchased at Roses 5&10 in Merchant Square. Instead of resembling the young geologist I aimed to become, I probably looked more like a scarecrow.

In front of Bryan Hall, standing apart from the fraternal order of resentful classmates, I waited in the early morning dew for Dr. Miller to arrive. He pulled up in his ancient 10-seater jalopy. We jumped in, tossing our gear and shovels in the back, and off we rambled.

The cliffs along the James River were located on private property, with plans for future development into an exclusive golf community. The owner gave Dr. Miller carte blanche when it came to admitting students, even as we ran up and down the bluffs with our feet eroding the muddy strata into the James. The cliffs were, as my father had explained, composed of sediments, with not a rock in sight. The unconsolidated sands and clays of the Yorktown

Formation were choked with fossils, mostly bivalve and gastropod shells, bleached white when exposed to the sun. The shells were composed of their original calcareous material, so they did not look like fossils to me. I was disappointed and found them rather unimpressive. The fossils I had seen at the museum were petrified, and those remains looked like they had withstood the test of time. These looked like seashells from a modern beach. Finding out that they were millions of years old barely appeased me. But one worked with what one had.

Each of us selected a research project based on the Yorktown fossils. My project started small, literally, since I decided to do a paleoenvironmental study of *Venericardia granulata,* a thumb-sized clam that was, as far as I could tell, ubiquitous throughout the Yorktown Formation. Carnivorous snails had found these clams to be tasty and the shells were often marred by round boreholes or as Dr. Miller quipped, "they were bored to death."

After working all morning on our various projects, we sat in a loose group on the grass to eat our lunches. A variety of breakfast left-overs were stuffed into our knapsacks—apples, muffins, hard-boiled eggs, anything portable. I remained contentedly on the periphery of the group, and although no one particularly welcomed me, the snide comments seemed to have quieted. I was like a marble pillar, noticed yet ignored.

By April, I had accumulated hundreds of tiny shells. I gathered up my bounty, bags labeled according to stratigraphic zones, and carried them across campus to the dorm. That evening, after spreading newspapers on my desk, I carefully strewed the carapaces across the paper.

Delilah, ensconced at her desk with her philosophy textbook, looked up.

"What on earth are you doing, Henrietta?" she asked.

Holding a set of calipers in one hand, and a shell in the other, I glanced at her over my wire-rimmed glasses.

"Measuring clams," I said.

Cigarette smoke wafted upward from her ashtray as she studied me like a lab specimen.

"Fascinating," she said. "Maybe tomorrow we can go to the Sunken Garden and watch grass grow."

Although *Venericardia* was not a particularly thrilling animal, I wasn't exactly bored to death with it since I drew some interesting conclusions based on my admittedly limited study. I detected an overall increase in clam carapace size from the bottom of the Yorktown Formation to the top. As the sediments became younger, the organism had evolved to become consistently larger—about twenty percent larger. This small study whetted my appetite for collecting and analyzing data. In my final paper, I shared my conclusions with Dr. Miller, and although he praised my efforts, he shelved my results in the jam-packed labyrinth of his office. Perhaps some archeologist would discover it one day, behind the jars of whalebone shards and shark teeth, and under the crates of whelks. Still, I had witnessed evolution along the tranquil shores of the James River. I considered it a beautiful confirmation.

CHAPTER 19

1961, Olduvai Gorge, Tanganyika, Africa

A short hike from basecamp brought us to a steep, excavated outcrop. The Leakey Quarry. A staircase of flat levels and sheer cliffs revealed the distinctly colored earth layers and clearly defined contacts. Maggie led me over to the base.

"The strata here at Olduvai Gorge are divided into four beds." She pointed at the bottom level with a stick, her voice flat. "This lowermost bed, known as Bed I, is about 60 meters thick and is early Pleistocene in age. We've discovered a lot of mammal fossils in this layer."

"It sounds like you've given this speech before," I ventured.

She nodded. "Yes, it's part of my stipend. To show guests around. I try to do my research in-between visits."

We wandered over to a pile of half-excavated bones spread over the ground.

"Here's the skeleton of the elephant that Mary mentioned. It's a *Deinotherium*. This genus had no upper tusks but had tusks in the lower jaw that pointed back and downward. You can see part of the enamel here." She pointed at a cylindrical shape in the dirt. "The curious thing about these elephant bones is that they look like they may have been broken and scratched as if gouged by stone tools to dig out the marrow. And we've found primitive tools around the skeleton and in its stomach cavity.

"Do you think the elephant was killed by early man?" I asked.

"Either killed by man or butchered by him. We still don't know if the hominids from Bed I were hunters or scavengers."

She grabbed several rocks from a sieve. Fist-sized, the stones had a few knicks along one side.

"These are the choppers and cutting tools found around the elephant. They are examples of the oldest Paleolithic tools. They're known as Oldowan technology and were first recognized by Louis as being manmade. Being from Kenya, he'd collected them since he was a child. Other anthropologists searched all over the gorge for tools but were looking for flint. They had preconceived notions of what the tools would look like. But here, in Olduvai, there is no flint."

I held one of the choppers in my hand. If I found it on the ground, I would not have recognized it as anything except a rock.

"These 'pebble tools' are made from quartzite, basalt, or other volcanic rocks. They can be found in Bed I and the lower part of Bed II," she said.

As I held the smooth stone with a sharp edge, in my hand, I tried to project myself back to the early Pleistocene when survival depended on this technology. Perhaps I would have starved. How had early man confronted and killed an elephant with only these tools? Or had an already-dead elephant been butchered with them?

"Bed II sits above Bed I. It is about 30 meters thick and consists of several formations, separated by an unconformity, or buried erosional surface. Below this missing time datum, we find Oldowan industry tools. Above the unconformity, the tools change and become much more sophisticated," she continued.

She reached in a different sieve and passed two stones to me. They appeared chipped and faceted. As I held the tools, the flaked edges scraped across my hand.

"These are hand-axes and cleavers. You can see the sharp edges around these tools. These are known as Acheulean industry tools."

"Wow, these edges are really sharp," I said.

"Yes, even after being buried for one and half million years," Maggie said, nodding.

She continued her instruction, her British accent mesmerizing. "Bed II is middle Pleistocene in age. In Bed II, the mammals we find have become quite large. There is a giant antelope, a giraffe with a flatter head and longer horns than today's, and hippos twice the size of today's hippo, with elevated eye sockets on top of their head. We've found fossils of a massive lion, wildebeest, leopards, and hyenas. The existence of hyenas is probably why the fossils of early man are so scarce," she said.

The taxidermied animals in the Mammal Hall flashed back to me. The hippo's teeth and hyenas' grins appeared in my mind. My face flushed in the morning heat. I wiped my brow.

"Beds I and II consist of volcanic ash and lava flows, intermingled with fluvial sediments, as streams flowed down from volcanoes. The streams drained into an alkaline lake occupying the bottom of the gorge. We've found lots of fish fossils from the lake beds. You'll be working at that site. We've already dug out a few for you to take back to the museum," she said.

"That's great, thank you. I know my father will be excited to get them," I said.

"Your father?"

"Yes. My father is a fish expert. At the Smithsonian."

"Oh, I see. Interesting," she said, with something in her tone I could not quite interpret. After a moment she continued her litany.

"Next are Beds III and IV. Combined they can reach about 30 meters thick, but they are only distinct to the east of here. Here in the quarry, they comprise that top bed, up there, and consist of stream deposits. Bed III dates to the late Pleistocene."

I stared up toward the top of the quarry.

"Are you interested in the different genera of hominids? Or are you just interested in fish and pollen?" Maggie asked.

"Oh, yes, I'm very interested in early man."

She sighed. "Ok then. Just last summer, toward the bottom of Bed I, Mary discovered the *Zinj* skull."

My smile radiated across my face. The exhilaration of actually being there, knee-deep at the site of these rare finds, could not be matched by any classroom discussion.

"Yes," I said. "We studied her find in my anthropology class."

"I guess the news is even reaching the American universities," she said, lifting one eyebrow. "*Zinj* has a small braincase, a large sagittal crest, a deep face, and massive chewing teeth. Mary and Louis named him *Zinjanthropus boisei*, a new australopithecine. He was found at a site thought to be a 'living floor,' meaning a place where early man camped and butchered carcasses of animals near the lake."

She continued, "After *Zinj*, by the end of last year, the Leakeys made several more discoveries in Bed I. They found some teeth and skull fragments, hand bones, leg bones, and foot bones. Everyone's very excited about Louis' discovery of a massive skull at the top of Bed II. It has brow ridges but a substantial brain capacity. The Leakeys are still studying this specimen, but for now, he is being called *Chellean Man*."

I nodded, picturing photos from *National Geographic Magazine* in my mind.

"This summer, the team is focusing on Bed I. I know you're here for the fossil fish, but as Mary said, Ray wants to photograph us digging. You need to be included in the photos since you're from the National Museum. Publicity, you know?"

"What do you mean?"

"When more scientists get involved in the work, more people hear about us. A future sponsor might see that the Smithsonian is involved, which will lend credibility to the project. There's a chance that person will want to become a benefactor to the dig."

"I never thought about that aspect before."

"Yes, drumming up funding can be dodgy." We walked over to the elephant fossil. "When we work on the *Deinotherium*, I'll show you what to do and make sure you don't ruin anything. The bones are fragile and you have to work meticulously. And when we go out in the field to search for fossils…don't get your hopes up. It takes practice to find anything."

I clamped my jaw shut and heaved an inward sigh of frustration. I had hoped for other women's support, not indifference. Maggie considered me a burden rather than a colleague. Perhaps I would win her over. But I was determined that her lack of acceptance would not impede my mission. Or my professionalism.

CHAPTER 20

The summer after my Freshman year, I returned home to Arlington. Nothing had changed, and yet, as a college girl, much had, at least internally. No longer under my parents' thumbs but still living in their house, I felt less accommodating toward my mother's moods. Still, I had little desire to branch out except to my beloved museum. When my father announced he had procured me an internship for the summer, I figuratively leaped with excitement.

"You won't be paid much, Henrietta, but you'll be doing some preparatory work for Dr. Falcone. You remember him, don't you?" he asked. "He studies microfossils. You'll learn how to sieve the samples, prepare them, and how to select them under the microscope to make slides."

"Yes, of course, I remember him. Thank you so much! I know you must have gone out on a limb for me, and I won't let you down," I said.

My father brushed off my words. "He's happy for you to be working for him. You know, Henrietta, several women in Australia have made a name for themselves studying microfossils. Initially, they had many critics but now their work is widely used in the oil industry."

My heart swelled with gratitude at his encouragement.

Once again, the mighty elephant in the museum rotunda raised its trunk in welcome. I skirted around it and headed to the creaking back stairs. Descending to the museum basement, I entered the immense preparatory lab, my new home for the summer. Wooden work tables with overhanging winches resembled oversized carnival claw machines. Tools ranging from rock saws to dental picks, sieves and shakers, magnifiers and microscopes gleamed from shelves and cabinets. Along the back wall, wooden desks were arranged between sinks and fume hoods for acids and organic compounds.

To me, the men who worked in the lab as professional preparators appeared as old as fossils themselves. Most months they did the slow, meticulous work of extracting fossils from the encasing rocks and preparing them for display. But once field season commenced they sprang into action, packing crates with shovels, picks, trowels, buckets, burlap, and bags of plaster. I entered the lab on that first morning to the ringing cacophony of metal tools slamming into boxes.

One of the preparators, a gentleman named Tom Thomas, called out to me.

"Hello, Miss Ballantine. I hear you're going to be working in the lab this summer."

Nicknamed Tom-Tom, for obvious reasons, he was a bulky man, short and muscular from lifting rocks and crates.

"Good morning, Mr. Thomas. Yes, I'll be working on forams."

"Your desk is over there. I've cleared it off for you. I figured you'd want to be as far away from the fume hoods as possible."

"Oh, thank you. I don't want to be anywhere near the hydrofluoric acid," I said. "That stuff scares me."

"Yeah, it's pretty corrosive. It can burn human tissue down to the bone."

I shuddered. "Where are you headed?"

"Down to Florida. We've started a big dig down there. Pleistocene camels and mammoths mostly. It's fun, but man, is it hot down there. And the summer's just starting," he said, smiling.

Hand trucks slipped under the crates and headed to the loading dock. The lab doors swung back and forth, over and over. By the afternoon, the preparators were gone, off to the Florida heat and the Ice Age mammals. The morning's noise seemed to echo into the descending silence.

Into this breech stepped my boss, Dr. Falcone, an overfriendly man, reasonably young, with dark hair and a trimmed beard. He studied foraminifera or 'forams,' the shells of single-celled organisms. About the size of a pin-head, forams evolved rapidly and therefore were called 'index fossils,' valuable markers of geologic time.

Although of similar height to me, Dr. Falcone's eyes rarely met mine. All of that microscope work must have warped his vision because his eyes always seemed to be concentrating below my neck. He had connections with an oil company, and through them had acquired a storage room full of sediment cores. Our first order of business was to retrieve the elongate cardboard boxes filled with core, setting them end-to-end on the lab tables. This task required a lot of lifting, stretching, and bending.

"Here, Henrietta, let me help you with that," Dr. Falcone said, reaching around me, brushing against my shoulder. "You shouldn't be lifting anything that heavy by yourself."

"It's not that bad. Just bulky," I said, as I grabbed one end, accidentally jabbing him with my elbow as I slid the box along the table. Dust motes rose in the air, illuminated by the overhead fluorescent lights.

No matter my best efforts, I continued to be in Dr. Falcone's way. He seemed to have some kind of sensory issue because he constantly bumped into me or reached across me. By day's end, covered in debris, sweaty, my plait coming undone, and my hair sticking out at odd angles, I was tired of figuring out how to maneuver around him.

The next day, Dr. Falcone showed me how to describe the sediment—who knew that 'buff' was a color?—and measure the cores.

We scooped a two hundred milliliter sample into a beaker for sieving and fossil extraction.

"Look Henrietta, you stack the sieves like this, with descending screen sizes, largest to smallest, gravel to clay," he said. "Now put the tower of sieves on the electric shaker."

As I reached up to place the tower on the shaker, he stood behind me, reaching his arms around me to lock the sieves in place, trapping me against the work bench.

"Now pour the sediment sample in the top...good, good... put on the lid and turn the shaker on, like this," he said, flipping a switch.

Vibrations rattled through my fingertips which were pressed against the table as sediment particles fell through the progressively smaller holes of each sieve, segregating according to grain size. He switched the power off.

"Now we'll pull the tower down and separate the sieves."

We both reached for the tower at the same time, laughing awkwardly. He moved out of my way so that I could reach up.

"Now pour the sample from each sieve in separate beakers and weigh each one on that triple beam balance. Record the weight here in the log book," he said. "The microfossils accumulate in this sieve. Let me show you how to do a soap float."

From a high shelf, he grabbed a large metal bowl, filling it with water in the sink.

"Come over here, Henrietta, and grab that bar of Ivory soap. Put it in the bowl and make a lather with it in your hands."

I bent over the sink, stuck my hands in the bowl, and rubbed the soap between my palms to create a bubbly lather. Standing next to me, Dr. Falcone dipped his fingers into the bowl and cupped his hands around mine.

Weird. Did he think I couldn't figure out how to make soapy water?

"Drop the sediment from that sieve into the bowl and swish it around gently," he said. "The sand will sink to the bottom and the forams will float to the top." He removed his hands, soap glistening on his hairy knuckles. "Voila!" Now we'll skim them off with a spoon and put them on a tray to dry."

———◆———

The cores and sieves became my constant companions that summer. Measure, sample, sieve, weigh, document, soap float, day in and day out. The monotony felt worthwhile when I poured the tiny dried fossils into test tubes for Dr. Falcone. He checked on my progress most days, looking over my shoulder, both proverbially and literally. It felt a bit disconcerting.

After a month, I received a nice surprise one morning, as Tom-Tom arrived from Florida to deliver a truckload of crates. He stacked the boxes of treasures in a storage room, loose dust swirling in the air.

"Mr. Thomas, what did you bring back? Can I take a peek?" I asked.

"Sure, come look," he said.

He grabbed a crowbar and pried off several lids. Most of the crates were filled with plaster jackets.

"That's part of a mammoth in there. And over here is a skull of a glyptodont."

"That's so exciting!" I said. "I think glyptodonts looked like giant armadillos."

"Yes, they did," he said, chuckling. "Wait till you see this." He unwrapped a burlap-covered fossil.

He handed it to me. "A mammoth tooth."

I held the massive tooth in both hands and ran a thumb over the enamel.

"You see all of those linear ridges on top? That pattern shows that mammoths were grazers," he said.

He lifted another lid and reached into the next crate.

"And look at this," he said, unwrapping some burlap. "This is a claw from a ground sloth."

I exchanged the mammoth tooth for the claw.

"It's hard to imagine that these animals lived in Florida," I said.

"Yep, now it's all alligators, snakes, and mosquitoes," he said. "I can't wait to get back to it."

More weeks of sieving followed. By the end of the summer, I yearned to learn more, so I hauled myself out of the prep lab to visit Dr. Falcone's office on the second floor. He was perched over his binocular microscope, concentration on his face. Sun poured in through his window illuminating his spartan desk. Books were arranged neatly on shelves. His wife and his two young sons smiled from a framed photo. I cleared my throat and knocked on the door jam.

"Henrietta, what a nice surprise. Come in, come in," he waved me in.

"Dr. Falcone, do you think you could show me how to make the slides and identify the forams?" I asked.

"Of course! You're doing such a great job of extracting them. Let's grab that chair," he said.

Reaching over, he rolled a chair from the corner and positioned it next to his.

"To make a slide you pour the fossils from the test tube onto this small black tray and then look at them under the microscope. When you have selected the one you want, you take this tiny paintbrush, dip it in water like this, and reach in and grab it. The surface tension of the water will lift the foram and you place it on the slide. Here, you try it."

I slid the chair over to peer through the lens. Adjusting the focus for my eyes, exquisitely shaped shells came into view—spheres, coils, spirals, grape-like clusters. An amazing minuscule world. I dipped the hair-thin brush into the beaker of water, wetting the tip. Selecting a tiny pitted sphere, I lifted it with the brush and placed it on a slide.

"Excellent," Dr. Falcone said. "Now let's look at the foram you picked." He leaned in to look at my slide.

"That is *Orbulina*, a fairly common planktonic genus. The planktonic forams—the ones that float rather than live on the seafloor—are generally spherical in shape."

He reached on his bookshelf and grabbed a thick volume titled *Lexicon of Foraminifera*.

"You can look up any species in here. It's updated every other year. This is essentially the encyclopedia for forams," he said. "Let's look at some others."

Pushing the slides around the stage plate, he referenced the fossils in the gridded, numbered squares. We took turns staring through the eyepiece at the tiny hyaline shells.

"You see here, Henrietta? In square 21? This genus lives only in offshore Texas today, but we find it in cores from the Miocene in Maryland. This fossil indicates that the Miocene climate was warmer than today. We use this type of data to determine paleoenvironments."

Caught up in learning about the fossils it took me a while to realize he was leaning uncomfortably into my shoulder, with his arm draped around the back of my chair. His face hovered right next to mine, his breath warm on my neck. Aware and nervous, I pulled rigidly upright, leaning away from him as much as I could without toppling over. Perhaps picking up on my discomfort, he gave my shoulder a little squeeze. Bringing his arm back around, he patted my thigh.

"Great job. You're getting it." We rose from our chairs. "If you play your cards right, maybe I'll take you out into the field next summer," he said with a Cheshire cat grin.

"Thank you for your help," I squeaked. I turned and fled. I wasn't sure what cards he was referring to, but I felt a bit queasy.

Did I have a reason to be uncomfortable? Was he just being enthusiastic? After all, I had been the one to ask for his help.

That summer, I learned many lessons about micropaleontology. Unintentionally, Dr. Falcone taught me another lesson, yet I was too naive to know what to do with it. I filed it away in my mind, like an itchy wool hat, and decided not to mention it to anyone.

CHAPTER 21

MIDDLE PLEISTOCENE, THE RIFT VALLEY, AFRICA

The wild olive trees growing on the volcano's slope stared down upon the group of women as they descended. The distinctive fermented smell of the leaves mixed with the odor of rotting grass and dried clay. Hearing the shrieks of other, more primitive primates in far-off African redwoods, the women stayed alert, clustering together. Ifa's bare feet scuffed the red oxidized soil, her toes stained like rust. She straggled at the back of her new familial group, allocated to the periphery. The women in the new tribe watched her with hooded eyes, wary of her foreign dialect and bizarre facial expressions.

The cloudless sky pressed down, heat entering every pore. In the dry season, food was elusive. Today the women hunted for the fish-that-sleeps, bundled in cocoons of dried mud. They approached a small stream, the water stagnant and murky. Thirsty, they knelt to drink. Ifa gulped a mouthful of the milky water, opaque from weathered volcanic ash, gritty between her teeth.

After satiating their thirst, all eyes concentrated on the stream banks as the women meandered downslope.

"Look. There. Holes." Kalama pointed to the breathing holes alongside the creek.

Eager to be useful, Ifa waded in. She jabbed her sharpened stick into the earth next to the hole.

"No. Stop. Farther out. Watch."

Pushing Ifa away, Kalama demonstrated her digging technique, punching pits in a distant circle around the breathing hole. Ifa, chastised, watched silently, arms at her sides. Wedging into the dirt with her hand axe, Kalama pried out a mud-encrusted sac. She peeled open the cocoon, revealing the flat-headed fish with tiny twig legs. Exposed from hibernation, its eel-like body flopped limply in her hands. Stunned, its beady eyes stared blankly.

"Pole. There." Kalama pointed. Ifa reached for the long pole on the top of the bank and handed it to her.

With deft hands, Kalama stabbed the fish through the head, crunching through cartilage. Speared on the carrying pole, it wriggled and gasped open its mouth. The women hooted in celebration. Moving along the bank they searched for more holes, gouging at the dirt, elated with each catch. After filling the pole with skewered fish, they headed back to their home camp.

The moving target of fishy smells reeked enticingly, catching the attention of hungry hyenas. Canny hunters, the size of lions, short-faced hyenas easily pierced through bone with their powerful jaws. Padding on cat-like paws, the hyenas approached from the rear. Ifa, in the back, heard the low cackle. The women panicked, crowded together, the pole of fish held high in the air. Ifa turned just as the pack of carnivores lunged toward Kalama. Brandishing her pointed digging stick and with a piercing war cry, Ifa stabbed at the snarling animals.

"AAAAHHHHHHHH!"

The frightened women, emboldened by her action, joined her, yelling and stabbing at the eyes and throats of the attackers. Jabbing over and over at the snapping jowls, Ifa landed a lucky strike down a hyena's throat. Eyes wide, it fell backward, wounded, choking on the stick. Ifa charged, shoving the stick farther back into its throat. Blood burst from its mouth. The other hyenas, immediately sensing its struggle, turned, and the target changed. Snarling, the pack ravaged the downed predator, now turned into prey. The women rushed away, feet pounding, muscles screaming. They reached the forested volcanic slope and began to climb. Kalama, winded, gasped for air, and Ifa grabbed her with one hand. Pulling Kalama uphill, Ifa stooped to grab a sharp stone off the ground. Adrenaline coursing through her, she prepared to fight if threatened again.

That evening, the women offered a central spot to Ifa around the hearth. Kalama presented her with a chunk of roasted fish. Ifa bit into the gift, the baked skin greasy on her tongue, the flesh tasting of reward. And respect.

CHAPTER 22

1958-1959, SOPHOMORE YEAR,
WILLIAMSBURG, VIRGINIA

After my unnerving encounters with Dr. Falcone, I was ready to return to college. Delilah and I moved to the sophomore women's dorm, bringing Little Debbie and Carolyn with us as suitemates. The building was as ancient as Barrett, but without the quaintness. On my arrival, I found Delilah crouched in our bathroom with an aerosol can. She was dressed in a poncho constructed from a colorful mola, a type of Central American applique. The fabric colors swirled around her when she moved like a brilliant carousal.

"Henrietta, you're back! How was your summer?" she smiled. Opening her arms wide, I found myself enveloped in her cloaked embrace, which I stiffly returned.

I pointed to the can of bug spray.

"What are you doing? Are you poisoning us?" I asked.

"There are roaches in here! One scurried by me this morning."

"Ugh, they're disgusting. Make sure you kill any spiders too," I said, wrinkling my nose and glancing around.

"Will do," she said. "I'm on a mission."

I shuddered. "Do you have any coffee?"

"You know I do! Help yourself," she said, pointing. "It's on my desk—*Coffea arabica*! Of course, from Guatemala—the best!"

The summer had felt like a coffee drought. Delilah had spoiled me to anything inferior to our dorm-brew. We toasted to our new room where the mold and roaches would be our bane for the year. Little Debbie and Carolyn heard our voices and came through the pesticide-infused bathroom to partake in our first coffee klatch as sophomores. Little Debbie appeared as serene and unblemished as ever. Carolyn was sporting a sparkly engagement ring, and we congratulated her and tried to be supportive, although I thought her crazy, and Johnny a drip. To each his own, I told myself. So far, no one had tugged at my heartstrings, and an 'M.R.S. degree' was nowhere on my agenda. I could barely find a college boy who was civil, much less interesting. Any future boyfriend of mine would have to be smart, kind, and courteous. Mannerly. A gentleman. Of course, it would not hurt if he was handsome also.

Classes began with their usual abruptness, and soon we were in full swing. This academic year I would take chemistry, mineralogy, paleontology, anthropology, archeology, and my second, and final, year of Russian. Once I finished with the stupid 'two years of a language at the college level' rule, I would be done with Russian forever. *I hoped.*

I spent a lot of time in labs this year—removing caffeine from tea leaves, doing titrations, identifying hundreds of minerals and fossils. Even anthropology had a lab of sorts; being in Colonial Williamsburg, the lab consisted of hiking down DOG street to the CW preparation lab and viewing what the staff archeologists were digging up. Pottery, pipe stems, Native American artifacts, even an ear wax remover from colonial times, all fascinated me.

One Saturday, our archeology class traveled back in time along the asphalt of Jamestown Road to a dig site. Each of us was assigned a 2-foot by 2-foot square of earth sectioned off with string in which to dig and sieve—*baby archeology.* You would think that by now I would have had my fill of sieving, but I loved it, digging into the fresh earth with tiny trowels, fingertips sinking into the sandy loam. Spooning the dirt into the sieves, shaking, sifting, combing through the remains. I did not find anything remarkable. In fact, I did not find anything at all. It did not matter. The glorious prospect of discovery, the 'what if?' would be my companion whenever I excavated.

Of course, paleontology was my favorite class, especially the required fieldwork. Saturday mornings found me back at the James River, and these trips became both educational and social outings. The hysterical-geology boys were maturing at the rate of evolution and still could not put two kind words together, but several biology-oriented natural science majors joined us, enlivening the group. Dr. Miller had upgraded to a station wagon. Seat belts did not exist—we just piled in. I never knew anything about Dr. Miller's personal life—one did not ask—but over the summer, he had married, and his new wife, Patricia, was just as vivacious as he. A graduate student at VIMS—the Virginia Institute of Marine Science—she also had an affinity for sharks. Tiny, with blonde hair tied up in a high ponytail, she would join us most Saturdays and would bring copious numbers of peanut butter sandwiches to share. We all adored her.

Once at the riverbank, we conducted our various research projects, whether biology- or geology-oriented. Dr. Miller demonstrated how to measure the section and collect samples in grids for population counts while we scrabbled up and down the cliffs. Occasionally I would be lucky enough to discover one of the black phosphatic shark teeth lying on the sand. Bull sharks, sand tigers, snaggletooth sharks, hammerheads, lemons, angels, threshers, all lost teeth in the Miocene sea, their multiple rows of teeth at the ready for replacement.

One Saturday, I found myself sitting next to Dr. Miller's wife, Patricia, at lunch. I garnered my courage.

"Mrs. Miller, do you mind me asking, when you were in college and graduate school, did you ever have to deal with naysayers? You know, people who told you that you wouldn't be able to succeed?" I asked.

She laughed. "Oh, you mean *men*? Yes, all the time." She looked at me with raised eyebrows and added, "Let's take a walk."

We stood up and walked along the top of the bank. The river meandered below in a lazy current, the sapphire water shining in the sun.

"No one could believe I wanted to study sharks," she said. "But I'm from Florida, and I've been swimming in the ocean my whole life. I've even gone scuba diving. I was always fascinated with sharks—how they breathe, sleep, detect blood in the water. No one was going to deter me."

"I feel the same way about fossils," I said. "Uncovering one for the first time, being the first person ever to see it. It's just a thrill you cannot describe."

"Yes, that's it exactly. Why do you ask? Have you come up against some resistance at William and Mary?"

"Honestly, no one has come out and said I couldn't study geology. But there have been a lot of insinuations. Mostly from older professors and fellow students. Even my mother thinks that girls shouldn't become geologists. And I'm the only girl in my geology classes."

"I was the only woman on a research ship that sailed from Woods Hole to Bermuda. We were at sea for two months. Do you know how I applied for that research position? I listed my first name as "Pat" instead of "Patricia" on my application. They were expecting a man, and I showed up," she said with a laugh.

"Really?! What did they do when they saw you?" I asked.

"They tried to deny me the position, but I had already accepted the money and used some of it to take the train to Massachusetts. I was standing right there, in front of them, and I wasn't going away. First, they told me there was nowhere for me to sleep on the ship since the researchers bunked together in close quarters. But I still stood there. They told me there wasn't a lady's lavatory on board. I suggested putting a sign on the door of one of the existing lavatories. They were stumped. But I kept standing there. Eventually, they allowed me to board, and put me up in the infirmary, with a sign that said 'Women Only' on the door."

"How were you treated once you were on the ship?" I asked.

"There were a lot of sideways glances and halted conversations at first. The crew members were overly friendly if you know what I mean. But I persevered. I worked hard to be there and was accepted based on my qualifications. After a few weeks, everyone seemed used to me. I simply continued my work."

"How did you even think about stating your name as Pat?" I asked in a low voice. "I would never come up with something like that."

"There are going to be stone walls built in front of you. You are going to need to find a way around them to reach your goals. Use your brain and your connections." She paused, and added, "And remember this, you have to be careful in ways men don't. On the ship, I did my research, but I did it quietly and methodically. I didn't brag or attempt to outshine anyone. I ate in the communal dining room and was polite but did not try to become buddies with anybody. And I kept my cabin door locked all of the time."

Patricia looked at me, "Henrietta, do me a favor. Stop referring to yourself as a girl. We are women. No one is going to take a 'girl' seriously. But women can quietly change the world."

CHAPTER 23

Toward the end of the Spring semester, one of the young men in the group took a shine to me. Who knew I would find my first date while scrounging in the dirt? A senior, Keith Turner studied wildlife biology. Taller than me and thin, he had a beaky nose and a tiny mustache. At the river, he patiently hunkered under a tree for hours observing squirrels while writing in his journal. He also loved reptiles, especially snakes. Once he learned I detested them, he took particular delight in pointing them out to me.

"Look, Henrietta, there's a water moccasin. Or is it a garden snake?" he teased me.

"You tell me—you're the biologist!" I shuddered and stepped back. Before this, I had not noticed how many snakes inhabited the James riverbank.

After Keith mentioned he liked coffee, I brought a thermos-full, bartering for extra beans with Delilah in exchange for washing, drying, and folding her laundry, which she hated doing. I would make a pot each Saturday morning, adding several liberated packets of sugar from the dining hall to tote in my knapsack. Sharing coffee with Keith, sipping from the communal cup unthreaded from atop the thermos, became a cozy, albeit unsanitary, ritual.

"Ah, my coffee mistress," he said, "you do make an excellent brew."

How scandalous.

One sunny morning, the dew evaporating into the warming air around us, Keith squatted down in front of me.

"Henrietta, m'lady, would you do me the honor of being my date at the Pi Theta Alpha Spring formal?"

"Yes, of course," I stammered.

"Excellent," he said, attempting to wink and twirl the end of his wispy mustache at the same time.

That afternoon, I raced back to the dorm in a panic. I had no experience with dances or dressing in formal wear. Fortunately, the first person I saw was Little Debbie.

"You have to help me," I pleaded. "Keith invited me to go to his fraternity dance. I don't have a dress. Or shoes. Or stockings." I started to hyperventilate.

Little Debbie smiled at me. "That's wonderful. When is the dance?"

"In two weeks," I replied.

"First, stop panicking. You have time. Second, we'll go to Binns department store," she said as if it were evident.

My second problem was that I needed money for the new ensemble. I reversed the charges from the hall phone, calling home that afternoon when I thought my father might answer. No luck. My mother picked up.

"Henrietta, is everything alright?" she asked.

"Yes, Mother, I'm fine. I have been invited to a dance. By a boy. I'm calling because I have to buy a long dress."

"A boy? What's his name?"

"His name is Keith. He's a senior."

Momentary silence buzzed down the line.

"Oh, a senior? Well, I hope he's a nice boy."

"Oh yes, he is. He's a biologist. He's studying the habits of squirrels."

"Squirrels?"

"Yes. I need some money deposited in my bank account for the dress. And some new shoes too."

She heaved a deep sigh.

"Alright, I'll let your father know. Pick out a lovely dress, dear. Nothing too revealing. You don't need to show all of your assets if you know what I mean."

I knew what she meant, no thanks to any instruction from her. Thank goodness for dorm talk.

Later that week Little Debbie took me in hand, not just literally, and dragged me to Binns department store, a fixture in Merchant Square, the door of which I had never darkened. The selection of dresses seemed daunting, matching shoes a mystery, stockings a misery. How did one manipulate a garter belt? Exiting the dressing room, clad in a long emerald-green dress, I twirled around, hem ballooning.

Little Debbie clapped her hands, her moon-shaped face lighting up.

"Henrietta, that color looks fantastic on you. It complements your complexion," she said.

Was that even a thing?

The night of the dance I felt like a princess in my newly-purchased gown, the skirt billowing over the crinolines. Walking hand in hand, Keith and I crossed the lawn in front of the Wren Building. I skipped up the steps in my ballet flats to the second floor, where crepe paper streamers wafted from the ceiling of the dimly lit Campus Center ballroom. The band played songs by Perry Como and shockingly, Elvis Presley. We danced until I thought my feet would fall off. Not that either of us knew how to dance, but we managed to lurch around. The dance floor was so crowded no one could see us anyway. Drunken frat boys splayed about, hiding flasks in coat pockets. Girls giggled in corners.

Sweating after a set of dances, Keith took my hand and pulled me outside on the second-floor balcony. Pinned in by the wrought-iron balustrade, we watched the traffic merge onto Jamestown Road. Unexpectedly, he leaned over and kissed me. My first kiss was a bit like a smack, and tickly from his feathery mustache. Although not overcome with romantic notions I found it to be a memorable moment all the same.

Perhaps this might develop into something more...?

A few weeks later, I had my answer. Keith matriculated with the class of 1959, moving on to other passions that did not include me. He never bothered to say goodbye.

CHAPTER 24

1961, Olduvai Gorge, Tanganyika, Africa

The next day, as the sun colored the sky in a yellow-orange glow, I joined the paleontology parade to the Leakey Quarry. I held my rock hammer and Maggie carried a broom and a box of brushes. Kimaru slung a rifle over his shoulder while Ray followed with his camera bags strapped around his chest. Bringing up the rear were Mary Leakey and Philip, each with a wooden sieve and scraping tools. Sally and Victoria added a canine component to the procession.

I watched, dumbstruck as a wildebeest calf joined us, his hump swaying. He offered a low moan. Sally barked back at him.

"This is Oliver," Mary said, seeing my startled glance. "He was abandoned by his mother. He likes to run with the dogs."

Along the way, I received my briefing on the dangers of field-work in Africa.

"Animals wander into the gorge, especially at night. Lions come near the camp and they are very protective of cubs. Never get between a lioness and her cubs," Kimaru said. "There are stray rhinos and buffalos and either of these could charge at you."

"Don't forget the cheetahs," added Maggie. "They're solitary, but can attack quickly."

"That's why I pen up Oliver at night," Mary said, patting the calf.

Ambling along, I stared ahead in contemplation. I had already circumvented danger in traveling here, by not missing airplane connections, not being stranded at the airport. However, this was a whole new level of risk, the lethal kind.

"Watch the ground for snakes. If you see a snake, assume it is poisonous," Ray said. "And steer clear."

I shuddered, my fear of snakes still prevalent after my time on the James River.

Kimaru continued. "Before we start on the elephant, I'll broom the ground to get rid of ants. We'll be kneeling in the dirt. The ants will bite, especially the driver ants. There are also spiders and scorpions. They like to lurk under the brush or rocks, in shady spots. And they can be venomous. Be careful where you place your hands on the ground. Or where you sit."

Arriving at the quarry, Kimaru whisked the ground surrounding the bones.

"I'm going to place you for the photographs," Ray said. He pointed. "Mary here. Maggie and Henrietta over there. Philip next to your mom. Kimaru, I'll take a photo of you with your rifle separately."

We followed his directions, splaying ourselves around the elephant, holding picks and brushes in our hands. *Would my rock hammer become famous?*

Ray snapped away with his cameras. Only later did it occur to me that we were never in the same frame as Kimaru.

———

In the tent after sundown, with the earlier discussion of danger on my mind, wild and semi-wild noises reverberated in my ears. Sally and Victoria barked and Oliver lowed. Maggie snored lightly. I swore I heard lions growling in the distance. Between all the roaring, rustling, barking, and bellowing, real or imagined, I had trouble falling asleep. Bugs buzzed around my head despite my mosquito netting.

Wrapping the blanket around me in fear of crawling arachnids, I resembled a sweating mummy.

Later that night, sleep intermittent, I awoke to the sound of roaring, frighteningly close. I sat straight up in my cot. The dogs began to bark and whine. Voices carried across the camp.

Bang, snap, crack!

Fizzing explosions boomed through the air.

Maggie awoke. "The lions must have come close," she said, rubbing the corners of her eyes. "The diggers throw firecrackers at them to scare them away."

She turned over with a nonchalant sigh.

After that, sleep eluded me. The noises increased to their pre-explosion levels. My chest clinched in fear. I flung off my blanket and rolled over and over on my cot, unable to settle. The air became stagnant and suffocating.

Heat seared behind my eyes and grit filled my mouth. I carried a heavy load, my heart raced. The volcano was erupting! Panicked, hyperventilating. Time to rush. Where were we headed? The ash. The ash rained down. Smothering us. I grasped my bundle. Precious cargo. We must leave. Run. Now!

Lurching awake, I panted in terror. The top of my tent came into view as the dream subsided like mist into my subconscious. Remnants of panic remained on my skin. My fingers gripped my crumbled blanket.

Slowly calming, I heard the monkey hoots of Simon, the clattering of breakfast dishes, murmured voices. Maggie's cot stood empty. Alone in the tent, I shook off my nightmare.

CHAPTER 25

MIDDLE PLEISTOCENE, THE RIFT VALLEY, AFRICA

Agony stabbed through her belly as her water gushed down her legs. Ifa squatted, panting and sweating, her brow ridges furrowed. Now was the time of magic, exclusive to the women's realm. Sheltered in the shade of a thorn tree, reeds placed beneath her, she moaned. Kalama and the other women took turns supporting her, soft murmurs of comfort offered, incantations chanted in low voices. A steady verbal throng.

Kneeling on the reeds, she howled, pushing, grasping at the dirt until her nails were caked. Time stretched, at once immediate yet seemingly eternal. Crying out, a final surge and the baby emerged, dripping, covered in creamy chalk. A gift from the earth. The scent of blood tinged the air. Exhausted, through her ache, Ifa heard her son's cries, his first squalls a delicious melody. Collapsed on the blood-stained reeds, she reached for her son. Dark hair covered his head, back, and arms. Piercing midnight eyes stared belligerently as if interrupted. Cradled to her breast, she watched as he lifted his face, his tiny hand grasping for her hair.

He was perfect.

They named him Khoam, after his father.

Ifa would kill for him. To protect him. To feed him. To survive, she must.

CHAPTER 26

I returned to my Arlington home after my sophomore year in a generally grumbly mood. In no way had I developed a crush on Keith—certainly not—but I felt a bit jaded by his ease of disappearing.

Our house had undergone its summer preparations. The 'winter' rugs were rolled up and stored in the eaves, and the summer grass rugs gave the house a lighter air. The screens were inserted in the windows, theoretically to let in the summer breezes, but instead increased the stickiness of humidity. My mother even acted happy to have me home, but experience taught me not to put too much stake in her early moods.

As it always did, the idea of my upcoming summer work at the museum perked me up. My father informed me that Dr. Falcone would be on sabbatical this summer, spending time in the field with his precious forams. What I overheard on the sly from Mr. Thomas was that Dr. Falcone and his wife were divorcing, and he was spending time with someone else precious as well. I felt nothing but a sense of relief. Last summer's dealings with him had left a bad taste in my mouth.

Since I would not have an internship with Dr. Falcone this summer, my father offered me the opportunity to clean fossil fish for him, which I happily accepted. Huge slabs of fossil-bearing rock were currently being quarried from the Green River Formation in Wyoming and trucked to the Smithsonian. The Green River Formation consisted of calcareous fine-grained shales and limestones deposited in tiny layers called 'varves.' These laminations had built up in the bottom of ancient lakes during Eocene time, about 50 million years ago. One particular layer was chock-full of fish fossils. A few other animals were discovered rarely in the rocks—turtles, stingrays, crocodiles, and even a horse.

My job this summer would be to chisel out the debris from the top of the bones. It was meticulous work, chipping at the rock grain-by-grain with a sharp knife, my back bent over the table, the slab of rock under a large magnifier. One slip of my blade could fling a fish spine into the dust bin. I learned to work with Elmer's glue next to me and brushed a diluted glue solution over each delicate spine, fin, or scale. The unrelenting dust glazed the room like fine-grained winter snow. I even found it beneath my clothes and nestled between my toes under my socks and shoes.

One excursion that summer stands out in my mind. It was all well and good for me to be uncovering the fish locked within the rock slabs. But someone else collected them. I told my father I wanted to collect fossils, 'real' fossils preserved in rocks instead of in loose sediments. On a Saturday morning, we started early on this quest, first driving to Oakton, Virginia, to a store called Allegheny Outfitters.

"You'll need something better for your feet than tennis shoes where we are going," my dad told me.

The store was located in a rambling colonial-era cottage, shaded by a huge live oak tree. We ducked our heads under the door jam and trod across the sloping wood floors. The store displayed equipment needed for camping or hiking—tents, tarps, lanterns, cookstoves, sleeping bags, backpacks. A salesman with a long flowing beard approached us.

"Good morning, sir. Can I be of help?" he asked my father.

My father cleared his throat. "Yes, my daughter is looking for some work boots," he said.

The salesman noticed me and seemed taken aback.

"What for?" he asked.

"Hiking, working in quarries…that sort of thing," my father answered.

"I'm sorry. We don't have boots in ladies' sizes," he said.

I raised one eyebrow. "Do you have boy's hiking boots?" I asked.

"Oh, yes. I didn't think of that. Right over here," the salesman said.

The boots I selected were huge monstrosities with a deep tread, in a boy's size seven. They reeked of a glorious mixture of sewn leather and waterproofing oil. The laces were thick rawhide, tough to knot. I lifted my foot; the boot felt heavier than I imagined. It was love at first sight.

After selecting my boots, we moved over to a wall display of climbing equipment. Included in the display were rock hammers. I had not thought about buying a rock hammer. I used a shovel to collect fossils from the Yorktown Formation.

"Dad, they're so expensive. Are you sure I need one?" I asked.

"We'll be dealing with much harder rocks today than what you're used to. To be a proper geologist, you need a rock hammer," he insisted.

Holding my new hammer by its sturdy oak handle I felt a jolt of happiness as I turned its metallic head to gleam in the light.

My dad paid for our purchases, and we continued driving farther out into the country. A glorious day, the sun shining brightly overhead, we rolled down the windows to collect the breeze. Over the next hour, the terrain rose as the foothills came into view.

"We are now in the Shenandoah Valley," my dad said, "in the Valley and Ridge province. The valleys are formed by streams wearing away erodible rocks such as limestone, and the ridges are held up by resistant sandstones."

We approached the quaint village of Strasburg, with its Victorian homes, a mom-and-pop restaurant, and small antique shops. We pulled into an Esso gas station, and a teenaged boy with a cheeky grin headed toward us to fill our tank and wash our windshield. As I headed to the back to use the facilities and stretch my legs, I stared at the Appalachian foothills along the western horizon, covered in deciduous forests, silent sentinels of Paleozoic upheavals.

Jumping back in the car, my dad handed me a packet of Planter's peanuts from the gas station store.

"Almost there," he said, popping some peanuts into his mouth. "This will hold us until we get there and eat our sandwiches."

Heading south, we rambled next to the meandering North Fork of the Shenandoah River, its glistening currents tumbling in its circuitous march to the sea. On the other side of the road, farm fields showed off their straight rows, the scent of hay and manure drifting in through the windows. A little farther and my dad pulled off the side of the road and turned off the ignition. The sounds of rushing water and cascading waterfalls provided a peaceful backdrop. An outcrop extended down the other side of the street, as long as a city block. Thick beds of blocky tan and gray rocks dipped at a high angle, the colors darkening down the roadcut. We exited the car and stood back to view the entire section.

"These strata are a result of millions of years of deposition. This is interpreted as a carbonate bank, so we should look for limestones and shales. The sediments were deposited on the seafloor during the Ordovician Period," my dad said, gesturing toward the rocks.

"Why aren't the layers horizontal if they represent an ancient seafloor? What about Original Horizontality?" I asked.

He replied, "They've been tilted by forces within the earth. Exciting work is being done in the field of structural geology. Continental drift is only the tip of the iceberg. Trust me, textbooks will need to be rewritten because of the new data being published."

We crossed the road and walked along the outcrop, gripping our rock hammers. The section ascended five meters above our heads.

"Here you have evidence of a series of cataclysmic extinctions, Henrietta," my dad said. "Let's look at the lithologies. Try the acid on these rocks." He handed me a plastic bottle of hydrochloric acid. I dutifully placed several drops of acid on the massive, tan rocks. The acid reacted effervescently, popping with tiny bubbles, releasing carbon dioxide gas in a chemical reaction.

"These are limestones," I said.

"Yes, this is part of the carbonate bank."

I plucked a brachiopod from a weathered piece.

"This lived in the lime mud," I said, holding it up.

He nodded. "Let's walk up the section and look at the younger rocks."

Walking farther along the road, the rocks transitioned, appearing smoother, darker in color, with a more layered appearance.

"The rocks here are less crystalline and the color changes. I think these are muddier," I said.

"Go ahead and test your hypothesis," my dad said.

I dripped acid on the rocks. No reaction occurred.

"This is shale; compressed mud turned to rock," I said.

"Excellent. Use the pick end of your hammer and pry the layers apart. You can see the fissility here, where the rock splits along smooth planes."

I jammed my shiny new hammer between the layers, a baptism of sorts. Of course, I had learned about limestone and shale in my Physical Geology class. Still, I had no experience with consolidated rocks in the field.

Within the shale layers, a thick yellow-tan stratum, indented from weathering, caught my eye. "See this lighter layer here? That mustard yellow one that looks weathered? What's that?" I scraped my hammer along the crumbly surface. My blade became coated in a yellow residue. "Wow, this layer is powdery," I added.

"Yes, that's bentonite, which is solidified volcanic ash."

"It looks like there are a lot of layers of the ash throughout the section. See it, here and then again there, up-section?" I asked.

"What does that indicate?" my dad asked, always the teacher.

"That there were volcanoes nearby, I guess?" I said.

"Yes. Back in the Ordovician Period, there were volcanoes to the east of here. The ash covered the area many times. The fossils you collect here—corals, brachiopods, crinoids—lived in an ocean known as the Iapetus Sea. They were smothered by ash repeatedly, and life reestablished itself on the ocean floor after each eruption."

Fascinated by the bentonite, I poked again at a weathered ash layer. The ash coated my fingertips, and as I rubbed them together, the fine-grained dust filtered down through the air. The falling flakes triggered a memory at the fuzzy edge of my consciousness. Mesmerized, I dug my rock hammer through another ash layer, picking up more crumbled bits in my fingers, releasing them in front of my eyes so that the flakes cascaded down in front of me.

My horizontal view expanded on both sides, filling with the ash, blocking out the outcrop, the road, the river. The ash showered down in the atmosphere, surrounding me, a thick poisonous rain. Staring through the fog, I glimpsed smothered grassland. More extensive than a farm field. Vague outlines of volcanoes appeared in the far distance. Someone was next to me, a hand on my shoulder.

I felt myself choking, gagging. I staggered back.

"Are you alright, Henrietta? Here, let me get you some water," my dad said. He loped across the road and grabbed the thermos from the back seat of our car.

The image snapped away, leaving me staring at my ash-covered hands. The air was clear once more. The river burbled in front of me, the rock face stood behind me.

My dad returned with the open thermos, concern on his face.

"I'm alright, thanks," I said, brushing my ash-laden hands on my legs, coating my pants. I reached for the water, taking a large swig. "I swallowed some ash, that's all."

"You must be hungry. We need to eat our sandwiches," my dad said. "I didn't realize how late it was getting."

He led the way back to the car, opening the cooler in our back seat, and grabbing our lunches. We made our way down a well-worn path to the river, likely trampled by fishermen. Traversing across cobbles on the point bar, we climbed up on a boulder at the water's edge.

"Olive loaf?" he asked, handing me a sandwich.

Still foggy and a little shaken, I nodded. Deep in my psyche, I felt I had touched a story buried just out of my reach. I took a bite of the sandwich and watched the river, the water flowing downhill over its bedload. A kingfisher rattled its song from the far bank. "Dad, do you believe there could be such a thing as a guardian angel? Someone or something who looks out for you? Protects you?" I asked.

My dad turned and stared at me. He took a moment, considering. "I've never experienced anything like that myself. But, in many cultures, people believe their ancestors stay around to watch over them. Why?"

I shrugged. "It's just something I've been wondering about."

He looked up at the sky while he chewed. "I guess to believe in guardian angels would be to believe in an afterlife. And that would lead to a belief in a higher power. Many scientists do believe in a creator. Even Albert Einstein says he's trying to figure out how God created this world."

I persisted. "What do you think?"

He paused. "I'd say I am keeping an open mind."

CHAPTER 27

My social life would undergo some upheaval in my junior year. Two weeks before the start of the semester, Delilah, Little Debbie, and I all received, by mail, engraved wedding announcements from Carolyn. She and Johnny had tied the knot in early August. On the back was written in pencil, "Will not be back to school this year." I was floored. She planned to graduate with us, or so I thought. I could not imagine why anyone would choose to drop out of school to get married, especially not to someone like Johnny. What possible reason could she have? I was flummoxed.

"Oh, for heaven's sake, Henrietta," Delilah said when I ruminated over it in front of her. "She probably got knocked up. Don't be so naïve."

This honestly never occurred to me. What about all that Bible reading?

None of us heard anything else from Carolyn. She disappeared into the ether like an ephemeral cloud.

Little Debbie was notified in late August by the Residence Office, although she neglected to inform either Delilah or me, that Carolyn's spot was assigned to a transfer student—*a stranger*. They gave her the option of moving into one of the Lodges. The Lodges were adorable tiny bungalows, planted right in the middle of campus in an idyllic wooded setting, like tiny mushrooms in a glade. Most housed fraternity men, although each could only accommodate seven students. The Lodges were in a state of transition, fraternities moving elsewhere to larger spaces, both on- and off-campus. Half of the Lodges had been reserved for women this year. At this late date in August, a spot opened in one. Little Debbie, our adorable snack cake of a suitemate, chose the Lodges over us. Perhaps in her position, I might have preferred the Lodges too. But she could have told us.

Delilah and I arrived at the junior women's dorm, moving one more residence hall down the sidewalk, like slipping to the next rosary bead. Strangers were in our shared bathroom. Two students from a community college in southern Virginia transferred into our suite. They both sang in the college choir. There was a lot of singing at all hours, our bathroom reverberating with lyrics. It was torturous. If I heard *Shenandoah* at midnight, one more time, I was going to scream. Between Delilah and I, we had not one musical bone in our bodies. Other than the musical annoyances, no real reason existed for our incompatibility. But we were like puzzle pieces that would not quite interlock. We belonged to different tribes.

This year I studied petrology, the study of rocks—igneous and metamorphic in the Fall and Sed Pet in the Spring. Having described all those cores for Dr. Falcone in the Smithsonian lab saved my bacon in the Spring semester. Geomorphology. Stratigraphy. Since I wanted to be a paleontologist, I took Biology.

I was interested in living things but wanted them dead when I examined them. I did not want anything to bleed on me or to stink. I was out of luck on both accounts. The biology lab reeked of formaldehyde, which turned my stomach. The cow's eye and the fetal pig proved to be both fascinating and disgusting at the same time. On the day we were instructed to prick our fingers and type our blood, I declared I already knew my blood type, although I did not, and picked one at random. I skewed the class data with only a glancing regret.

One fortunate outcome of the class was my introduction to botany. I had never given much thought to plants. The dusty philodendron in our dorm room barely survived my pathetic caregiving attempts. Between semesters and at the beginning of each summer, I carried it dutifully over to the Greenhouse, where someone— probably a biology graduate student—perked it up until I returned to collect it. No one in my family had ever gardened. I learned about xylem and phloem, stamen and pistils, and pollen. Plant sex?! Who knew? A whole new world blossomed, literally.

I took a step back from going to the river this year. Freshmen and sophomores in the natural sciences department needed to do their Historical Geology or Paleontology projects, but I was finished with these. To be truthful, I was a bit tired of clams and scallops by my junior year. I would still seek advice from Dr. Miller—he was both my Sed Pet and my Stratigraphy professor—and would stop to chat with his wife Patricia if I saw her in the department. Still, my worldview was expanding, and stomping on snakes did not fit into it this year.

Since I had given up the river, Delilah inferred my Saturday afternoons were open. "We're going to the football game this weekend," she declared.

Did she know me at all?

"No, thanks, I don't have any desire to go," I told her.

Yet resistance proved futile and on Saturday a group of girls from our hall scooped me up to attend my first William and Mary football game. Pounding across the arched Crim Dell Bridge, we traversed the stagnant, inky pond below. Trees swayed and leaves fluttered like nature's applause in a chilling autumnal breeze. Red maples, *Acer rubrum*, lived up to their name in shimmering scarlet, tulip poplars, *Liriodendrum tulipifera*, in veined goldenrod and the oaks, all manner of *Quercus*, already leaned toward their winter sepia. Uphill, past the Lodges, through the square brick battlements surrounding the stadium, we entered like victors and scaled the bleachers.

Our team was called the Indians. After all, we were right down the road from Jamestown, home of Pocahontas and John Smith lore. Our mascot, a student dressed in full Native American regalia, rode onto Cary Field on a pony, whooping, at half-time. Kegs flowed in the stands and a hotdog sold for fifteen cents. Wearing my green and gold sweater, I cheered at any small victories, watched others down the beer, and smothered two hotdogs with ketchup to make them palatable.

The team lost. William and Mary was known for their academics, not football, as hard as they tried.

"Mary was on the field today, and William stayed home," a voice snidely remarked behind me.

By the end of the game, between the squalling devotees, lubricated fraternity men, and ingested nitrates from processed meat, my head beat like a kettle drum. Walled in by the crowd, I felt like all of my nerve endings were exposed. Thankfully, attending this competition satiated any perceived need I might have had for the comradery that comes from observing a contact sport with several thousand non-participating strangers.

During a particularly cold spell in January, Delilah traipsed into our room and unwrapped herself from her coat and scarf.

"We need to join the Philomathean Society. Both of us," she declared.

"What's that?" I asked.

"It's a group of women who meet each week to debate different topics. I've gotten to know some of the Philomatheans in my philosophy classes. You'll love them. Always ready to jump in and give their opinions. No blending into the walls for them."

Delilah had finally selected a major and decided on Philosophy. What she planned to do with it was anyone's guess.

"Don't you think I'm the sort that blends into the walls?" I asked her.

She tilted her head, considering. "No, not at all. You're just odd. You know...unique."

"Gee, thanks," I replied.

"Sorry. I meant that in a good way. After all, who wants to be the same as everyone else?"

Words to live by, I thought. '*Who wants to be the same as everyone else?*'

Now she was full of purpose. "What do you think about joining?"

If interested in joining the Philomatheans, one had to put an application forward and be voted in. There were mystical criteria to meet and an interview. Knowing a member helped, which I did not. Once in, there were monthly dues and responsibilities, such as bringing food to the debates. The Philomathean Society even had their own house, right on Richmond Road, on the edge of campus, in which the senior girls resided.

"Sure, why not?" I said. I figured I could use some expansion to my limited friend circle, and maybe there would be some debates on natural history topics.

We were both accepted, Delilah on her merits and me only by some miracle, I thought, and this became our primary activity for Saturday evenings. The debates resembled glorified wine and cheese parties. When we arrived at the Philomathean House, the evening's topic was posted at the front door. We were expected to mingle around to the different clusters of coeds, discussing our opinions on it. A fair amount of cheap wine and beer was imbibed. Men were invited to join in the discussions, by member invitation only. If a male student misbehaved at a debate, the other members could blackball him from future events. It was a closed democracy.

Through the Society, I became friends with Laurie from Texas, with her big ideas on literature—which I did not give a hoot about—and her bigger twang. I discussed the emergence of colonial-era ideals with bookish Mary Alice and the merits and drawbacks of the death penalty with smart-as-a-whip Charlotte. If the potential energy stored in those rooms was ever allowed to fully convert, it would compete with the power locked within atomic nuclei.

Natural history topics were seldomly discussed, the number of female science majors being limited. One evening, however, the topic was Evolution versus Creationism. Because of my background, I became the center of attention that evening as I politely clashed with some of the religion majors over the creation account in Genesis and the meaning of the Biblical 'day.' It was heady stuff.

As the Spring semester progressed, I noticed Delilah spending a lot of time with one man. His name was Kelvin Ford. He was a student, but an older student, who decided in his thirties to return to school to finish his degree in philosophy, which had been interrupted. He planned to attend seminary after college. I found his grooming suspect, his shaggy brown hair and long scruffy beard neither in fashion nor appealing. I kept these opinions to myself. He and Delilah spent a lot of time drinking coffee in the downstairs lounge, deliberating over whatever philosophy majors cared about, and generally mooning around. They used a lot of our coffee beans that semester, the mornings' grinding now taking twice as long. I still considered the beans to be ours, even though Delilah had fired me from doing her laundry after I had shrunk one of her mola shirts. I suspected there was another kind of grinding going on as well. Men were still not allowed in the dorm rooms, but Kelvin, being older, had an apartment. I stayed mum, but the situation worried me.

Toward the end of the Spring semester, Delilah received a telephone call from her father informing her he was being reassigned by the State Department, effective immediately. She needed to cancel her summer plane tickets. Her parents were moving back to Washington, D.C. It caught Delilah by surprise, as she planned to spend the summer again in Guatemala.

"Back to Washington?" she moaned. "Is there anywhere more boring?"

Having grown up right next door in Arlington, I found Washington, with its museums and monuments, a pretty exciting place. But it was not exotic. I tried to explain the city's advantages. One I was unable to point out, however, was that I would be nearby. Because I would not be. That summer, I would be joining a field excursion with my father. We would travel to the Green River Fossil Quarry in Wyoming to dig for several months. *I could not wait.*

CHAPTER 28

The summer arrived in a flutter of excitement and nerves. My heart raced as I imagined our upcoming jaunt to the Green River Quarry. And we were flying there! I had never flown in an airplane and pictured myself as an intrepid world traveler. We would fly from Washington, D.C., to Chicago, change planes, and continue on a smaller plane from Chicago to Salt Lake City. A geologist from Princeton University, a colleague of my father's, would pick us up and drive us to Wyoming.

The day arrived for our departure. My dad dressed in his suit and hat. I wore a skirt and cardigan over a white blouse and my ballet flats from Binns. I felt quite sophisticated. We set off in our spiffy attire for National Airport in a taxi cab, each with our suitcase. My boots and rock hammer were stowed in mine, along with my dungarees and work shirts.

After checking our luggage and boarding the airplane, my stomach began to churn nervously. *How did it feel to soar high off the ground?*

A stewardess, in her uniform and nurse-like hat, came down the aisle and handed us each a piece of gum. I stared at it. "It's for your ears," she informed me.

With silent apologies to my mother, I chewed on the gum like I was masticating a rhino, staring out the window, breaking out in a sweat. Then we were away from the gate, engines revving, tearing down the long runway, lifting up, up. I counted the seconds in my head, "one one-thousand...two one-thousand...three one-thousand," because I had heard that most crashes occur in the first two minutes after takeoff. My father tried to lean over me and point out views from the window. "Look, Henrietta, there's the 14th Street Bridge!"

Was he crazy? I had to count! And why would I want to look down when I could imminently crash? We finally leveled off, my heart stopped pounding in my throat, and the captain turned the Seatbelt Sign off. We were free to move about the cabin. And to smoke. Passengers lit up all around us. Perhaps I hadn't been the only nervous person on the flight. My father patted my hand, "Just remember the Bernoulli Effect, Henrietta," he said. "Air rushing over a foil produces lift." Ah, well, I hadn't taken physics yet—that 'pleasure' still awaited me—so I figured I would hedge my bets and ask for assistance from my guardian angel, just in case she was listening. I appealed to her throughout the flight, and if Bernoulli was in effect, that was fine too.

We were served a hot lunch on the flight to Chicago, the tiny trays with individual compartments holding salad, biscuit, chicken, and rice. There was even a compartment for a warm brownie. All washed down with a Coca-Cola. Afterward, we were given a warm towel for our hands. We landed in Chicago with only an hour between flights, which suited me just fine. Our landing had been uneventful, but I wanted the next take-off to be over.

Our next plane was smaller and looked more flimsy to me. There were only two stewardesses on this flight. The take-off was bumpier, but I breathed through it. This flight lasted another two and a half hours, during which we were served a large snack. Processed cheese in tiny individually wrapped wedges, crackers, peanuts, and pretzels—all washed down with another Coca-Cola, which I accepted although I preferred RC Cola. Other passengers imbibed alcohol and many puffed away on their cigarettes, leaving the air in the small cabin like a deadly combination of noxious fumes.

Staring out the window as we approached the Salt Lake City airport, I cannot say that I was impressed with the view. Surrounded in the distance by high mountains, the city, such as it was, looked like a postage stamp set in the middle of an endless desert of tumbleweeds.

"Welcome to Salt Lake City," the stewardess intoned after we touched down. "Please remain in your seats until we are at the gate. The local time is 3:15 p.m."

It was much later, according to my watch.

The tiny airport had only one gate. The good news was that the suitcases were pulled out of the plane quickly and set on the carousel. The bad news was that my bag was not among them. My father's case arrived but mine did not. The harassed airline counter attendant apologized. There were telephone calls. More waiting. No one could locate my bag. It became apparent that my suitcase did not make it onto our second flight. Had I asked Delilah for advice on flying, perhaps she would have told me to carry one change of clothes or pack one in my father's suitcase for emergencies. But I had not asked, and here I was—in my best dress clothes and shoes— standing in the blowing desert sands of Utah.

While we waited in vain for good news, a gentleman of medium height, with graying hair and a ready smile approached. Dressed in field khakis, he held a banded hat in one hand. He and my father greeted each other.

"Henrietta, I'd like you to meet Dr. Glenn Jensen, from Princeton," my dad said. "Glenn and I worked on a mastodon site in New Jersey together."

"Hello Henrietta," Dr. Jensen said. "That dig was a long time ago. The mastodon skeleton is now at the New York State Museum."

A three-hour drive to Kemmerer, Wyoming loomed ahead of us. My father left our address at the Kemmerer Hotel with the counter attendant and we left. Since it was the airline's fault, my luggage would be delivered to me. Or so we were told. I stared balefully out the window of Dr. Jensen's pick-up truck as the scenery zipped past.

"Henrietta, Kemmerer is famous for being the site of the first J.C. Penney store. You should be able to buy some replacement clothes there," Dr. Jensen said.

I neither wanted to spend money on new clothes nor liked shopping. I spent the drive grousing to myself in the back seat. Finally arriving at the Kemmerer Hotel, a saggy three-story stone building on Pine Street, I slumped upstairs to my closet-sized room, located next to my father's, with the bathroom down the hall. Throwing myself on the twin bed, I slept immediately, waking only to accept a sandwich he brought up, and falling back into a coma-like sleep until morning.

I awoke when my father knocked on my door. I had slept in my clothes and looked like it.

"Time to get up, Henrietta. Come down to the dining room for breakfast when you're ready."

After meandering down the hall to use the facilities, I arrived in the dining room to be introduced to a group of geologists—all men of course—who were in the process of devouring breakfast. I needed my coffee, but this being not-the-end-of-the-earth, but close-to-it, the only coffee they served smelled burnt and tasted worse. I drank it anyway. The crowd appeared in high spirits, but I concentrated on my clothing predicament. Shockingly, no one from the airline had shown up with my suitcase overnight. I wolfed down some fried eggs and sausage.

"Dad, I need to buy some clothes. Do we have time to go to Penney's this morning?" I asked, my face turning red in mortification. I did not want to be the cause for the group's delay.

He looked around the table—after all, we were riding with others having no transportation of our own—and there was general agreement, so we pushed back from the table.

"I'll be as quick as I can," I said to no one in particular.

The J.C. Penney 'mother store,' as the sign proudly proclaimed, was founded in 1902, and looked as if it hadn't changed one iota in all of that time. However, it still served its purpose. I was able to purchase undergarments, socks, shirts, and a pair of overalls. Shoes proved problematic. No women's boots were stocked in the heat of the summer—not that I wanted to spend money on new boots. I purchased a pair of flimsy tennis shoes, in an awful shade of olive green, which fit poorly, but they were certainly better than my ballet flats.

"Hopefully, I won't drop a rock on my foot," I grumbled.

Changing in the dressing room, I tossed my slept-in clothes in a bag and headed to meet my dad at the cash register.

On the lengthy drive, we rumbled down gravelly dirt roads, washed out in places. Riding with one of the quarry workers, our heads almost knocked against the pick-up truck's roof as we bounced along. We slowed several times to traverse across cattle gates. At one point, we climbed out and pushed the truck from a deep rut. I was thankful my stomach had time to settle after breakfast.

All my discomfort melted away, however, as we arrived at the Green River Fossil Quarry. My heart lodged in my throat as I stared upward. The quarry was simply immense, the walls soaring upward. Gigantic piles of rocks baked in the sun. A bulldozer, creating wide tread marks in the mud, scooped up huge rock slabs, like a massive game of dominoes. We parked near a construction trailer and Dr. Jensen met us for a tour.

"The workers are concentrating on what is called the 'split fish layer.' Most of the vertebrates are found in this 6-foot-thick layer," he said as he pointed. "See that enormous pile of rock over there? That's discarded rubble. The bulldozer had to dig through all of that to reach the fossil-bearing layer. There's a much smaller layer, about 18 inches thick, and higher up in the section, there." He pointed higher. "That layer also contains vertebrates, but the rock is blockier and harder to split. Last week the bulldozer was working on an upper terrace, driving across the top of the 18-inch layer, and it ran over a crocodile fossil, smashing it into a million bits."

I thought my father would cry over that story.

"Henrietta, you can work on those small piles over there. They all contain fossil-bearing rock. We have them drying in the sun because it rained here last week," he said, gesturing to several piles over which someone had set up a canvas canopy.

I traipsed over to the canopy, picking up a rock hammer and chisel off the ground. Kneeling in the dirt, I reached for a slab and began to split it along the layers. Chips flew and a damp earthiness wafted into the air. Although experienced at cleaving the powdery rock in the museum prep lab, working at the source felt more satisfying. Outdoors, breathing in the fresh air, the heat from the mid-day sun washed over me. The fish were scattered about and plentiful—heads, fins, tails, scales, whole, halves, a petrified seafood buffet.

After six days, my suitcase finally arrived at the hotel. I changed out of the now-encrusted overalls into my clean dungarees, happy I could finally wash the week's clothes at the laundromat in town. I had never appreciated my boots more than after that week of trying to avoid a crushed foot. And I learned my flying lesson—dress in clothes I could wear for days. Anything else was just ridiculous.

On our fourth week in Kemmerer, a van of geology graduate students arrived from Princeton University. Driving from New Jersey, they had been on the road for a month, studying geology on a cross-country traverse. They were now meeting up with Dr. Jensen who had scheduled them to work a few weeks at the quarry before continuing. My dad and I tagged along to meet them at the town's campground. Arriving, we found the students unloading tents, sleeping bags, a camp stove, lanterns, and duffels from their van. A tall, thin man with a scraggly beard sauntered over.

"Henry, Henrietta, let me introduce you to my colleague, Dr. James Eddy. He's the professor who has been leading this motley crew," joked Dr. Jensen.

"Dr. Ballantine, pleased to meet you. I'm familiar with your work," he acknowledged my father. "Well, hello," Dr. Eddy turned to me as I stood in my field clothes. "Are you working here, or are you someone's wife?"

I did what I did best and kept silent, managing to raise one eyebrow at him.

"This is my daughter, Henrietta. She is a geology student at the College of William and Mary," my dad said, jumping in to fill the silence.

I reminded myself that Princeton did not admit women, so Dr. Eddy did not deal with any in his classroom. Fortunately, our introduction was interrupted by the five Princeton men ambling toward us.

"Gentlemen," Dr. Jensen called to the students, "come over and meet Dr. Ballantine and Henrietta."

The Princeton men introduced themselves, a crew that looked bedraggled from riding, disheveled from camping, and hungry. They shook hands with my father and nodded dismissively to me, turning their backs to set up their tents. I sensed snickering and noted a few stolen glances. Their attitudes reminded me of an analogous subset of the men from my Historical Geology class. I hoped to be proven wrong.

CHAPTER 29

SUMMER 1960, WYOMING

The Princeton men had been trained in the Socratic method, which to me meant they were constantly arguing. About everything. They joined us hammering on the quarry rocks, splitting them along bedding planes to find fish. Once we found promising slabs, we sawed them in situ, with a circular saw, and lifted them out of the ground. I preferred the intricate work which I did in the afternoons, sitting with a magnifying glass under the awning, chipping away large flakes of the substrate with a knife. The truly delicate dissection would come later in a lab.

All the while, the discussions raged. One of the men was especially argumentative. He was tall, with short brown hair, a muscled physique, and an angular, handsome face. A graduate student, his name was Frank Bailey. And he loved to bait me with his questioning.

"Why do you think all of these fish are preserved intact when others are disarticulated?" he asked while examining a slab containing multiple fish skeletons.

"Perhaps these were buried quickly," I said.

"What difference would that make?" he asked.

"Maybe predators started eating the fish if they weren't buried. Turtles or crocodiles could have gnawed at them. Those fell apart because they were partially eaten," I said.

"Seems like a lot of partially eaten fish. Why were some buried quickly and others not?" he asked, a smirk on his face.

"Sedimentation rates change."

"Why? Explain that to me."

"Perhaps some were buried in volcanic ash. That's why there are many in one place, like a fish kill."

"If the whole lake was buried in ash, wouldn't all of the fish be dead in the lake? Why are there fish in the layers above?" he asked.

"How does anything survive after being covered in ash? Maybe fish eggs were buried but hatched the next season," I answered.

Frank stood back and looked at me, hands on his hips, a haughty grin on his face. "Maybe."

He was infuriating.

Again he would start, others joining in the debate.

"Do you think the lake was deep or shallow?" Frank asked.

"Shallow," answered Burly Abe, who looked like a bear.

"Why? Give your evidence," said Peter the Owl, staring through his immense oval glasses.

"Because limestone forms in shallow water," answered Edwin the Stork, who stood on spindly knock-kneed legs.

"Always?" asked the Insufferable Brian.

"Hmmm...maybe not. What do the fossils tell us?" asked the Owl.

"Henrietta, what do you think?" Frank put me on the spot.

"Maybe the lake was deep and anoxic and that's why many of the fish did not disarticulate. They couldn't rot on the bottom without oxygen," I answered.

"But a lot of the fish did disarticulate. There are piles of bones and scales. As you said before," Frank said, circling back, with a smug look on his face.

The jerk.

Being an experienced debater it galled me that Frank always maintained the upper hand. Exasperated, he drove me mad. If my father noticed our arguing, which I'm sure he did, he didn't comment on it. He spent a fair amount of time chatting with all of the

Princeton students, including Frank. Eating lunch together as a group, there was constant debating, chastising, joking. I was either ignored or challenged. At least to my face.

One afternoon I perched at the picnic table attempting the finer extraction of a fish with a small scraper. Tired from stacking rock slabs on pallets all morning, the sun beat down on my sore back. The smell of machine oil and clay reached my nose. Frank hunched over the rock saw, trimming excess limestone from around individual fish. Dust clung in the air, the gritty mist acting like tiny prisms refracting the sunlight around him. I glanced sideways, watching him as he wiped the sweat off his forehead, tossing the discarded rock into the waste pile with his muscled arms. A pretty impressive sight, I admitted to myself.

He sauntered over and deposited several fossils in front of me, a silt cloud wafting around the table.

"Here are some specimens that might clean up nicely. You can see half of this one exposed on the surface," he said, pointing.

"Yes, that's *Piscacara*. You can see its long, spiky dorsal and anal spines," I replied, setting down my scraper.

I immediately pursed my lips and my face reddened. Did I just say that out loud?

Frank, of course, noticing my discomfort, capitalized on it. "*Anal* spines, you say?"

He grinned expansively and called out. "Hey guys, come over here. Henrietta wants to show us some *anal* spines!"

The Insufferable Brian and Edwin the Stork meandered over, snickering.

"I'm dying to see those *anal* spines. Where are they, Henrietta?" Brian said.

My face blushed in mortification.

"They are partially covered in rock," I stammered.

"Ah, Henrietta's anal spines are covered in rock," the Insufferable said, sneering.

What dolts. Were they twelve?

Ignoring them, I examined the slabs Frank had set in front of me. Holding a piece up to my eye, I spied something interesting along the newly-sawed edge.

"Wait, look at this slab," I showed it to Frank. "See this pattern of brown dashes aligned parallel along this bedding plane? I think these might be the radiating ribs of a stingray! Do you have the piece you sawed off?"

Walking over to the waste pile, Frank scrounged through the discards and held up the missing piece. A stingray was a rare find. Could this be one?

The entire next day I chipped at the stingray, gently scraping the limestone away from the bones with a fine-bladed knife. It was meticulous work, and my neck and back ached with the effort. At lunch, the Princeton crew crowded around to see my progress.

"Can you tell what it is yet, Henrietta?"

"Keep going, Henrietta. I can't wait to see the ray!"

My dad looked at it, a dubious expression on his face. He hesitated.

"I guess it *could* be a stingray," he said.

Over the next few hours, as the sun lowered in the sky, the specimen revealed itself bit by bit. At the end of the workday, I peeled back a final plane of lamination with a flourish, revealing the entire fossil. There it was. A pile of fish bones in a mashed-up heap. Not a stingray. Not even a whole fish. Randomly arranged smushed bones had created the dashed pattern on the rock edge.

The echoing laughter of the Princeton men as they climbed into their van burned into my brain. Frank had the grace to pat my shoulder.

"Next time, Henrietta, next time," he said.

I wasn't sure which was worse—the laughter or the pandering.

CHAPTER 30

The booth containing the pay phone stuck on the side of the hotel, appeared as if it had not been cleaned since its installation by Alexander Graham Bell himself. Calling collect was expensive, but I did not have enough coins to pay for the call. My mother accepted the charges.

"Henrietta, is that you? Are you alright? Is your father okay?" she asked.

"Yes, everything's fine. We're having a good time and digging up a lot of fish," I said. "But I wanted to let you know I have been invited to join a university field trip with other students so I won't be flying home with Dad. I'll be driving back across the country with them."

I had gone over the words in my head beforehand.

There was a momentary silence. I could feel the temperature rising.

"Dad thought I should call you to let you know," I added. Which of course was not technically true.

"What university? What students?" she asked.

"Princeton University. Dr. Jensen is here with his truck, and another professor came from the university with a van of students. They've been here for three weeks working in the quarry. But they're leaving tomorrow and asked me to join them. There's room with Dr.

Jensen. We'll be heading to Utah to dig for trilobites, then driving back across the country. They'll drop me off at Auntie Hilda's house in Harrisburg. Dad will pick me up from there," I said.

Another moment passed. I tapped my toe in anticipation. My dad had approved me going on the trip, as long as my mother agreed. I had been surprised by the invitation and I really wanted to go. Even with the snooty Princeton men. It was an opportunity to see more Western geology and I did not want to pass it up.

"Isn't Princeton University all men?"

"Yes, but I'll be fine. I have a separate pup tent. And Dr. Jensen will look out for me."

"Absolutely not! You get yourself on that plane with your father! Where is he? Is he there?"

"Not right now. But it will be fine. I'll call you when I get to Harrisburg," I said.

My mother sputtered something.

"Love you!" I said as I hung up the phone.

Poor Dad. Wait until he got home.

The isolation of Utah revealed itself as we drove down two-lane macadam roads, the van and pick-up truck in tandem, through tiny rundown hamlets, alone and secluded. Back to the airport, we dropped off my dad. I gave him a quick hug as he exited the truck.

"Have a great trip," he said to me. "See you in a few weeks."

As he grabbed his luggage from the back, I heard him say, "Take care of my girl, Glenn."

And then we were off, skirting the Great Salt Lake, its distant waters shimmering like a mirage across the monotonous desert. I lost count of the prairie dog colonies, curious heads bopping up and down in their holes. Knowing nothing about Mormonism, the trip gave me an education in names. Nephi, Ephraim, Jericho, Deseret. Like a Who's Who of *The Book of Mormon's* scriptural significance.

Reaching the town of Delta, we pitched our tents in a campground behind a local park. Known for incarcerating Japanese-Americans during World War II, the town was now a quiet amalgamation of rock shops, Mexican restaurants, and decay.

The next morning after an unappetizing breakfast of Spam fried on a camp stove, we headed north, turning eastward off the main highway onto a bumpy gravel road leading toward stark unforested mountains. After a long ride during which my teeth almost rattled out of my skull and my breakfast was in danger of reappearing, we stopped within sight of a nondescript foothill. Craggy mountains rose as an abrupt backdrop in the distance, ivory and gray strata disappearing into talus slopes below.

I let most of the Princeton men hike ahead of me across the gravelly terrain. They were welcome to be the first to encounter anything venomous. Dr. Jensen, ever the gentleman, walked last, keeping an eye on us. Reaching the outcrop, we looked up to see layers of black shale from bottom to top, stretching up into the sky. The sun glanced off my glasses as I tilted my head.

"This is the Wheeler Shale, middle Cambrian in age. It's at least 500 meters thick and was deposited within the House Embayment. There is some Burgess Shale-type preservation in here, mostly carbonaceous films. But most of the fossils are trilobites. There are three abundant species and some rare ones. Let's see what we can find," Dr. Jensen said.

I was all set with my hammer, ready to dig for my favorite fossil, the trilobite, those cockroaches of the sea. I would have been happy to collect in silence, filling my sample bag. But no. The debates began at once.

Dr. Eddy began, "These rocks have been interpreted as landslide deposits off a carbonate platform. What would be the evidence for that?"

The Stork jammed his hammer into the outcrop. "These rocks look horizontally bedded. Wouldn't a landslide deposit have bedding that's sloped at an angle?"

"Perhaps. Where are the carbonates? What would we look for?" asked Dr. Eddy.

The Insufferable answered. "They would be located around the edge of the embayment."

Burly Abe joined in. "How would we know they were contemporaneous?"

"Facies changes perhaps? Some evidence of limestone and shale interfingering?" answered the Stork, examining a piece of the shale.

Frank stood with his back to the outcrop, his arms crossed and a glint in his eye. "If this was a deep embayment, how did these rocks end up at almost 10,000 feet? What do you think, Henrietta?"

I knew he was baiting me again.

"Well, I guess it was a geosyncline. That's how these thick sequences were deposited…" I said.

"Yes, maybe, but how did they end up at this elevation? Here in the middle of the continent?" he persisted.

I waited for someone else to chime in, but no one came to my rescue. No theories about mountain building popped into my head. I would not take Structural Geology until next semester. I tried to turn the tables.

"What do you think, Frank?" I shot back.

He answered with another question.

"Have you ever heard of tectonics, Henrietta? The continents moving?" he asked.

"Yes, I know about continental drift," I replied.

"Not just continental drift. Orogenies. Earth deformation. How about seafloor spreading?" he asked.

When he mentioned seafloor spreading all of the hammers became quiet. The men exchanged glances.

"Seafloor spreading…?" I said, looking around.

"Seafloor spreading is the idea that the plates are pulling apart at the mid-ocean ridges, spreading apart like a conveyor belt. Lava is erupted there, adding material to the oceanic crust and pushing the rest of the seafloor away. Eventually, the seafloor is recycled at the trenches. This drives the movement of the continents. And the uplift of the mountains," Frank said. He was on a roll.

Dr. Jensen spoke. "Frank, those data have not been published yet. Professor Hess has shared his theory with us at Princeton, but it is not common knowledge."

At least someone was kind enough to point that out. Still, at that moment, my cheeks burned and I felt like a complete fool. I could not help myself, I blurted an especially nasty curse in Russian under my breath, and added, "*Ehte lyodeh edeohteh.*" *These men are idiots.*

I turned and walked away, using all of my fortitude not to stomp on Frank's feet with my boots as I passed him. Far down the outcrop, almost out of sight, I stared at the shale layers and the debris that had fallen at the base, willing myself to calm down.

"Kingdom Animalia, Phylum Arthropoda, Class Trilobita," I recited silently in my head.

When I spotted a large trilobite, I wordlessly staked my claim and started splitting the rock along its laminations. Trilobites popped out along the bedding planes. Their stony eyes stared at me from their entrapment. Filling my bags with specimens, I ignored the Princeton know-it-alls for the rest of the morning.

When we compared our fossils after lunch, my collection was the most varied. I collected four species of trilobites—*Asaphiscus* with its prominent tail section, *Elrathia* with its pin-prick eyes, one spiny *Olenoides,* and a clutch of tiny barbell-shaped *Peronopsis.* I had some brachiopods, worm tracks, and what I thought might be a sponge fossil.

"Good show, Henrietta! You must have had the best spot," Dr. Jensen proclaimed.

I smiled, gathered up my treasures, wrapped them in toilet tissue, which I called 'paleo paper,' and placed them gently back into my sample bags. With a thick black marker, I wrote 'Property of H.B.' in big letters across each bag.

Dr. Eddy strolled up next to me.

"You know, Henrietta, *Ya gavaro nimnogo Paruski*," he said. *I speak a little Russian.* And he smiled.

Oops.

✦

From tiny trilobites to gigantic dinosaurs, we rambled on to Dinosaur National Monument. Playing tourists, we rode on a tram up the hill to the exhibit hall to view the skeletons half-exposed in the massive quarry wall. I ran my fingers down the gigantic femur of an *Allosaurus*, imagining life in the late Jurassic.

From there we crossed the majestic Rocky Mountains, my ears popping across the Continental Divide. After donning helmets and heavy jackets, we crammed into a mine elevator and whisked down a shaft to tour an underground gold mine at Cripple Creek.

Camping outside of Cripple Creek that evening, I stared into the darkest of skies, the stars twinkling like drusy sugar over my head. Now that the men were used to having me around, they reverted to their neanderthal manners. Burping, slurping, cursing, farting—I had never experienced anything like it. The behavioral bar was set low.

Our campfire roared and a hearty scent wafted from the propane stove. Beef stew from a can, I discovered, tastes delicious when you are ravenous. Peter the Owl brought over two tin mugs of stew, handing one to me, and plopped down next to me.

"Here you go, Henrietta. It looks like you could use this," he said.

"Yes, I sure can. Thanks, Peter," I smiled.

We chomped along in companionable silence, the smoke stinging my eyes.

"Did you always want to be a geologist?" Peter asked, the flickering from the flames reflecting off his glasses.

"I always wanted to be a paleontologist," I said. "Ever since I saw fossils in the Smithsonian. What about you?"

"I was going to be a doctor," he said. "Until I took a geology course. After that, there was no turning back."

We continued chatting, about nothing in particular, back and forth. I happened to look over and saw Frank's face. He was staring straight at us, his eyes hard, his face a stone. The second our eyes met he turned his head and stared into the fire.

What was that about?

On to Colorado Springs, we arrived at Garden of the Gods, the site of towering hogbacks tilted vertically in grand salute against the backdrop of the Front Range. The deep reds and sand-dune whites of the Lyons Sandstone stood in juxtaposition to the pink coarseness of the Fountain Formation's alluvial clasts. American flags fluttered as we gathered in the parking area. It happened to be the Fourth of July. As we surrounded Dr. Eddy, he handed out topographic maps.

"We're going to make geologic maps today on top of these topographic base maps. I've divided the area into three sections. Grab a mapping partner and pick a section. We'll meet back here around four o'clock and see if your geologic interpretations match at the edges," he said.

I looked around. There were six of us, an even number. Would this be like kickball team selection? When no one wanted me on their team?

Frank turned to me.

"Do you want to map with me, Henrietta?" he asked.

Really?

"Sure," I answered, incredulous, yet a bit grateful.

Hiking across the scrubby landscape, with Frank in front of me, we traversed between the hogbacks. Pebbles crunched monotonously beneath our boots. The sun scorched the back of my neck, and I pulled the brim of my hat down to shade my face. Nature's color-coding of the rocks helped us with our mapping. I had to admit

Frank was skilled at recognizing the lithologies, marking the formations and contacts on our map. He could interpret the big picture, seeing the proverbial forest, rather than the metaphorical trees.

Our conversation was limited to our work.

"What formation do you think this is? How about over there? Where should we head next?"

Until mid-morning, when Frank blurted out, "He's engaged, you know."

I took a swig from my canteen. "Who?"

"Peter."

"Oh. That is nice. I mean he's nice."

"I just thought you should know," he said.

"You know," I said, tilting my head to see him from under my hat, "some people are just thoughtful. Or friendly."

He startled. "I'm thoughtful. I'm friendly."

"Yeah, to who?" I asked.

He gave me a long look. "Let's eat lunch," he said.

We sat on the gravelly ground in the diminishing shade of a hogback, the sun high in the sky. As we pulled our sandwiches from our knapsacks, I tried to make up for my bluntness.

"Did you grow up in Princeton?" I asked, thinking the answer would be no.

"Yes, since first grade," he said.

"Oh? I figured you just went to school there."

"No. My dad works at the Princeton Medical Center."

"Do you have brothers and sisters?"

"Two brothers. They're both older than me. Both married. No kids." He took a bite out of his sandwich. "How about you?"

"I'm an only child."

"Was that lonely?" he asked.

I considered. Had it been lonely?

"Yes, at times," I answered.

We had our first real conversation. I told him about my mom and what it was like to grow up in Arlington and have a tutor and not go to school. He told me about his childhood as the youngest of three boys and described how his older brothers picked on him, although he chuckled when he said it. It was the first time I had seen a genuine smile on his face.

After lunch, we hiked toward a distant ridge and wearily, our target did not appear to be getting any closer.

"What do you usually do for the Fourth of July?" I asked. "Do they shoot off fireworks in Princeton?"

"No, but we have a big block party," he said. "We cook a whole corned ham from the butcher. It comes from Philadelphia, where they corn them. My mom bakes it all day in the oven, and it's the best thing you've ever tasted."

"I've never heard of corned ham. Is it like corned beef?" I asked.

"The same process, but the taste is different and delicious. You can shred the meat off the bones with a fork, it's so tender."

We skirted down a deceptively gentle-looking slope. The thought of the ham and the rhythm of Frank's voice pulled my attention from my feet.

"I'd love a taste of that right n-" I began.

Loose talus rolled under my boots. I started to slip downhill on the scree. Crying out, I fell to the ground, sliding, bracing with my palms. Frank turned and stooped down, trying to catch me, but I slid too fast. Skidding on my hands, and scraping the backs of my arms along the ground, I rolled to a stop.

"Are you alright?"

"Yes, I think so." Tears welled in my eyes.

"Here, let me see your hands."

Frank took my skinned hands in his and turned them over. Removing his canteen from his knapsack, he poured cool water over my bleeding palms. He gently patted them with his bandana.

"Your hands are a bit scraped up. Can you stand? Are your legs ok?" He pulled me up and brushed the dirt off my back. Taking the bandana, he poured some water on it and dabbed it on my face.

"I'm ok," I sniffed. "I don't think anything is broken. It mostly just scared me."

As I attempted a wobbly smile, my hands began to sting.

"I don't have any bandaids with me. It's up to you, should we continue or go back?" Frank asked.

I looked forward at the ridge and back toward the parking area, our van a distant dot, weighing my options.

"I don't know," I said, my chin quivering now, my voice shaky. "It's hard to judge distances out here."

Taking a long look at me, Frank reached around me, hugging me to him. He gently rocked me side-to-side. "It's ok, Henrietta. We'll go back and put something on the scrapes. We've done enough mapping."

I nodded, raising my face toward his. Before I could form a coherent thought, he pulled me closer and kissed me. A long slow delicious kiss. And I kissed him back, raising my bleeding arms around his neck. Suddenly, nothing hurt at all.

CHAPTER 31

SUMMER 1960, CROSS-COUNTRY TREK

Alternatively stand-offish and covertly affectionate, Frank's attitude seemed to change toward me with each geological province we traversed. Heading across the Great Plains, he ignored me, bored and grouchy. Nothing to see but a monotony of corn stalks. My arms stung as the scrapes scabbed over, my elbows, now a shade of purple, feeling bruised and sore. None of this helped my mood.

Detouring to the south of Chicago allowed us to accept the hospitality of Dr. Eddy's mid-Western friends who lived on the outskirts of Peabody, Illinois. Past the VFW hall and the bowling alley, we blinked once and traversed the entire town. Hosting us for dinner and offering their backyard as a campsite, the sun-toughened couple emerged from their farmhouse as we pulled up. After nights of canned food warmed over a camp stove, our spirits lifted when they presented us with that evening's dinner. Buttery corn-on-the-cob picked from their garden, fingerling potatoes, fat hamburgers cooked over an outdoor fire pit, homemade cherry pie. We ate like starved baboons.

The yard backed to acres of corn fields, the setting sun casting a low shimmer on the silks. Fireflies appeared, their bioluminescence pulsing in the darkness. Drawn by childhood memories, I meandered toward the corn, reaching up, catching a bug in my fist, feeling its tickling feet. Opening my hand, I watched its tiny flickering before releasing it back to the heavens.

Frank walked up beside me, his features barely visible in the twilight.

"Look, lightning bugs!" I said. "I used to catch them in a jar, with holes in the lid. I would keep them until morning and let them go."

"Lightning bugs?" he laughed. "You mean 'fireflies.'"

I sighed. "Must you disagree about everything?"

"Well, not everything," he said, raising an eyebrow.

Reaching for the insects, we trapped them in our cupped hands. Holding them out to each other, we released them, one by one. Once liberated, the flies coasted lazily away, tail lights throbbing, advertising for mates. As darkness fully descended, crickets and treefrogs trilled a backdrop of discordant harmony.

Our eyes met and Frank reached for me. Wordlessly, we crushed together between corn tassels, arms around each other, kissing with a hunger that could not be satiated. Stalks bent and snapped. Overhead, meteors streaked across the sky as the earth's orbit crossed the Perseids, debris from a comet that could not hold a candle to the sparks in the corn.

"There but for the grace of God...," Frank said, nodding out the window, a somber expression on his face.

I nodded, eyes wide open.

After a marathon sprint across the Appalachian Plateau, we had pulled off the highway onto a rutted back road. Bouncing over the potholes through Appalachia was like traveling back in time. The poverty smacked us in the face, weathered dilapidated shacks with tin roofs, yards full of rusting cars. Trailers with busted windows decayed at the end of dirt tracks. Small children crouched in mucky yards.

The open-pit coal mine emerged before us, appearing as a giant chasm scorched by dragon fire. *National Bitumen—No Trespassing* warned a rusty sign. We pulled into the parking area. The air was tinged with black particles and smelled of sulfur. A foreman waited for us in a soot-covered trailer. After asking us to don hard hats and filthy orange safety vests, he noticed me in the group. He paused, staring for a moment.

"Women are bad luck in a coal mine. Nothing personal. But she'll have to wait in the parking lot," he nodded his head toward me.

"Henrietta is a geology student," Dr. Jensen said. "Can't you make an exception?"

"I'm sorry, but no. The miners are a superstitious lot. She can wait here, or we'll have to cancel your tour."

An awkward silence prevailed for a moment. All of the men intensely studied their boots.

"Go ahead, I'll be fine here," I said, not wanting to make a fuss. "I can see the operation from the parking lot. You can fill me in later."

The men traipsed down the packed dirt road into the bowels of the gigantic pit, morphing into Lilliputian versions of themselves. Frank led the group, chatting with the foreman, the angles of his face captivated, gesturing with his hands. Appalachian stratigraphy was his bailiwick, and he was in the middle of it. As I paced in the lot, I ogled the gigantic dump trucks and excavators, monstrous even from a distance.

Viewed from my perch, I found the strip mine appalling. The gaping maw of the mine had wrenched out the pines, displaced the woodland animals. Habitats destroyed. All of the wildlife, from the nematodes in the soil to the blue jays, box turtles, white-tailed deer, decimated. Acres of black, sooty devastation loomed, a bituminous-coated wasteland.

Stooping to examine shards of coal and shale flung from overflowing trucks, I spied a group of miners tramping up the road from the mine. Coal dust blackened their faces, hands, and overalls rendering them indistinguishable. Their chatting ceased immediately as they spotted me. It was their turn to ogle. I climbed into the van to wait.

Passing next to me, one of the miners leaned his head through the open window.

"Are you lost, lady?" he asked with a grin. His youthfulness startled me, his face streaked with grime, sweat, and dust. Even his teeth looked black.

"No, I'm just waiting," I replied.

"You're welcome to come wait with us," another replied, cackling.

"No, thank you," I said.

They moved on, snickering and backslapping each other.

An hour later, the tour ended. I climbed out of the van as our group returned to the parking lot. Frank walked over to me, grinning from ear to ear, happy as a magpie.

"The tour was incredible," he said. "The amount of coal they take out of the ground from strip mining leaves the old subsurface mines in the dust. No pun intended." He chuckled at his own humor. "The efficiency is amazing."

"Efficiency? Don't you see the destruction?" I said to him. "The trees cut down. All of the animals are dead. It's a wasteland."

"I'm sure the company will remediate when they're done. Plant trees…" he replied.

"How will the trees grow? The soil has been stripped away. The water is probably poisoned with sulfur."

"You don't know that," he said, frowning. I noticed the rest of the group backing away, stripping off their safety gear.

"The people here are probably too poor to complain. The mine has killed all of the natural beauty here," I said.

"Natural beauty?! Don't you see that the mine employs the people who live here? Without the mine, where would they work?"

"Where did they work before?"

He stared at me, incredulous.

"They worked in the underground mines, which were more dangerous than this," he said, waving his arm at the pit. "They dealt with cave-ins, poisonous gases, constantly breathing in the coal dust. Day after day. Bent over. In the dark. Backbreaking work.

They still do." He drew breath. "And where do you think your heat comes from in the winter, anyway?"

Glaring at him silently, I couldn't find any words. Yet, the strip mine had triggered an awakening in me, a spark in my consciousness, of environmentalism. The necessity of ecosystem protection. Frank saw profits, wages, and energy. Idealism versus practicality, we oscillated on different wavelengths.

After being ignored, abandoned, and the butt of jokes, I turned and climbed back into the van. Hot and hungry, I leaned back in the seat, folded my arms, and closed my eyes. The thought popped into my head—I was ready to go home. I had even surprised myself.

The cliff face loomed overhead the next day, the manmade highway-cut dissecting Pennsylvanian age strata, gritty siltstones and oily shales. Three hundred million years ago, lycopsid scale trees, giant fern trees, and horsetail rushes thrived here, sending down branching daughter roots beneath murky swamps. Dog-sized amphibians chased giant dragonflies and tiny, newly-evolved reptiles hatched from amniotic eggs.

Now stamped with white carbonaceous films and fractal imprints of long-dead ferns, the black shales interfingered with opalescent coal seams. Tree bark and whorled leaves pyritized the fissile rocks with glittering gold. I was spellbound.

"Oh look, *Calamites!*" I pointed to a fossil imprint of tree bark with distinctive jointed markings to Peter, who happened to be crouching next to me. "And *Lepidodendron!*" I added, pointing at the dimpled pits of a scale tree patterned in the rock.

"Trust the walking encyclopedia to come up with Latin names," said Insufferable Brian.

Frank noticed me lugging a heavy chunk of shale covered in lacelike ferns. We hadn't spoken since yesterday at the mine.

"Let me help you with that," he said.

"No, thank you," I replied grim-lipped, as I struggled with the oversized rock. "I can carry my own fossils."

Without a word, he leaned over, grabbed the slab from my hands, and carried it to the van. I followed him, wordless.

"Don't you think you have enough fossils, Henrietta?" he asked with a small smile.

I sensed his attempt to break through the ice and decided to meet him halfway.

With a straight face, I feigned shock. "Frank, there are never enough fossils in one's collection."

He reached over and squeezed my hand.

Sample bags full, Dr. Jensen's truck and the van overloaded with petrified ferns, twigs, and stumps, it felt like Christmas day. Testing the efficiency of our vehicles' shock absorbers, we drove through the wind gaps of the Valley and Ridge and limped on to Harrisburg.

My poor Auntie Hilda did not realize what she agreed to when my father asked if I could be dropped at her house. Auntie Hilda was my great-aunt, a reedy old lady who loved playing bridge and drinking manhattans. She downed one of the latter when she realized that seven smelly men wanted to sleep on her living and dining room floors for the night.

The following morning, after taking my hair out of its plait and plunging into a hot shower to scrub off the Appalachian dirt, I felt like a new woman. Downstairs, Dr. Jensen sat at the kitchen table as Dr. Eddy flipped pancakes at the stove, the last of our camping food. The Princeton men were packing their sleeping bags back into the van.

"Dr. Eddy, Dr. Jensen, thank you so much for letting me come on the trip," I said.

"It was our pleasure, Henrietta," Dr. Jensen said.

"You fared better than I thought you would," offered Dr. Eddy. "Pancakes?"

Breakfast over, the crew began to depart. Joining them by the van, I stood next to Peter as he stuffed his duffel in the back. "I guess you'll be glad to see your fiancée," I said.

Peter peered through his glasses. "What fiancée? I don't have a fiancée."

Frank strolled up behind Peter, giving him a shove into the van. "Let's go, jerkoff," he said.

I raised my eyebrows at him.

"I can be a real S.O.B. sometimes," he said with a smart-alecky grin. He leaned over and ran his fingers through my loose damp hair. "Write to me, Henrietta. Your dad has my address," he whispered in my ear.

"Okay, I will," I murmured back, with a wistful smile.

Giving me a quick peck on the cheek, Frank leaped into the van. Doors slammed, engines fired. I waved until he was a blur on the horizon. "Don't forget about me," I implored into the stratosphere.

CHAPTER 32

After working in the Leakey Quarry, posing for photographs, extracting the *Deinotherium* skull, and scooping and bagging pollen samples, the time arrived to dig for fish. Maggie, Kimaru, and I hiked to the fish site, several kilometers from basecamp. We lugged our usual equipment—brushes, hammers, picks, chisels, and shovels. Our canteens weighted with water, our knapsacks carried our lunches. Kimaru toted his rifle.

The Ice Age lake existed only in stratigraphic memory, the desiccated silts preserving the remains of the ancient biome, the planktonic algae, nektonic fish, thirsty mammals, and treacherous crocodiles. The unique diversity captured in these layers was a testament to the richness of prehistoric times. I imagined the lake as I trudged toward the fish site. What would it have looked like? Probably a lot like Lake Manyara. But the Pleistocene beasts would have been different than today. Gargantuan, ferocious, deadly. And hungry. Always hungry.

"Do you think we would have survived?" I asked Maggie.

"Survived what?" she asked.

"The Pleistocene," I said. "With the shovel-tusked elephants, the giant rhinos, the chalicotheres. The felids and the canids?"

"Well, some people did," she said. "Or we wouldn't be here, would we?"

"Good point," I said. "I appreciate you helping me, by the way. I know you didn't come to Africa to babysit visitors."

"It's fine," she said. "You know, part of the job."

But it didn't sound fine. She stared down at her boots, her frown lines deepening.

"What's your research about, exactly?" I asked.

She looked up in surprise.

"My research concerns the evolution of African predators throughout the Pleistocene. Including man as a predator. That's why I'm so interested in the marks on the elephant bones," she replied. "Thanks for asking. None of the visitors ever do."

"It sounds interesting. I guess your research doesn't include predatory fish?"

"No," she said. "I'm especially interested in saber-toothed cats. Felids, as you call them."

We scuffed along, our boots treading through the sisal which grew prolifically along our route.

"We'll pry up the slabs you want to take back to the museum, but we won't have to do all of the heavy lifting," Maggie said. "The diggers will carry the slabs to camp once we've extracted and marked the ones that you want."

"That'll be great. Thank you. And once Mr. Thomas arrives, he'll help me prepare them for transport. Or I should say 'if' he arrives. When I left, it still wasn't decided."

"Well, if he's coming, it will be with Kimaru's run to Moshi next week, I would think. Louis tries to schedule visitors to coincide with our supply runs. No waste of petrol," she said.

"That makes sense," I said. "You'll like him. Mr. Thomas, I mean. He's great at making jackets. Has years of experience. He goes by 'Tom-Tom' although I never call him that," I said.

"Why not?" she asked.

I stopped to think. "I guess it would be like calling your parents' friends by their first names. Just weird," I said.

She stared at me as if I had two heads, shrugged her shoulders, and walked on.

The fish site had been marked with wooden stakes. Dusky gray siltstone layers fanned out along the ground like playing cards. A few slabs had been pried out and stacked. Kimaru walked up from behind us.

"Watch where you step," he said. "The fish are under your feet."

Fragile bones peeked out of the earth. Fish scales were sprinkled like cornflakes on the top of the bedding planes. I knelt on the ground and began to brush at the loose grit. Maggie joined me, carefully clearing debris without disturbing the bones.

"There are a bunch of clam fossils here with the fish," I said, pointing.

"Yes, and these dark laminations are full of organic matter. They're probably from the plants that grew along the lakeshore. Maybe your palynology study will figure out what they were," she replied.

Straggly bushes offered little shade as we bowed under the relentless sun. Hours passed as my skin prickled from the heat and my knees became skinned. I constantly readjusted my hat to shade my face. Freckles bloomed on my arms. Still, I was in my element.

Leaning on one wrist, I chipped at a fish skull with a fine pick.

"Maggie, come look at this fish," I said. "It looks like an eel. See there? The sediment surrounding it looks like it's a different color. It's almost like it was enclosed in a sac."

She knelt next to me. "Hmm…keep digging around it. Can you see how deep the discoloration goes?"

Wiping the sweat out of my eyes, I reached for my fine-bristled brush.

"No. I don't want to dig too closely. Most of the skeleton is just an imprint. Here are the skull and the teeth," I said.

"So the rest of the skeleton might have been made of cartilage?" she asked.

"Yes, maybe."

I swiped away some of the finer debris.

"Look at this—at the impression here. I think this fish had legs! Perhaps it could have climbed out of the water," I said.

"You know, lungfish can breathe air and they move from pond to pond. I don't know if they have legs, but they might," Maggie said.

Grabbing my trowel, I gently plunged the tip around the strange fish, extracting it with the encasing discolored sediment.

"If I'm looking at this imprint correctly, this fish had an unusually bulbous head compared to its skinny body," Maggie said.

An image flashed in my mind. Fishes with rubbery skin. Flanking each other, hanging on a pole.

"Yes, round enough to impale with a stick," I said.

"What?"

I shook my head. "Nothing. I have no idea why I said that. It just popped into my head."

CHAPTER 33

For our senior year, Delilah and I moved into the Philomathean house. Our room was located next to the living room, which meant the noise level was high most of the time. However, as an upside, our room was spacious, having once been used by a house-mother. The college could no longer afford to place a chaperone in each specialty and sorority house on campus. We did not miss having one.

Our coffee habit took a hit this year. Delilah's parents' move to Washington meant the end to our Guatemalan coffee supply. There was nowhere to buy coffee beans except the A&P. Although a step up from the terrible coffee I had endured all summer, it was still a bitter pill to swallow, literally. I'd schlepp five long blocks north, to the grocery on Lafayette Street to buy coffee and cat food, and drag it all back once a week.

Yes, cat food. I was given the great honor of taking care of the house cat. Our house came with a big tomcat—a brown tabby, with huge paws and a crescent-shaped bite taken out of one ear. His name was Romeo. Each year, one of the Philomatheans took responsibility for the cat. It was portrayed as an honor, but I noticed I was elected for the post of 'Keeper of the Cat' when I was not around.

I did not mind. Romeo spent a lot of time outside, well, roaming, so it wasn't a huge job, but I had to buy his food. I took to him right away, although he was more enamored with Delilah, who could not stand him. He would lie on her bed in spite.

"Would you take that cat out of here? He's probably full of fleas," she said. "I bet he hasn't ever had a rabies shot. Cats belong in a barn."

I picked up Romeo and put him on my bed. The next time I came into the room, he was back asleep on hers.

Of course, when he left dead presents on the back step, it was my responsibility to dispose of them. That was gross.

I wrote letters to Frank and he wrote back. Mine cheery and newsy; his much more abbreviated. He was working on his dissertation on Appalachian stratigraphy and tectonics, a textbook worth of subject matter jammed into a thesis. Other than that, he was fine. His parents were fine. His brothers were fine. It was like squeezing blood from a boulder. The Philomathean house had only one telephone, and only incoming long-distance calls were allowed. Long-distance calls were expensive, which was why Frank never called me, I thought. No commitment forthcoming, no future plans ever mentioned. He did sign his letters—Love, Frank. Surely that meant something.

The Philomatheans proposed new debate topics, and our Saturday evening parties commenced, with subjects as diverse as the purpose of pointillism in art, the causes of the Civil War, and the comparative attributes of red and white wine. Delilah invited Kelvin to these, and many of the girls brought dates. The wine debate evening became quite a drunken debauchery to celebrate the end of Fall classes, right before final exams. On debate nights, Delilah and I always shut our bedroom door, but we didn't think to lock it. The night of the 'red versus white wine' event, sometime past eleven o'clock, I was tired and fuzzy-headed, so I opened the door to our room. I immediately realized someone was in there and backed out into the hall. Delilah saw me and the look on my face.

"What's the matter? Is someone in our room?" she asked.

I nodded, "Yes, I think so. On your bed."

"What?!" Pushing open our door, she turned on the ceiling light. The bulbs blazed. The couple on her bed, warned by my intrusion, had hastily pulled themselves mostly together. The girl was a new member, a sophomore.

"Get. Out." Delilah was emphatic. They scampered.

The next morning, a bit hungover and headachy, I tried to reason with Delilah.

"Maybe we should let it go. I'm sure they've both learned their lesson," I said, thinking to myself that perhaps Delilah would be more understanding, given that she and Kelvin might not have been strictly vertical all the time.

But Delilah was having none of it.

"They were on my bed, Henrietta. The cat is one thing. But this? I'm sorry, but no."

I could not blame her.

Delilah and I both voted to blackball the young man. Two days after the incident, it seemed all the coeds on campus knew the story. The young woman was probably mortified. It was 1960, after all, and a girl's reputation was paramount. She resigned from the Philomathean Society. Winter break, fortunately, interrupted the gossip over the episode. I heard not a whisper about her after that.

CHAPTER 34

DECEMBER 1960, ARLINGTON, VIRGINIA

Our metallic silver Christmas tree cast an incandescent glow in the front window, lights reflecting off the glassy ornaments. The angel on top winked at the wrapped presents stacked below. An advent centerpiece of candles and evergreens wafted a piney scent across the dining room. In the kitchen, displayed prominently on a pink depression glass cake plate, a newly baked coconut cake glittered with flaked icing and nonpareils. Our front porch railings, festooned with garlands, were frosted with natural snowy flocking.

I barely noticed any of this. I was a nervous wreck. Frank was coming for Christmas! Arriving in the afternoon, driving from Princeton, two days before the holiday. I had invited him and he had accepted, as easy as that. Or so I thought until I saw my mother pacing the house, eyes on high alert. Always setting ridiculously high standards for holidays, she was in a tither, adding extra volatility to the day.

"Henrietta, you need to sweep the front porch. Frank is going to think we live in a barn."

"Harry, you just tracked in a bunch of snow! Put your boots on the back porch!"

I had not seen Frank since the summer, an ocean of time. Dressing with care, I pulled on a skirt and cashmere sweater set. Would he even recognize me?

A powder-blue Cadillac pulled into the driveway, tail fins sprouting from the back. I slipped on my snow boots and scampered outside, hugging myself in the cold. When Frank stepped out of the car, a grin on his face, twinkle in his eye, I remembered what drove me crazy about him.

"Nice car," I said, a bit sarcastically.

"Yeah, it was my grandpa's. Beggars and choosers, you know," he said.

"I'm so glad you decided to come for Christmas."

"Well, I need to consult with your dad about some Appalachian fossils."

"I see," I said, in mock exasperation.

"And you did offer me a behind-the-scenes tour of the museum. I couldn't turn that down," he said, with his crooked smile.

He opened the back door of the sedan to reach for his suitcase. The backseat and passenger seat were stuffed with boxes.

"Are you moving in?" I asked.

"Well, not here…" he began.

My dad clattered down the porch stairs. "Frank! Welcome!"

We breezed into the house. My nerves steeled for interrogations.

━━━◆━━━

Gorging that evening on a lavish feast of roasted turkey, stuffing and gravy, my dad, Frank, and I reminisced about our time in Wyoming. The past summer was a touchy subject for my mother, however, since I had taken off with the Princeton men without her approval. She was uncharacteristically quiet, surreptitiously glancing at Frank under lowered eyelids, like a leopard sizing up its prey.

"When do you finish your degree, Frank?" she asked.

He turned to her with a brilliant smile. "I defend my dissertation in May."

"What will you do after that?" she asked.

"Actually, I've just taken a job. Henrietta is familiar with the company." He turned toward me. "National Bitumen advertised for a geologist and I applied. I start right away. That's why all the boxes are in my car. I'm driving there from here."

A glob of turkey stuck in my throat. Bitumen meant coal. Coal meant mining. Mining meant danger. "What will you be doing for them?" I croaked.

"Initially I'll be tracing the coal seams, making geologic maps, recommending new locations for tunnels and strip mines. I'll also be trained in mine safety and inspection."

"You'll be inspecting mines?" I asked.

"Yes, eventually."

"What about your dissertation?" my dad asked.

"I'm finished with my courses and fieldwork. I can finish my writing anywhere I can carry my typewriter," he said. "Which is in the trunk."

A leaded weight settled in my stomach. Frank knew how I felt about the coal industry.

"Where will you be working?" I asked.

"I start in a little town called Grandy. In southwestern Virginia. That's where I'll be trained. Then they might move me to another of their locations. In Appalachia."

"Do you have a place to stay?" my dad asked.

"Yes, the company has arranged for some kind of temporary housing for me."

"We can celebrate with dessert," my mom said, disappearing into the kitchen. Like an offering, she carried in the coconut cake, placing it in the middle of the table. My dad sliced it and handed pieces to each of us.

"This is the best cake I have ever eaten!" Frank said. "Absolutely delicious, Mrs. Ballantine. And I love coconut."

A smile reached across my mother's face. The ice broke.

Overnight, an additional inch of snow fell, covering our suburban sidewalks in a pristine glaze. I almost hated to ruin it with footprints, but the need to be away from my parents caused Frank and me to bundle out of the house for a winter walk. Old habits died hard and we set out on my usual path, heading to my aunt and uncle's house. Uncle Al lingered in the hospital with some ailment or other, but I wanted Frank to meet Aunt Esther. Miss Tiny now played ball in beagle heaven.

The wind buffeted us as we crunched through the snow in our hiking boots. Quiet reigned over the neighborhood, the streets unplowed, cars frozen in driveways. Stratus clouds blanketed the sky, the air saturated with the dampness of a low-pressure system stubbornly refusing to retreat. Turning the corner, out of sight, Frank reached for my hand, his warmth spreading through my loose-knitted glove.

"You'll love my Aunt Esther. We'll only stay for a short visit because I know she'll want to get to the hospital."

"What's wrong with your uncle?" Frank asked.

"Oh, who knows. He's always sick. Mother thinks it is all in his head."

Frank gave me a strange look.

"No diagnosis? The doctors must have run tests."

I looked at him and thought for a moment, our breaths condensing into tiny puffs in the frigid air.

"I…I don't know. I've always assumed he's just a hypochondriac."

"Does your mother say that in front of your aunt?"

"Hmm…probably not," I said. "I've never given it much thought , I guess."

"Maybe you should ask your aunt? You know, collect more data," he smiled.

"Yes, more data," I said, smiling back. "Excellent idea."

Swinging our arms together, hands clasped, striding along in companionable silence, I thought of my tutor, Madame Sekomova. She would be happy for me, I believed, in that quiet moment on our frozen nature walk. Perhaps this was part of the destination that she had spoken to me about.

"Maybe you can convince my mother to give you another piece of coconut cake at lunch today," I said.

"Please don't tell her, but I hate coconut," he said. "I was just trying to be polite. It seemed important to her that I like it."

I smiled at him. "That was nice of you."

"Yes, I am a nice guy. I distinctly remember telling you that," he replied, smirking.

I flashed back to the Garden of the Gods and that first kiss.

"You know, I wasn't sure you would come to visit. I couldn't tell if you missed me. Or if I was just, you know, a summer romance."

Frank stared down at me.

"Henrietta, I just couldn't figure out what to do with you," he said.

"What to do with me?"

"Yes, you are just in a category all by yourself."

I paused. "You mean you didn't know how to classify me?".

He grinned. "Exactly."

We turned through the gap in the boxwood hedges at my aunt's yard, the snowy branches scraping against our shoulders leaving deposits of powdery crystals. Slush-covered stepping stones led up to her porch.

"That's easy," I said. "Kingdom Animalia."

I leaped onto the first stone, pulling him with me, "Phylum Chordata."

We jumped to the next stone, "Class Mammalia."

Jump. "Order Primate."

He laughed. We jumped again. "Family *Hominidae*," I said. "Genus and species?"

"*Homo sapiens*," we recited at once, landing at the porch edge.

"Subspecies..." he said, staring at me. "Beautiful."

Months of uncertainty fell away as he kissed me at the last stone, our heartbeats synchronized. My Aunt Esther applauded sound-lessly from behind her storm door.

Two days later we bundled up to head to the museum. Not wanting to park Frank's car filled with his worldly possessions on a downtown street, we headed for the bus stop. The snow had turned into a dingy mush on the sidewalks. Cars zipped by spewing fountains of tire ejected slush. I shivered and wrapped my new Princeton scarf around my chin, my Christmas gift from Frank.

"Are you excited about your new job?" I asked as we loitered at the bus stop.

"Yeah, I'm excited to make money. And use whatever skills I've managed to pack into my brain."

"Promise me you'll be careful," I said. "Especially when you go into the underground mines."

He frowned at me. "I know you don't like the idea of my working for the coal company. You made it clear how you felt about that strip mine last summer."

"I just want you to be safe," I said. But it was more than that, and we both knew it. The memory of the destructed mountain stood between us. *Why would he want to be a part of that?* Yet I didn't want to ruin the day by starting that conversation.

Alighting from the bus, we traversed the National Mall, standing in the middle for a sightseer's view. Frank gawped at the Capitol at one end, the Washington Monument in the distance at the other. Then climbing the glistening marble steps of the National Museum, we entered the Great Hall. The echoes of tourist chatter boomed around the high dome of the rotunda, reverberating off the Doric and Ionic columns. I led the way to the Hall of Extinct Monsters, aware of Frank's hand clasping mine, the warmth of our shoulders touching. We wrenched our necks to gape at my old friend, *Diplodocus*, centered in the room. Children skipped along in front of us, staring and pointing at the *Triceratops* and the *Stegosaurus*. Their parents called after them as they raced ahead to the giant sea turtle shell mounted on the wall above the reptilian mosasaur skeleton with its piercing teeth and paddle-like flippers. We meandered behind the trail of sticky fingerprints left on the glass-topped mahogany display cases. Although I had wandered through this hall hundreds of times, the displays took on a new excitement as I shared them with Frank. I pinched myself to confirm I was awake.

Walking to the Ocean Hall, we stood beside the enormous replica of a blue whale.

"Makes you feel tiny and insignificant in comparison, doesn't it?" I asked.

"Yes, this whale and the *Diplodocus* are huge. On the other hand, we're the ones staring at them. Not the other way around," Frank said. "Henrietta, the place is amazing. I can see why you love working here."

"The storage rooms and prep labs will be empty today. No one comes in on Sundays," I said.

Through the camouflaged door behind the Neanderthal exhibit, I used my key to enter the work areas. The sudden silence of the interior hallway reverberated against the muffled cacophony of the exhibit halls. Plodding along, pulling Frank by the hand, my heart echoed in the quiet. I opened the door to the ammonite storage room. After all, Frank had been promised a behind-the-scenes tour. And I was ready to give him one. Not a complete tour, mind you, but an excursion to the more interesting bits.

CHAPTER 35

I set off for my last college semester with the knowledge that Frank was closer to me geographically than he had been at Princeton. Nonetheless, he could have moved to the Moon since I had no address or phone number for him. I consoled myself by plunging into the last classes required for graduation. Structural Geology. Physical Anthropology. Botany. And Physics, which I loathed. I wanted to explore, to dig, to discover. I did not want to run toy cars down inclined planes or launch metal balls across a lab room. Didn't Newton figure all of this stuff out in the seventeenth century, for heaven's sake? Building circuits terrified me. I finally concluded that I simply needed to do the math, make the units come out correctly, and stop my whining.

My mood was generally whiny, however, and by mid- February, darkening by the day. Delilah turned from her desk and glared as I hunched over on my bed.

"What's the matter with you, Henrietta?" she asked, "You're snapping at me about everything. You're even yelling at the cat."

Tears pooled behind my eyes. "I'm sorry." My shoulders slumped. "I haven't heard from Frank. Not one letter. I'm worried that something's happened to him."

She got up from her chair, walked over, and sat down next to me on my bed.

"He's in Timbuktu, right? Working for the coal company?" she asked.

I attempted a smile. "He may as well be in Timbuktu. Yes, he said he'd write and let me know his new address. Then nothing," I said.

"He had to move into a new place and start a new job, right? And try to finish his dissertation? I don't think you have anything to worry about. He's probably just busy."

Romeo jumped up on my bed and I reached out to stroke his fur.

"See, even the cat's here to let you know that everything is okay," she said.

I appreciated her assurance, but an uneasy feeling settled in my stomach. I appealed to my guardian angel, but she remained stoically silent.

My father rang a few nights later, the call blessedly distracting. I hunkered down in the phone alcove with the receiver pressed against my ear to hear over the clanking of dinner preparations in the kitchen.

He began, "Henrietta, last night I attended a lecture sponsored by the National Geographic Society. Guess who the guest speaker was?"

"I don't know, Dad. Who?"

"Dr. Louis Leakey!" he exclaimed. "What a gifted speaker! His work has tremendous implications for the evolution of man. After the lecture, I spoke with him and he told me they've uncovered hundreds of fish fossils from the Pleistocene lakebeds at Olduvai. He's invited me to visit this summer to bring some back for the Smithsonian."

"That's great, Dad," I said. "Really terrific!"

And I meant it. In Physical Anthropology we were studying the evolution of man. The subject matter enthralled me. Learning about the discoveries made in East Africa, I became a devoted fan of Mary Leakey. She appeared in stunning color photographs in the *National Geographic Magazine*, digging for fossils alongside her famous husband, Dr. Louis Leakey, and their young sons in Olduvai Gorge in Tanganyika.

"Are you familiar with the Leakeys' discoveries?" my dad asked.

"Yes, I was just reading about Mary Leakey finding the skull of Nutcracker Man. He's the early hominin that's almost two million years old."

He chuckled. "And as astounding as that actual find was, the fact that the scientific community credits Mary with the discovery and not Louis is almost unprecedented. That alone should give you cause to be excited."

He had no idea.

"Listen, I'm working with the museum now to see if they'll pay my way to Olduvai. And I was wondering, if they do, would you like to come with me?"

Words stuck in my throat. It would be a dream come true to go to Olduvai Gorge. Scenes of me digging in the gorge with Mary Leakey bloomed in my mind.

"Henrietta?" he asked.

Finding my voice, I said, "Yes, yes, I'd love to go with you!"

"Of course, I'd probably have to pay your way. But it would be your graduation present."

"What does Mother think? That would be a pretty big expense."

"I haven't told her yet. Don't worry about that. I'll talk to her. I have to get my funding first."

Against my better judgment, I decided to ask. "Dad, have you heard from Frank at all?"

"No, I haven't. We finished up our collaboration over Christmas with the Appalachian fossils. Why?"

"Nothing. Never mind. I haven't heard from him in a while."

"Do you want me to call Glenn Jensen and ask if he's heard from him?"

"Oh, no! Please don't do that. I'm sure he's just busy with his new job," I said, echoing Delilah's words.

"Alright. How are your graduate school applications coming along?"

I crossed my fingers and lied. "Great, I'm working on them. I'm still deciding on a thesis topic."

"If you need any help, let me know."

As I hung up the phone, the words of Patty Miller came back to me—"Use your connections, Henrietta."

But there were limits. I would use my connections to get to Olduvai Gorge. But certainly not to check up on my boyfriend. Heaven forbid.

CHAPTER 36

Cloudless nights followed parched days in the gorge. Our cistern water dwindled, causing rationing. Bucket bathing allotments were reduced. My clothes, recycled several times, had been shaken and hung on a clothesline to air out between wearings. This did not do much to alleviate the odor. Or the dirt.

Extraction of the fish fossils completed, the slabs had been pried, split, and stacked. Ready for jacketing, they remained piled at the dig site awaiting the digger's strong muscles. Today was my chance to reconnoiter the gorge. My opportunity to search for new fossil discoveries, of the grazers, the carnivores, and if I were lucky, of ancient man. Within this ecosystem, he had carved out an existence, standing upright, creating tools, using an evolving brain to survive and thrive. I awoke early with anticipation tingling all over my body. I pulled on my stiff overalls, the denim embedded with grit, and headed to the banda.

Humming a tuneless song, Wawira handed me a teacup.

"Try this. A special treat for you today," she said. "Be careful, it is hot."

A rosy liquid filled the cup. The beverage carried a floral scent. I took a cautious sip.

"It tastes a bit like plums," I said. "What is it?"

"This is tea made from the coffee cherries. After the beans are extracted, the fruit is dried and used for tea. Do you like it?" she asked.

"Not bad," I said, sipping. "But it won't replace real coffee in my book."

Not wanting to insult her, I drank the entire cup, the brew sliding down my throat like drizzled syrup.

After wolfing down the morning's ugali, Maggie, Kimaru, and I set out for the day. The sun broke over the top of our destination, a craggy monolith in the distance. The landform was a monadnock, an erosional remnant left after the wind, rains, and long-disappeared river sculpted Olduvai Gorge.

"We're traversing across Bed I. Study the ground as you walk. Keep your eyes open for anything out of the ordinary," Maggie instructed. "Something darker, lighter, or bumpier than the surrounding sediment. Perhaps a shine or reflection, an odd shape. You know what Pleistocene enamel looks like—just like the elephant tusk."

We trekked in silence, three abreast, scanning the ground. Carefully placing our feet among the clods of clay, we slowly made our way across the dry, desolate landscape. Barking geckos and black crickets flitted out of our path. Vultures circled overhead, searching for carrion. Occasionally Maggie or Kimaru knelt to examine the earth. Nothing was found. It all resembled nondescript alluvium to me.

After a morning of staring at our feet, we arrived at the highland. The monolith extended skyward and stretched horizontally for a half-kilometer in two directions. Its vertical outcrops exposed bedded strata, the eroded edges knifing out like jagged stair steps. In places, talus slopes broke the lateral continuity of the beds. Maggie pointed to a dark brown layer, about eye height.

"The unconformity within Bed II lies just above this layer. Remember, below is Oldowan; above is Acheulean," she said, referring to the tool technologies.

I nodded as I traced the layer with my eyes along the hillside. Today's datum line.

My stomach rumbled. "Let's eat lunch," Kimaru said.

The three of us sat on the flattest stones that we could find and pulled out our lunches. Jars of cold stew. After the morning hike, it tasted like ambrosia. I chewed on a chunk of meat. I never knew what type of meat was in African stew; I never inquired. Best not to know.

I was feeling a little discouraged. Not that I thought I would find a vertebrate skeleton immediately. But there had been no evidence of anything, not even what we called 'float'—out-of-place, gravity-deposited bone shards.

"I didn't realize it would be so difficult to spot anything," I said, taking a sip from my canteen. "Whenever I've searched in sedimentary deposits there's usually something to find, even if it's a plant scrap or a shell fragment. I guess I've been lucky."

Maggie nodded. "Fossilized bone is tough to spot. It can be light or dark, depending on mineralization. It takes a practiced eye."

Lunch finished, we stood up, stowing the empty jars in our knapsacks.

"I'm going to climb up to the top of the hill, to keep an eye out for animals," Kimaru said. "Call out if you need me."

He climbed up a vertical gouge in the steep face, his rifle on his shoulder. Loose debris rained down under his boots as he disappeared from view.

Maggie turned to me. "Let's keep each other within sight, but not walk on top of each other. We'll have a better chance of finding fossils that way. I'll go to the left and you go to the right. Don't go gallivanting off. When you get a fair distance away, come back toward me."

In other words, she wanted me out of her way.

Turning in the opposite direction, she strolled away, her attention focused on the outcrop.

I crept along the hillside, my eyes trained on the dark layer for reference. I scanned methodically up and down the cliff, inch by inch. The African sun lifted higher and blazed. The temperature rose steadily and my arms seared in the heat. The knapsack weighed heavily on my shoulder. As I edged along, Maggie shrank in my peripheral view. My full concentration was on the hunt. Childhood colors came to mind—bittersweet, tan, desert sand, mahogany— the layered variation in hues representing changes in petrology and therefore in environments throughout time.

The relentless rays bared down, hour after hour. My head felt molten beneath my hat. No fossils emerged from the layered sedimentary rocks or ash-crumbly bentonites. Weary, I halted, my throat parched. Maggie appeared as a minuscule figure against the hillside. Kimaru was not in sight. Deciding to walk back toward Maggie as I had been instructed, I turned and took a few dispirited steps. Thirst overcame me, so I set down my knapsack to retrieve my canteen. As I bent to undo the buckle, a shadow loomed from behind me, a human form.

I turned slightly, squinting into the sun. The person's outline was back-lit with brilliant radiance, almost blinding me in a kaleidoscope of colors. A hand gripped my shoulder. Immediately, a sense of peace radiated throughout my body like liquid amber. I froze as in a trance. My heart rate and breath slowed. Time became irrelevant and began to warp, elongating into the ebb and flow of space. Words were spoken, the language foreign yet translated. Was it Russian? No, more primordial, and sensed rather than heard.

"I am here, my sister."

I replied into the air. "I don't have a sister. Who are you?"

"We are all sisters. Daughters. Mothers. You have met me before."

The presence exuded a gentle, motherly aura.

"Where did you come from?" I asked. "Wawira, is that you?"

"I am of the Spirit. We are kin, you and I. The same tribe. From different times."

For some reason, this made sense to me. I felt a profound connection. Tranquility surrounded me.

"Why are you here?" I asked.

"Our paths cross. I do not want to be lost. My bones left in the ash."

Straightening up, I tried to look over my shoulder at the person behind me, but the sun shone directly in my eyes, forming crepuscular rays in the cloudless sky.

"All is well. Keep looking. Do not turn back. You need to find me. I will guide you."

"Guide me where?" I asked.

"Where you were always meant to go. You are on the right path." Her tone changed. Sharply, she warned, "Stop. Stay still."

I heard the urgency in her words. My field experience told me to listen.

Arms wrapped me from behind in an embrace. I glimpsed ebony skin and muscled forearms; my back cushioned against soft breasts. As she pulled me backward away from the outcrop, I stumbled against her. She released me, and pointed from behind, her outstretched hand next to my shoulder. I glimpsed her broken, weather-worn nails, and bent arthritic fingers.

She called out. "A serpent! There! Quickly. Kick!"

I found my balance and focused on the ground. A monstrous snake, its body coiled, flicked its tongue at me. I swear I heard it hiss. I reacted without thought, swinging my booted foot back and propelling it forward, smacking into the snake, sending it flying into the sisal. I froze for a moment, in shock. Then I leaped back and screamed, over and over.

With a scuffling rain of talus, Kimaru slid down the slope from the top of the hill and hurried toward me.

"What's the matter? Are you hurt?" he asked.

"A snake, it was a snake!"

I shivered all over, motioning with my hand toward the brush.

"It was huge. I kicked it over there." Tears welled in the corners of my eyes.

He walked over and poked at the shrubs with the end of his rifle. "I don't see it. It must have crawled away. What did it look like?"

"It was light gray. Its mouth was open and was black inside. It was coiled, ready to strike..." I said, my voice trailing as I looked at him.

He nodded. "Maybe a Black Mamba. They're deadly. It's a good thing you saw it in time."

Maggie pulled up, breathless. "Are you alright? I heard you scream."

"Henrietta saw a snake," Kimaru said. "She kicked it. I think it's gone now."

"You kicked it? Why the bloody hell did you do that?" Maggie asked. "You should have backed away from it."

"Wawira warned me. She told me to kick it. I would have stepped on it if she hadn't!"

They both stared at me and then eyed each other. Kimaru shook his head. "Wawira is not here. I would have seen her approach from the top of the hill. She's back at camp."

"Well, someone did. There was someone here. I would have been bitten..."

They scanned the area as I leaned over, hands on my knees, gulping air.

"There's no one else here, Henrietta," Maggie said. "Maybe you're dehydrated, and you imagined someone? Perhaps you need to go back and rest?"

"Someone was here," I said with steely certainty. But I began to feel light-headed. The base of the outcrop swam before my eyes. I began to sway.

"Good heavens. Are you going to faint?" Maggie asked.

Kimaru grabbed my arm and lowered me to the ground. He pulled my knapsack toward him, grabbed my canteen, and unscrewed the stopper.

"Here, drink this," he said. "Slowly."

I swigged the tepid water. My head began to pound. I leaned my head back and poured water over my forehead, letting it drip down across my eyelids. My adrenaline-surged body shook.

Maggie hunkered down beside me. "Let's rest and then we'll hike back. You look zonked."

"Alright," I said, my heart rate settling.

"I think we'll work in the banda tomorrow. Kimaru has to drive to Moshi anyway. He'll be picking up your Mr. Thomas. We can use a day out of the sun."

I nodded in agreement, wiping my eyes with my sleeve.

But I needed to come back. I could not leave Africa until I returned to this place. My orders had been issued. And I intended to follow them.

CHAPTER 37

Anticipating another afternoon of tedium, I slid onto my stool in the Structural Geology lab and unwrapped myself from my coat. The damp February cold of the coastal plain infiltrated my bones. In class, we had been analyzing circular graphs known as stereonets, flat projections of the three-dimensional geometries of folded strata. My head fell on the table in utter boredom every time I looked at one. Frank probably excelled at this stuff. But I could not ask him, since I still had no address to write to, no word at all from him.

The other students filed in, one by one, mostly ignoring me. My lab partner, Michael, plopped down next to me.

"Good morning, Henrietta. Ready for more stereonet fun?" he asked.

"Oh yeah, can't wait," I said. By senior year, at least one of the geology men decided to be friendly.

Our Structural professor, bald as an exfoliation dome, waltzed in with a newspaper in his hand. He held up the headline. *Coal Mine Collapse. Miners Remain Trapped.*

"Did you hear about the mine collapse yesterday?" he asked the class. "This is why it's so important to learn about stress and strain."

My ears began to ring. All of the air left the room.

He turned to the board, drawing a diagram of mine pillars with chalk.

"The stress on mine pillars is calculated by four factors, the mine size to mining depth ratio, the..."

"Where was the mine?" I asked. All heads swiveled toward me.

He looked down and read the first lines of the article. *"A shaft in the Bluemont No. 5 coal mine in Grandy, Virginia, collapsed unexpectedly yesterday. A two-man inspection crew and five miners remain trapped farther down the mine. Rescue personnel are on the scene. A spokesman for National Bitumen announced that every effort..."*

I stared at him, starting to hyperventilate.

"Are you alright?" Michael whispered to me.

The ringing in my ears grew louder. Standing up, I walked to our professor and snatched the newspaper from his hand.

"Sorry, professor..." I began, my voice sticking in my throat.

I turned and escaped from the room.

Scurrying across campus, I barely glanced at the traffic on Richmond Road. A horn blared as I crossed. Plunging into the living room at the Philomathean house, my brain tried to assess what to do. Who to call? I had no phone number for Frank. I knew Frank's parents' names but had never met them. Did they even know I existed?

Delilah bounced out of our doorway, waving an envelope. "Guess who got a letter today?" she asked in a sing-song voice.

She half-handed it toward me as I ripped it out of her grasp, noting my name on the envelope. I nudged her aside and tumbled into our room, ripping open the seal.

"Good grief, Henrietta!" she said.

"There was a mine collapse," I said, distracted, shoving the newspaper toward her as I opened the letter.

Dear Henrietta,

I'm sorry it has taken me so long to write. I have been busy with my new job, which is great. Grandy

*is a small town, not much here. My training will be
over this summer and then I'll probably get moved
to another location. I hope you are doing okay.
I miss you.*

Love,
Frank

Six weeks I had waited for this. Shakespeare, he was not, but
at this point, I did not care. His address and phone number were
printed at the bottom of the letter.

Staggering to the phone, I stuck my index finger in the hole for
0 and dialed. The dial circled back, clacking into place.

"May I help you?" the operator intoned.

"Yes, I'd like to place a collect call. To Frank Bailey from
Henrietta Ballantine." I read her the number.

"One moment please."

The phone trilled distantly in the background.

"Hello?" a woman's voice answered.

"Collect call for Frank Bailey from Henrietta Ballantine," the
operator said.

"He ain't here right now," the voice said. The phone banged down.

I stared at the receiver. *Who was she?*

Isolated, with no means to communicate with Frank, his parents, or National Bitumen, I could do nothing but wait. Gloom settled over me as I set the receiver back on its cradle.

CHAPTER 38

Williamsburg Times
February 12, 1961

"Grandy, Virginia. The associated press reports that two men were rescued yesterday from a side shaft in the Bluemont No. 5 coal mine. The entrance to the shaft collapsed two days ago. Both men are reported to be in stable condition at the local hospital. Five miners remain trapped in a separate side tunnel isolated by the same collapse. Rescue crews remain on the scene. The drilling of an auxiliary borehole to provide air to the trapped men has commenced. Concerns about carbon monoxide gas concentrations are mounting. Families gather at the site and at the local Baptist church, where a spokesman for National Bitumen addressed the crowd yesterday ..."

I fretted while living in a daze. Had Frank been in the mine? If so, was he one of the men who had been rescued? I inferred that the two rescued men were the inspectors. And that the men still trapped were miners? Not inspectors? Or geologists? What if I were wrong? When would I know?

Enveloped by worry, my schoolwork languished. Graduate school applications teetered on my desk. Distracted, with no dissertation topic, I lacked the gumption to plow through them. Even with a topic, I needed an advisor to support me at a university that would admit me. The stars needed to align but at this moment my galaxy spiraled the wrong way, approaching entropy.

Williamsburg Times
February 13, 1961

"Grandy, Virginia. Five miners remain trapped in a shaft at the Bluemont No. 5 coal mine. The entrance to the shaft collapsed three days ago. Hope for a rescue remains high in this Appalachian town. An auxiliary borehole was completed yesterday, breaking through the roof of the shaft where engineers believe the men may be trapped. The borehole is designed to provide fresh air to the trapped men. Rescuers beating on the pipe in hopes of hearing a return signal have received none so far. Families remain cloistered at the local Baptist church..."

I tossed the newspaper into the trashcan.

"Henrietta, phone for you!" called out one of the Philomatheans.

I leaped from my room into the hallway, snatching the receiver from her hand.

"Hello?"

"Henrietta?" The connection was poor. A buzzing noise hummed down the line. Frank's voice came through muffled, but I could hear the exhaustion in it.

I sank to the floor, stretching the phone cord toward me. Tension drained from my body and pent-up tears spilled over.

"Frank! Are you alright?" I sobbed into the receiver.

"I'm okay. I guess you heard about the accident?"

"Of course, I heard. I've been worried sick."

"I wasn't in the mine when it collapsed."

"Thank God! Why didn't you call me?" I did not care about the neediness in my voice.

"We've been working to help rescue the trapped men. I haven't had any sleep since the collapse. I've finally come back to shower. And get some sleep."

"It's been four days!" I said.

The buzzing increased on the line, drowning out my words. "What?"

"It's been four days," I repeated, louder.

"Yeah, tell me about it," he said, voice raised over the static.

"Do you still want to stay there? In Grandy? After all of this?" I asked, incredulous.

"Henrietta, I can't get into that right now." I heard his exasperation. "Just give me a break, okay?"

A woman's voice sounded in the background. "I hope that ain't long distance!"

"Listen, I've got to go. I'm not supposed to use this phone."

"When will I see ...?"

The phone went dead.

My Valentine's Day gift. Frank was alive.

<hr />

Williamsburg Times
February 17, 1961

"Grandy, Virginia. This close-knit town mourns today as the bodies of five coal miners were retrieved from the National Bitumen's Bluemont No. 5 mine. After a rescue attempt that spanned a week, a prayed-for miracle did not materialize. Funeral services for the

men are being planned. A spokesman for National Bitumen pledged…

My letter to Frank was half condolence and half plea.

February 18

Dear Frank,

I read about the sad ending to the mine collapse in the newspaper this morning. I was so sorry to hear about the miners. I hope you are alright. Will you attend the funerals? If so, please express my condolences to their families.

I think about you all the time and worry about you. I wish you worked somewhere else. Once you finish your Ph.D., you'll have more options. Perhaps at a university? Or a museum? Or for the government? Won't you reconsider?

Love,
Henrietta

I popped the letter into the mailbox on the Philomathean house porch. In hindsight, my plea was unfair. Emotions were high, but I should have known better than to nag.

Frank did not reply.

The weather that Spring was especially warm, yet I hardly noticed. Meandering through the Colonial Williamsburg gardens served as both a diversion and a requirement for my botany class. With my *Guidebook for Native Plants* in hand, I blocked out thoughts of Frank by memorizing the Latin names of flowers. The stately tulips in the genus of, not surprisingly, *Tulipa*, jumped out of the ground, displaying myriad colors. Windflowers, with the genus name *Anemone*, did not look at all like sea anemones but resembled multi-colored buttercups. Purple bell-shaped Foxgloves, genus name *Digitalis*, waved their lovely yet poisonous blooms. The simple English Daisies were aptly classified with the genus name *Bellis*, 'bella' meaning beautiful.

Adding to my sullen mood were the Spring plumes of pollen grains. Virginia had no shortage of pollen. which blew out of the trees, especially the pines, dispersed as a green-yellow goo. I coughed, sneezed, wheezed, and dabbed at my itchy eyes. Although fascinated by flowers in general, monocots and dicots, and plant reproduction, at first it was difficult for me to see the beauty in pollen. Yet in botany class, when we examined pollen under the microscope, a whole world bloomed, literally, before me. The relatively new study of pollen, known as palynology, intrigued me. Minuscule pollen grains displayed an array of shapes and surface ornamentation—spines, netting, furrows, pores—each specific to its plant species. By analyzing these indescribably small structures one could surmise which plants released them. And more interesting, at least to me—pollen grains were preserved in the fossil record. By studying the pollen locked in sediments or sedimentary rocks, a scientist could discover which plants lived in the geologic past.

Inspiration flashed. I could take pollen samples in Olduvai Gorge. Analyzing the pollen grains would allow me to investigate how the African vegetation had changed throughout time. How had plants evolved during the time of early man? I had found my dissertation topic.

CHAPTER 39

MIDDLE PLEISTOCENE, THE RIFT VALLEY, AFRICA

The cavity in the vuggy rock enveloped the cone-shaped web hidden within. Kalama had no warning as she rested on the ground, tired from the day's trek. With an unlucky placement of her hand, the bite was painfully sudden. She cried out, yanking her hand away. Too late, she saw the scarlet slash on the black button body. Venomous. Kho reacted immediately, pulling his mother toward him, smashing at the spider with a rock.

Kalama rested by the fire as the people made camp around her. Ifa knelt beside her. Trying the earth magic, she reached for Kalama's hand and rubbed it with moistened mud, packing moss around the blistering wound. The treatment soothed, but the swelling began to work its way up Kalama's wrist. Ifa stood and began to pace, her eyebrows knitted. She beseeched to the Spirits for help, raising her arms to the sky and stomping a rut into the ground with her feet. Other women joined her in the quiet pleading, voices thrumming. The evening cooled and Ifa grabbed a softened hide and wrapped it around Kalama. Lying down next to her, Ifa reached over and embraced her tightly. Full darkness fell and the stars appeared as heralds in the sky on a cloudless night.

The finite blackness ended with the first hints of dawn. Kalama's arm, inflamed and swollen, had turned a purplish hue. Tears ran down her cheeks as she lay on her side and grasped her knees. Her stomach muscles cramped and stiffened. She groaned into the morning light as the women took turns rubbing her back. Low chanting continued around the fire. The weakness in Kalama's legs prevented her from rising.

She called Kho, Ifa, and Khoam to her. "Goodbye," she whispered in a faraway voice. As the sun perished for the night, her eyes rolled back in her head. Kalama was gone.

Cradling his mother's body to his chest, Kho rocked her gently, tears on his cheeks. Sobs choked Ifa's throat. She remembered Kalama's assuring smile, her soft touch, her comfort of little Khoam. Staring into the dying embers of the hearth fire, its flickering as ethereal as exhalations, the women wailed and pulled at their hair in mourning.

At daybreak, Kho carried the body and placed it under a blackthorn tree. Ifa covered Kalama's face with wildflowers, her body with cattail reeds. Surrounding her, the people, her children, and grandchildren wore the blood paint. Grief settled around the tribe like a tangible cloud.

Kalama departed the earth, her body to the African plain, her sighs were now the winds, her steps forever silenced became the echoes of hoofbeats, the crackle of heat lightning, the dance of her children.

CHAPTER 40

"Mother, what are you doing here?" I asked as I stepped off the train at Union Station in the District of Columbia. Usually, my father collected me, but today, my mother waved at me from the lobby. She hated driving in the city and only did so under duress.

"Your father couldn't pick you up. He's had an accident," she said.

Her face looked pale and dark circles underscored her eyes. I sucked in my breath as a hard knot formed in my chest.

"What? What happened?"

"He's broken his leg. In several places. He was in traction in the hospital, but he's home now. His whole leg is in a cast. His arm is pretty bruised too," she said.

My heart jumped into my throat.

"Is he going to be alright?"

"Yes, but it will take a while for him to recover. His kneecap was also cracked, so he may need to have surgery on that later."

We exited the station, me lugging my suitcase, and walked to the Chevy, which was parked parallel along the street.

"How did it happen?"

"A rock dropped on him at the museum," she said.

"When did this happen? How long was he in the hospital? Why didn't you call me?"

"Last Monday. He didn't want me to tell you and have you worry since you were coming home today anyway."

We loaded my suitcase into the car and climbed in.

"I wish you had called me. I would have come home," I said. "What happened, exactly?"

"A big hunk of rock slipped," she said. "You know, one of those rocks with the fish fossils in them that you worked on last summer? Of course, your father, not thinking, jumped in to try to catch it. It was way too heavy for him to lift, much less catch, and it slipped through his hands and landed on his leg."

I could not imagine my father thinking he could catch a rock slab. Some of them weighed hundreds of pounds.

My mother pulled away from the curb. She drove slowly in the right-hand lane, navigating down Constitution Avenue while I watched out for pedestrians and pole-mounted red lights. Traffic was heavy since I had arrived at rush hour.

"Henrietta, I'm so glad to hear that Frank is alright. We were very worried when we heard about the mine collapse."

"Yes, so was I," I said. "He called me afterward. But I haven't heard from him since."

"Not since then? That was two months ago," she said.

"Yeah. I might try to call him on your phone if that's alright with you? We can't call long-distance from either of our phones," I said.

"Sure, that's fine. You aren't chasing after him, are you?"

"Probably," I replied.

Across the Teddy Roosevelt Bridge to Wilson Boulevard, we pulled into our driveway after a shaky thirty minutes. I grabbed my suitcase, ran up the front steps, and slammed through the door. My dad sat on the couch in the living room. His leg, fully encased in a cast from toe to hip, rested on a footstool topped with pillows. Across the room, Walter Cronkite broadcasted the news on our RCA television, tin foil on the rabbit ears.

"Dad! What on earth happened to you?" I asked as if I had not just heard the story. I leaned over and hugged him.

He chuckled and grimaced at the same time. "I'm fine."

I set my suitcase down and dropped into the old recliner.

"I can't believe you didn't call me when this happened. You've been in the hospital all of this time?"

"Almost a week. The swelling had to go down before they could put me in a cast. We didn't want to distract you at school, honey. There was nothing you could do."

"I could worry."

"Yes, that's exactly what I didn't want you to do."

"Does it hurt?"

"Only when I breathe," he said, tongue-in-cheek.

"What were you thinking, Dad? You know how heavy those rock slabs are."

"Yes, well, Tom-Tom brought in the slab with the forklift, and just as he was placing it on the table, it slipped and slid toward me. It was just a reflex to reach out and try to catch the edge of it. All I could see were the fossils coming at me. But the rock pinned me to the floor. I was pretty scraped up."

"Yes, not to mention your bones and kneecap breaking," my mom quipped, arriving from the kitchen to hand us each a glass of iced tea.

"Well, at least the fossils are alright," I said with a grin.

He forced a laugh. "Yeah, how lucky."

I wasn't going to mention it then, but in my mind, our plans for Africa had just gone up in smoke. A brushfire of epic proportions.

Sitting there at that moment, I wished I could go back in time. Before Frank took the job with National Bitumen. Before my dad broke his leg. All I needed was a time machine. I guess I should have paid more attention in physics class.

───────

After failing to build a time machine in my attic bedroom, the next morning's hunger and the smell of cinnamon toast drove me downstairs. Grabbing a plate of toast and eggs from the kitchen, I discovered my parents sitting outside on the front porch. I sat down on the third rocking chair to join them. A white haze obscured the sun and low clouds built in the east.

"How is your leg feeling today, Dad?" I asked, swallowing a bite of toast.

"Like I'm ready to go waterskiing," he said, smiling.

He turned to me. "Henrietta, I don't know if now is the best time to discuss this, but obviously I'm not going to be able to go to Africa."

"Yes, it occurred to me." I took a bite of my scrambled eggs and stared across the front yard. A lone sparrow hopped along the top of our fence.

"I've been trying to come up with a solution so you can still go. I know how much you were looking forward to it," he said.

"Yes, and I was going to collect samples for my dissertation," I said, sighing inwardly. "I've decided to study palynology, and thought I could take pollen samples in the gorge."

"That will be a great topic! We need to figure out a way for you to go. I thought perhaps Dr. Falcone could travel in my place. You've worked for him, and I know he'd be happy to go. He's quite unencumbered these days."

The shock of his suggestion caused my chest to tighten. I pictured Dr. Falcone's face next to mine in my mind's eye.

"No, Dad," I said, shaking my head.

"No? I thought it would be a good solution. You have the field expertise with the fish, and he has the credentials with the museum." He looked at me, curiosity brimming in his eyes.

Ironically, it was my mother who understood the look on my face.

"Harry, I think Henrietta would be uncomfortable going with Dr. Falcone," she said. "After all, he's a divorced man. It wouldn't be right."

"Yes. I'm sorry, but I could not go with him," I said.

We sat for a bit in contemplative silence.

"Another solution might be for you to go in my place. You work for the museum, albeit as an intern," my dad said. "We could get you reclassified as a laboratory technician. You'll be a college graduate. I would have to convince the powers that be, but perhaps they would substitute you for the funding. After all, we weren't going to have time to study the fish in the field. We were just going to dig them out. You could certainly do the digging. And perhaps the museum would send Tom-Tom, or another lab tech toward the end of your trip, to help you build the jackets and transport the fossils back here."

My mother spoke up. "Henrietta cannot go to Africa by herself. Traveling across the country with a bunch of men was one thing. Africa is quite another."

But I was tired of people telling me '*no.*' Tired of people assuming I would fail. Tired of being underestimated. And tired of worrying and waiting.

"Of course I can go to Africa by myself. All I need is a ticket. It'll be just like flying to Utah, but longer. I can do the digging. And get my pollen samples. If Mr. Thomas can help me with the jackets for the fossils and help me transport them back, then I'd certainly be able to do the rest. Dad, please see if the museum will agree to send me. I want to go."

I thought my mother would faint off the porch.

———

I procrastinated over my week at home, staring at the telephone, a long-distance call now within my grasp. I finally succumbed to its siren song. Rates were cheaper after five o'clock and on weekends, so I waited until Saturday evening. After an eon of TV viewing, my parents retired for the night. The phone resided on the sideboard in the dining room, within earshot of their bedroom.

I dialed Frank's number, the repeated return of the dial fracturing the quiet.

On the other end, the phone rang several times.

"Hello?" A woman's voice.

"May I speak to Frank Bailey, please?" I asked.

A deep sigh. "Hang on."

I counted dollar signs in my head as I waited. Finally, his voice came through.

"Hello?"

"Hi, Frank. It's Henrietta," I whispered.

"Oh. Hi. How are you doing?"

"I'm okay. I'm calling to see how you are."

"Why are you whispering? I'm fine. Busy. Hey, I heard that your dad broke his leg. Glenn told me. Is he alright?"

"His leg is in a cast. It's broken in a couple of places. His knee-cap's broken too. And I'm whispering because I'm at home."

"Oh, right. Did you come home because of his accident?"

"No, it's my spring break. No one told me about the accident until I got here."

"Oh. Well, I'm glad he's okay."

Teeth were being pulled here.

"How is your dissertation coming?"

"Almost done. I just mailed the last version to Glenn this morning."

"How is your job?" I asked.

He snorted. "Well, you've made it pretty clear that you don't want to hear about that."

I heard a rustling sound down the line. A child whined.

"Frank, can you read me a story?" asked a tiny disembodied voice.

"Who's that?" I asked.

"Listen, Henrietta, it's obvious you don't approve of what I'm doing here. That you don't support me. But this is my job. And I like it."

"You can't have liked it when those men died," I said.

A pause came down the line, followed by a terse reply.

"Of course not. That was awful. You have no idea. But now that the weather is better, I'm able to get out and do field mapping. Believe it or not, I'm good at it."

"I'm sure you are. But to what end? To level the mountains?" I said, my voice cracking.

Frustration crackled in his voice. "Henrietta, this is not going to work. Us. At least not right now. I think maybe we should cool it for a while."

How much cooler could it get?

"Alright," I said, my voice a choke.

"Gotta go."

The click resonated through my ear, across my chest, and stabbed at my heart.

CHAPTER 41

The skull of the *Deinotherium* rested on the table in the banda, almost covering the entire surface. The cranium, partially crushed in places, had a low, flattened profile, unlike the dome shape of modern elephants. The mandible extended downward, attached to two lower tusks that curved backward. The ivory was cracked and discolored. A sieve filled with bone shards took up the rest of the table.

Maggie and I perched across from each other, bent over, examining the shards one by one. We painstakingly attempted to assemble the three-dimensional prehistoric jigsaw puzzle. Maggie reached over with her pair of tweezers and plucked a bone fragment out of the sieve.

"Oh, here you are, you cheeky bugger," she said, her clipped British syllables bouncing like boomerangs. "Look here, Henrietta, under the magnifier. This piece fits right there."

She handed the shard to me, her tweezers to mine. I eyed it under my magnifying glass while she pointed to a spot above the eye socket.

"Yes, it looks like it might fit there," I said.

She grabbed it back from me and applied glue to the edge. It slipped smoothly into place as she attached it to the rest of the skull.

"And that's how it is done!" she crowed.

Still shaken from the previous day's encounter with the mysterious visitor and the snake, I welcomed a day working at basecamp. Kimaru had driven off in the lorry after an early breakfast. He was headed to Moshi to load up more supplies. He would drive back tomorrow and bring new guests arriving at the airport.

"Louis usually shows up around now," Maggie said. "He tries to bring potential investors with him. If there are extra people to transport he'll follow the lorry in his Jeep."

Excitement buzzed around the camp, and I settled into the chaos to calm my nerves. The diggers joked and whistled as they erected new tents. Hammers clanged against stakes. Poles were assembled and inserted into canvas loops. Cots were constructed, dragged into the tents, and draped with mosquito netting. Simon wandered the camp, chirping and climbing onto the diggers' backs.

Wawira bustled around the banda, singing in her flat monotone. She wiped the empty shelves with a cloth while rearranging the canned goods. We were all ready for an influx of fresh food. And we needed water. Especially if more people arrived. Kimaru promised to bring water-filled jugs. Still, it wouldn't be enough for me to wash out my shirts. Or my hair.

"Wawira," I asked, "what was in that tea you gave me yesterday?"

She turned and looked at me, her head tilted sideways.

"Coffee cherry tea," she said. "Remember? From the husks of the coffee beans?"

"There wasn't anything else in it?" I asked.

"No." She shook her head, and turned back, humming.

Maggie reached across the elephant skull for another rock chip. She held it in front of her eye.

"If you don't mind me asking—if your dad is a paleoichthyologist at the Smithsonian, why didn't he come to Africa? Why did he send you? she asked. "No offense, of course."

"We were both supposed to come. But he was in an accident right beforehand and broke his leg. So here I am."

"Oh, that's a shame." She continued her examination of the fragment. "So, do you have a boyfriend?" she asked.

Now we were doing girl talk?

I sighed.

"I did. We broke up right before I came here," I said. "It's a long story."

"Well, I don't have anywhere to be," she said. "Unless you don't want to chinwag about it."

I sniffled and rubbed at my eyes. And then I told Maggie and Wawira, who eavesdropped, about Frank. How we met. How he took the job with the coal company. About the mine collapse. And the subsequent collapse of our communications.

"So, you see, I think it's over. I have no idea if he's even thinking about me anymore," I said. "He could have moved on by now. Married some country girl. Who knows?"

And then I choked and tears poured forth. Wawira grabbed a cloth and handed it to me, patting me on the back. Maggie looked pained.

"I'm sorry, Henrietta. I shouldn't have been so nosy," Maggie said.

"Oh, no, it's alright. I guess I've had all that pent up for a while," I said, wiping my eyes. I gave them a watery smile.

In the afternoon, fat, gray clouds moved in, an unusual occurrence during the dry season. The remnants of a storm off the Indian Ocean managed to survive the orographic descent over the caldera, bringing much-needed rain to the gorge. Wawira located every available bucket and bowl, and we scurried around, setting them outside as catchment basins. Brief, but heavy, the rains forced us to hunker down in our tents. The repetitive patter on the canvas felt like a balm to me and I relaxed on my cot. I closed my eyes and thought of Frank. *What was he doing now? Was he thinking of me? Did he ever?*

"I didn't ask about you, Maggie," I said. "Do you have someone special?"

"Oh, I have my eye on someone," she said. "I'm not sure he sees me in the same light."

She rolled over and ended the conversation.

So much for girl talk.

After the deluge, the water levels rose in the cisterns, and winged ants floated in the rain-filled pots. I grabbed one of the buckets for a badly needed sponge bath. I scrubbed the ground-in dirt from my skin and from under my fingernails. Unbraiding my hair, I dipped my mane into the water and squeezed shampoo through it. My scalp tingled and my skin cooled as I massaged away the silt and sweat. My whole body felt revitalized as if washing away the grime had decreased the downward pull of gravity.

As I bathed, I reflected upon how we took water for granted at home. We turned on the faucet, and water flowed out, plentiful and drinkable. Here, every beast and fowl competed for the same watering hole. Every elephant, hippo, and crocodile wallowed in the same pond and every lion and cheetah drank from the briefly-replenished wadis. Africa was a land of extremes. Thirst. Hunger. Danger.

I swear the bucket was half-filled with dirt when I finished.

CHAPTER 42

E ver since the Noah's Ark debacle, as I now thought of it, attending church ranked low on my list of priorities. Below such activities as attending sporting events. Or cleaning up Romeo's hunting trophies. However, one of the Philomatheans, a girl named Layla, sang in the choir at Bruton Parish Church. She would be singing a solo on a Sunday morning in May and had invited all of us to attend the service.

Outwardly I projected a refreshed and driven persona once I returned to school. I expounded eloquently on my graduate school applications, stamped and posted them. I delved back into my classes. Inwardly it was another story. Preferring to be a hermit in my room, but wanting to support Layla, and egged on by Delilah, I strolled with the contingent of Philomatheans to church. The historic Bruton Parish Church building, its steeple visible up and down DOG street, dated back to the early eighteenth century. The cemetery, with its elevated tombs and weathered monuments, provided a spooky backdrop for meandering tourists. We entered the sanctuary, our footsteps echoing off the stone floors, the wooden high-backed pews, the priest's high pulpit.

The priest entered the narthex, swinging the incense. I swore I smelled a hint of ozone as he passed. The robed choir followed, leading the opening hymn. The service was a mystery to me, with lots of chanting, kneeling, standing, sitting, and singing. Tucked in the pew were the Bible, of course, a hymn book, and a prayer book. The regular congregants responded on cue with the Gloria Patri, the Apostles' Creed, the Doxology, but I had to look them up in the books. I did at least know the Lord's Prayer—I wasn't that much of a heathen—but the one I learned in Sunday School was a bit different—debts or trespasses? And why did the Apostles' Creed suggest that Jesus descended into Hell? I had not heard that before. But despite the confusion, sitting in the pew, I lifted up my heartache to the Lord and prayed to be soothed. It couldn't hurt to try, I figured. A measure of well-being drifted over me as I knelt next to my fellow Philomatheans.

Layla's solo was lovely, heavenly even. The light filtering through the arched windows highlighted her hair as she sang. I cannot remember anything about the sermon, but the whole experience left me feeling lighter.

Trekking back to the house, I marveled at the catalpa trees on Palace Green, the white-washed cottages, the clopping of the horse-drawn carriages. Chatting with the Philomatheans, I realized I felt at ease with this special group of smart, talented young women. We were right on the cusp of becoming full-fledged adults. You could almost hear us roar.

That afternoon I returned to my Physical Anthropology notes. My final exam was in two days. *Australopithecus. Zinjanthropus. Robustus. Neanderthalensis.* Several million years of evolution. After the morning in church, I felt like a living oxymoron.

Graduation seemed so far off and then suddenly it arrived. My parents would not be attending because of my dad's accident. Delilah's parents would bring me home. With our graduation gowns billowing out in the light breeze, Delilah and I crossed Richmond Road to the Wren Building. We joined the line to ring the bell in the cupola, its tolling continuing all morning.

After the graduation ceremony, the time arrived to say goodbye to Romeo. The Keeper of the Cat honor passed to a girl who would be taking summer school classes. I had purchased a can of albacore tuna for our last meal, feeding him on the back steps. He slurped it up like manna. Afterward, I picked him up and stroked his head, and told him he was a good kitty. I would miss him. He fussed to get down, looked at me with baleful eyes, turned his back on me, and stalked away without a backward glance. *Stupid cat.*

CHAPTER 43

Riding the downtown bus in the middle of the day felt freeing, no one crowding, pushing, or standing over me, clinging to the overhead rails. Alone, my father still on medical leave, I exited at the National Mall in a gust of exhaust. Already sticky with humidity, the morning air pressed on my lungs. The famous cherry trees were past their prime, the blossoms withered and scattered. At the Smithsonian Castle, Dr. Westmoreland's secretary held my visa and plane tickets, for I was headed to Africa, approved and scheduled. Arriving early for my appointment with her, I decided to check in with Mr. Thomas in the prep lab. I was hoping he had been approved to travel to Africa also, either with me or joining me later.

I strode across the rotunda to reach the curving stone steps that led to the basement. I grasped the wrought iron railing, descending, letting the familiarity of the museum sink in. Having not been to the prep lab for half a year, the hallway seemed narrow and claustrophobic. Turning the corner, I shouldered open the swinging doors to the lab.

"Henrietta, is that you?"

Of all the people I could run into, I had not counted on seeing Dr. Falcone.

"Yes, hello, Dr. Falcone. How are you?" I said as politely as I could manage, not quite myself.

Looking side to side, he stepped toward me.

"Funny you should ask. I was just thinking of you," he stepped closer. "I have a bone to pick with you." He grinned a clenched-teeth smile.

As he moved forward, I stepped back against the counter. Pressing his hand on the wall next to my head, he leaned his face toward mine until it was an inch away. Lowering his voice, he hissed, "I understand you are going to Olduvai Gorge. I was planning to go, but all of a sudden, you're going in my place. Can you explain that?"

Caught off-guard, I sputtered, "Yes..."

"Well, it must be nice to be Henry's daughter. You've managed to step on everyone's toes for this prime assignment," he said.

My face burned, and I started to apologize, "I'm sorry..."

But something happened. I stopped mid-sentence. *Who did he think he was?* My debating skills with the Philomatheans kicked in. I pulled myself to my full height—he wasn't much taller than me—and looked him straight in the eye.

"What do you mean, Dr. Falcone?" I asked, flint in my voice. "I have field experience digging fossil fish, which is what I'll be doing in Africa. I thought you studied foraminifera. There certainly aren't any of those at Olduvai Gorge."

He pulled back, startled, gape-mouthed as a flounder. Elbowing him out of my way, I marched out of the lab, heart thumping, head held high. The lab doors swung closed behind me. I burned that bridge spectacularly, but it was worth the flames.

"Hello. I'm here to see Mrs. Marsh," I said. "Henrietta Ballantine. I have an appointment."

Dr. Westmoreland's office was located on the second floor of the Smithsonian Castle. Constructed of red Seneca sandstone, the original Smithsonian building resembled Dracula's medieval hideaway mixed with Rapunzel-like towers. I had an appointment with the secretary of the Secretary, if that made sense. A receptionist perched at a desk, gnawing on her thumbnail and staring with a jaded look at her typewriter. Her expression relaxed when I walked in.

"Oh yes, just a minute," she said. She disappeared down a hallway and returned a few moments later, followed by a woman with hair lacquered into place in the latest beehive style. High heels clipped the floor as she walked toward me.

"Hello, Miss Ballantine. I'm Mrs. Marsh. Dr. Westmoreland has asked me to tell you that he would like a word with you. Could you please wait?" She indicated a chair by the door.

"Oh yes, of course," I said. *What else could I say?*

"I'll let him know that you're here. It may be a few minutes," she said, peering over her reading glasses.

I twitched in the uncomfortable chair, crossed and uncrossed my legs. The stern countenance of James Smithson frowned down upon me from a portrait on the wall. I should have brought a book. The receptionist tried to look busy, pecking away on her typewriter, answering an occasional call. She glanced over at me apologetically. I felt bad for her and I'm sure she felt bad for me. After forty minutes of tedium, Mrs. Marsh returned.

"Dr. Westmoreland is available to see you now," she said, defying gravity with that hairdo.

I followed her into the back hallway, through a glass door, into a spacious office. An arched window overlooked the grassy expanse of the Mall. An enormous wooden desk occupied the center of the room.

"Dr. Westmoreland, this is Miss Ballantine," she announced as if I were mute.

Dr. Westmoreland, distinguished as always, suit and tie immaculate, rose from his desk chair and extended his hand.

"Miss Ballantine, please come in. Have a seat. How is your father?"

Mrs. Marsh left, closing the door, her self-importance fading away with her.

"He's healing, thank you," I said. "His cast is off and he's walking with a cane. He's getting his strength back, trying to exercise. But he may still need knee surgery. The doctors are waiting to see if the kneecap will knit back together."

My, wasn't I verbose all of a sudden?

"That's good to hear. Excellent. Well, I'll get right to the point. The reason I wanted to talk with you is that I realize you have been led to believe that the National Museum has chosen you as a representative..."

"Yes, and I am thrilled to have been chosen," I said. "I've studied at the museum since I was a little girl and worked here for the past three summers, both as a volunteer and a lab technician. The museum is in my blood, you could say."

"Yes, that's all well and good." He cleared his throat. "You see... I'll just come out and say that I have some deep reservations..."

I cocked my head and examined him as a crow might look at a grasshopper.

"About my going to Africa? Or representing the museum?" I asked.

"Both actually," he said. He seemed relieved.

I let a moment pass.

"May I ask why?" I asked.

"Well, first is your inexperience." He rested his elbows on his desk and steepled his index fingers.

"I realize that I don't have years of experience. But the job is to dig and prepare fish fossils for transport. I've spent two summers working specifically on fish fossils. One summer in the prep room and one summer at the Green River Quarry," I said.

He studied me. "You lack qualifications," he said, finally.

"I have a bachelor's degree in Natural Sciences from the College of William and Mary," I said.

"You're very young," he said.

"Yes, I am," I replied evenly. "And strong. I have the stamina to work long hours in the field. In the sun and the heat."

"Your position with the museum is tenuous. You're only classified as a lab technician."

"Yes. I was under the impression that another lab technician might be sent to help with transport?"

"That has not been approved," he said. "There are several scientists at the museum who outrank you who wish to go in your place."

Ah, now we were getting somewhere. Someone had complained. And I could guess who.

"Scientists who have worked on fossil fish? Who have experience cutting the slabs from the ground? Making plaster jackets for them? Who have done the intricate work of extracting fossil fish from the substrate? Without damaging them? These fossils will be truly unique, coming from Olduvai Gorge. And important, since this is a collaboration with the National Geographic Society. I'd hate to see them damaged by inexperienced handling."

Dr. Westmoreland started to look uncomfortable. His face turned a bit red.

"I don't know...I...Africa is just not a safe place for a young woman," he stammered.

"Dr. Westmoreland, sir, let me assure you that I will represent the museum professionally," I said, sitting up straight in the chair and leaning forward. "I can do the job and I'll do it well. I will not be an embarrassment to you. I will be a credit to the museum. I am packed and ready to go. And I would think that Dr. Mary Leakey might have some ideas about a young woman's place at an African dig site. Should we call the National Geographic Society and inquire?"

I hummed a little tune as I crossed the Mall to the bus stop, visa and airplane tickets firmly ensconced in my purse. I was ready to fly.

CHAPTER 44

MIDDLE PLEISTOCENE, THE RIFT VALLEY, AFRICA

Opening like the yawning jaws of a prehistoric beast, the rift valley tore apart, each side diverging from the other as eastern Africa attempted secession from the rest of the continent. Tectonic forces caused the crustal slab to thin over underlying mantle rocks, already heated at great depths. This thinning and subsequent pressure release allowed the mantle rocks to melt, forming underground magma as viscous as hot tar. Less dense than the surrounding solid rock, the molten fingers oozed upward through existing cracks, causing the earth to quake along this Great Rift.

The scent wafting on the breeze was unfamiliar, more sulfurous than smoke. Fire was a constant threat and the tribe, already wary, scanned the horizon with flinty eyes. The ground shook repeatedly under their feet, sending the tribe into a panic. The patriarch issued a command and the frightened people gathered a few belongings, blades, tools, pelts, and scurried off the mountain to the savanna below. A sudden explosive whoosh thundered down the volcanic slope behind them. Thick black-crusted lava poured out of the volcanic vent. Lava runnels streamed down the flanks. The intense heat turned the ground into an inferno, consuming the surrounding forest. Trees crackled like tinder, their trunks deforming before succumbing in a tilting blaze.

Herds and predators alike began a thunderous retreat. Kho grabbed Khoam in his arms, and he and Ifa escaped across the savanna. They pushed through the reeds, away from the terrifying visage of the lava, fire, and smoke. They knew instinctively in which direction to flee, following the herds. Fine particles of volcanic ash spread out as a choking blanket across the landscape, falling on the people as they sprinted away. The pyroclastic powder fell like dry rain, sticking to their faces and in their hair. The ash coated the grasslands, poisoning the grain. Then behind them, the grasses caught on fire as lava reached the volcanic base. Smoke rose in the air, the vegetation now smoldering.

The people sprinted on, children carried in arms. The elderly fell behind, some lost in the chaos. Animals mooed, snorted, brayed. Hooves thundered and trampled. Dust rose, mixing with the smoke. Ifa and Kho sped onward.

"There! The lake!" Ifa called above the clamor. Kho nodded. They headed toward the relative safety of the water.

They ran across the long expanse from the volcano, finally reaching the lakeshore. They slowed, sweating, ash-covered. The lake water was turbid with rock flour. The ash mixed with the marsh mud, forming a sticky quicksand underfoot. Khoam cried in his father's arms, terrified from the tumult. Kho patted his back and rocked him back and forth. They moved toward the water but the boy's wails caught the attention of a crocodile, submerged in the muck. Just in time, Ifa spied its glassy, predatory eyes.

"Run!" she called, pointing at the creature.

The gargantuan reptile raced up the bank after them. Opening its giant maw, its knife-like teeth flashing, it lurched toward the family. The mighty jaws snapped shut just as the humans careened out of reach.

Panting, exhausted, Ifa and Kho pressed on. Side-by-side, cautiously traversing along the edge of the lake, they left paired footprints in the sticky mire.

Their migration route was engrained in Ifa's memory. She was heading *home*.

CHAPTER 45

1961, Olduvai Gorge, Tanganyika, Africa

The firelight flickered in the African sky punctuated with equatorial constellations. Yesterday's rain now a memory, the typical high pressure had returned, marked by an absence of clouds. The diggers had constructed a pyramid of our precious firewood and lit it to smoldering. We assembled ourselves in a hearth circle, seated on rocks, waiting in anticipation for the late arrival of the lorry. Philip tossed pebbles into the fire causing sparks to spew. Simon peeped from the banda, swinging from the roof with his long prehensile tail, unhappy with the flames. Oliver rustled in his pen. Mary Leakey paced and the dogs would not settle.

"I wonder who will arrive," Mary said. "Louis has been lecturing in England, and you never know who he will round up. Scientists, sponsors, or potential investors? Richard and Jonathan may travel with him, although I'm not sure Jonathan will be joining us this season. He may stay in London with his grandmother."

Insects buzzed, seemingly increased in number after the rain. A bleating sound came from the near distance.

"What was that?" I asked.

"An aardvark," Maggie said. "They're nocturnal. Don't worry—they eat ants. I wonder what spooked it."

As if in answer, a lion roared.

Mary sighed. "He doesn't sound too close. But just in case, we'd better get the firecrackers."

One of the diggers got up, his rifle on his shoulder.

"I'll take a look around the camp, ma'am," he said.

We sat in agitated quiet, staring at the embers. The roaring of the lions became muffled as they meandered away. Even they seemed to respect our anticipatory mood. Just as I was about to nod off, headlights appeared on the distant road.

Sheathed in their own light, two vehicles pulled up, the lorry, followed by a well-worn, dusty Jeep. We stood up to greet the newcomers. Mary sprinted over, the dogs at her heels. From behind the wheel of the Jeep, a stocky man emerged, his signature coif of white hair sticking up from his head. He opened his arms wide and engulfed Mary in a hug. The infamous Dr. Louis Leakey. I recognized him from *National Geographic Magazine* photos. Behind Dr. Leakey, a young man extracted his long legs from the back seat. Mary walked over and hugged him, a big smile on her face.

"That's Richard," Maggie murmured to me, with a nod. "Their oldest son."

Two other men materialized from the Jeep. Louis introduced them to Mary. Ray approached and shook hands.

The doors to the lorry opened. Kimaru stepped down from the driver's seat.

I walked over. "Hello, Kimaru. Welcome back," I said.

He nodded and smiled, as the far door of the lorry slammed. I stepped toward the hood to greet his passenger.

"Mr. Thomas!" I called. "Welcome to Africa."

The passenger stepped around the hood into view. But it was not Mr. Thomas.

It was Frank.

His clothes rumpled, his eyes shadowed with dark circles, he smiled his crooked grin at me.

I stopped mid-stride, my body registering shock.

"What are you doing here?" I asked. "How did you get here?"

"Nice to see you too, Henrietta," he said. "I flew into Moshi and rode here with Kimaru."

"Yes, I figured that out. But why?"

"I'm the muscle, sent to haul your fish fossils. On my own dime. And I'm here to see you. Obviously."

He stepped forward and grabbed me, planting a kiss that made my anxiety melt away like an underground river. I wrapped my arms around his back and clung to him.

The whole crowd cheered. Someone gave a wolf whistle. I muffled my face in his shirt and began to cry.

"Don't cry, Henrietta," he said. "Aren't you happy to see me?"

"Of course, I am, you idiot," I said, into his shirt. I pulled back and swiped at my tears with the back of my hand. "I've been waiting for you for an epoch."

<hr />

The two gentlemen from the National Geographic Society were afforded every courtesy, since, after all, their organization funded the expedition. Introductions were made. I was introduced as 'Henrietta Ballantine, from the U.S. National Museum, who is here for her father, Dr. Henry Ballantine, paleontologist.' Frank had already met the men in Nairobi, traveling with them from there. He was now referred to as 'Dr. Bailey.'

The next morning's air smelled of soot from the previous night's fire. Too small for all of us, the banda now served as a dining room for the special guests, and as a serving station for the rest of us. Frank and I perched on rocks around the charred logs in the firepit. Frank looked revived, having slept in the tent he shared with the Leakey sons. Balancing our breakfast plates on our knees, I marveled at the boiled eggs, bread and butter.

"Finally, something fresh for breakfast," I said.

"What have you been eating?" Frank asked.

"Boiled cassava. Which tastes like wallpaper paste. And this cornmeal mush called ugali. You scoop it up with your fingers like this," I said, shoveling some into my mouth.

Frank followed suit. A grimace crossed his face.

"That stuff is awful," he whispered to me. He gulped some coffee. "Thank God the coffee is good."

I nodded. "Congratulations on your degree," I said. "How was your defense?"

"It went well," he said. "I stopped to see your parents on my way up to Princeton."

"You did?"

"Yes, you'd already left. Your mother was in quite a state about you coming here."

I smiled. "Yeah, I know. She wasn't thrilled. How did my dad seem?" I shoved some bread in my mouth.

"OK. Hobbling around. He's worried about you too, but didn't want to show it."

I turned to him. "So how, exactly, did you end up coming here?"

We were interrupted by Mary Leakey, rising from her seat in the banda.

"We will be leaving for the tour of the quarry in a few minutes. Fill your canteens and make sure you have your sturdy shoes on," she announced.

Chairs pushed back. Plates were scraped and piled.

"You should go to the quarry to learn the stratigraphy of the gorge. It's fascinating. And you'll see examples of the tool technologies," I told Frank.

"Are you going to go?" Frank asked.

"No, I want to uncover the fish slabs and sort them. They're stacked over there, under that tarp," I pointed. "You and I can start making the jackets when you get back."

The two dignitaries, dressed in pressed and spotless safari clothes, joined the Leakey clan as they gathered by the firepit. Oliver sauntered over with the dalmatians and the newcomers looked askance at the wildebeest. Mary, topped by her enormous sun hat, laughed and stroked the calf, explaining his status as a pet. The whole menagerie hiked away, Louis Leakey, in his signature white coveralls, leading the procession. Maggie hovered by Richard Leakey's elbow, while he presented her with polite indifference. Frank, looking suitably crumpled in his field clothes, caught up with Philip. My heart gave a small leap.

Simon, left behind, climbed up my arm for a piggyback ride, his long monkey-tail wrapped around my shoulders. I reached up and patted his back while he pulled at my braid.

Actions speak louder than words, or so they say. But I still wanted to hear what in the world Frank was thinking.

As the afternoon heat simmered across the gorge, Frank and I unpacked supplies from the lorry. We carried aluminum foil, rolls of burlap, heavy-duty scissors, bags of plaster powder, and what Maggie referred to as 'loo paper.' These had been shipped by the National Museum as I left for Africa and had finally arrived in Arusha. I had unveiled the stack of fish slabs from their tarp. We dropped our equipment on the ground next to them.

I retrieved the special wooden box containing the odd, eel-like fish, which I had stored in the banda. We pried off the lid.

"Take a look at this fish," I said. "It's mostly an impression, although you can see the skull bones. It looks different from the other fish."

"Yeah, it looks pretty weird. And delicate. Let's start with this one," Frank said.

Frank grabbed a metal bucket and filled it with water from the cistern. Kneeling on the ground, I cut open the top of the bag of plaster and dumped some of the powder into the bucket. Dust cascaded up and coated my arms. I slopped the mixture around with a paint stirrer to judge its consistency. Frank knelt beside me.

"Now you'll get to see my amazing jacket-constructing abilities," he said. "Can you hand me that foil?"

"How is it that you know how to make a jacket?" I asked.

"One of the paleontologists at Princeton gave me a crash course before I left," he said, ripping off a sheet. He gently laid a sheet of foil over the fish.

"Next, the toilet paper," he said.

"You mean the 'paleo paper?'" I asked.

He grinned. "Oh yeah, that's right."

He wrapped the whole slab, end-over-end, with the paper.

"See, this will keep any loose grains away from the jacket. I know what I'm doing," he said.

He unfurled a length of burlap from the roll and started to cut it into long strips.

"So how exactly did you end up here?" I asked.

He sighed. "Well, to be honest, I decided I overreacted with you on the phone."

"You mean the call where you said it wouldn't work out between us. The one where you said we should 'cool it for a while?'"

He stared at me from under his hat. "Geez, did you memorize what I said? Yes, that one."

He looked properly chagrined. I almost felt sorry for him.

"Anyway," he said, "I was hiking around, doing fieldwork, in the middle of nowhere, and all I could think about was you. And it hit me. 'What was I doing?' The minute I could take leave, I drove up to see you at your parents' house. But you'd left already."

"I thought you were on your way to defend your dissertation when you stopped in."

"I was. I couldn't take any leave before then."

"So it was a two-for-one trip? How convenient for you," I said. "I hope it wasn't out of your way."

"You aren't going to make this easy, are you?" he asked.

"Nope."

He sighed, handed the burlap strip to me, and began to cut another one.

"I couldn't take any leave until I'd worked for six months. And I had already asked for the time off to go back to Princeton. If it makes you feel any better, I was pretty miserable."

My heart melted a little.

"Who was the woman? And the kid?" I asked.

He looked at me, his eyebrows raised. "What?"

"The woman. Who answered the phone. The kid who wanted you to read him a story. I could hear through the receiver, you know."

"Oh for heaven's sake. That was my landlady. And her son. I told you I was in temporary housing. I rent a room in a board-ing house."

I dunked the burlap strip into the bucket. My voice caught as I stared down into the glop.

"I thought you'd found a mountain woman with a ready-made family."

"Seriously? No. Of course not."

"Well, since we're being honest, I guess I overreacted a little about you working for the coal company. Although that accident at the mine really scared me," I said.

"Yeah, I was scared too, believe me," Frank said. "It was terrible, seeing all those families standing outside the fence. And I was there in my National Bitumen shirt."

"It wasn't your fault."

"I knew that, rationally, but it felt like I was the enemy."

I pulled the plaster-coated burlap strip from the bucket and wrapped it around the fossil as if it were a mummy. Then I grabbed the next strip and plunged it into the bucket.

I looked up at Frank, my eyes shiny. "But how did you get here? To Africa? Other than on an airplane, I mean?"

"Your dad arranged it. The museum wouldn't fund another per-son. So he talked to someone at National Geographic. I'm sort of a liaison from Princeton to the museum. They didn't question it too much since I'm paying my own way. So here I am."

He dipped his hands into the bucket and grabbed mine. The goopy plaster squeezed up between our fingers.

"How about this, Henrietta? I'll work for the coal company while you're in grad school. After that, I'll find something else."

"What are you saying, Frank?" I asked, my eyes glistening brighter.

"Look, I know you are a determined woman. You have a master plan. But I want to be included in your plan. I want to be part of your life."

I pulled my hands out of the bucket and threw my arms around his neck. My momentum knocked him over, and I spilled on top of him. Plaster bits flew. I gave him a long intense kiss. Coming up for air, Frank stared into my eyes.

"Henrietta, you have to get off me."

"I didn't hurt you, did I?" I kissed him again.

He squinted his eyes. "No, but I landed on an anthill and they're biting my ass."

The moment killed, I laughed and helped Frank up off the ground, brushing at the ants with my goo-encrusted hands.

Over the next few days, the plaster would harden into protective jackets, protecting the fragile fossils from breaking. While my heart, once fragile and broken, softened and mended.

CHAPTER 46

Jacket construction completed, I was allowed to return to the monolith, with the understanding that Frank would accompany me and be armed. A driving need called me to go back. My guardian angel, or whoever she was, had given me a mission. To find her. I felt compelled to do so.

The rocky mesa towered above us as Frank and I hiked along, his hand gripping mine. A rifle was slung on his shoulder.

"Do you know how to use that thing?" I asked, dipping my head toward the gun.

"Sure. You aim and pull the trigger. How hard can it be?" he said.

"So, the answer is no, I would guess?"

He laughed. "I know how to shoot a rifle. I've been duck hunting with my dad and my brothers."

"Well, I guess we're safe from vicious ducks then," I said.

I gulped in lungfuls of dry air, my heart rate high from our hike. Basecamp was visible in the far distance. Almost mid-day, the sun gave us the usual punishment with its rays.

"That's the unconformity," I said, pointing to the dark layer. "Separating Bed I and Bed II. And the two tool technologies."

"Let's move down this way," Frank said, rounding a corner.

I giggled as he pulled me after him.

"What a shame, the camp is no longer in view," he said, smirking.

He led me along the base of the cliff. Talus scuttled as we wedged against the hill. His body pressing into mine, he lifted my chin and met my lips with his.

"Maggie would call this snogging," I said, breathlessly.

"Let's not talk about Maggie," Frank said. "Let's not talk about anything at all."

I was having trouble coming up for air. Or thinking. Together, we slid down to the ground.

"Did you bring protection?" I whispered in his ear.

"Honey, I didn't travel across an ocean and two continents to not come prepared," he said, reaching into his pocket.

Soon, partially clothed, our bodies found the ancient rhythm, going back generations, millennia, ages. A tempo shared by all humans. Back through the geologic periods, the same carnal beat across the ancestral mammalian clades. Desire waxed and waned. Our cries lifted into the air, wafting toward the Serengeti Plain to mix with the pant of the cheetahs, the plunge of the hippos, the song of the sacred ibises. Sex was as necessary as feeding, as natural as breathing, as Darwinian as surviving. So why was it so much more spectacular?

Clothes retrieved, hunger satiated, lunch consumed, we continued to ramble along the cliff. The sun poured down like infrared citrine. I leaned into Frank's shoulder as we walked, hand in hand. If I were a cat, I would have purred.

"This reminds me of Utah," Frank said. "Desert, scorpions, and snakes. Nothing to see for miles. Although you weren't as friendly back then."

"Haha. Nope. And you weren't as friendly either," I retorted.

"Touche."

I spotted the location of the landslide Kimaru had made when he slid down the cliff to my rescue.

"This is where the mysterious woman appeared to me," I said.

I had told Frank about my vision. To his credit, he believed me. Or at least pretended to.

"Where did you kick the snake?" he asked.

"Over there, into the sisal," I said. "Let's keep walking. The woman told me that I was almost there. That I needed to find her."

"I'm game." Frank looked up to the sky and called out. "Lead on, oh mysterious one."

"Stop joking around."

"Sorry, beautiful woman. I will remain serious from here on out," he said, with a mocking smile.

I sighed and shook my head. We strolled on, eyes alert. His hand pressed comfortably into mine. Black flies buzzed. As I slapped at one of them, a reflection on the side of the slope caught my eye. I released Frank's hand and moved in for a closer inspection. Leaning against the hill, I brushed loose wisps of hair out of my face and stared at the strata, just above the unconformity.

Sunlight refracted off the patina of ancient enamel. A tooth peeked from the ash-softened earth. I pulled off my knapsack and reached inside it for a brush.

"Frank, look at this!" He leaned in.

Carefully sweeping loose dirt from around the tooth, several more teeth emerged. The pitted porosity of brown-black bone cropped out of the rock.

My heart thumped in my chest. I could feel the sweat running down my back underneath my shirt. Elation coursed through me.

"Look there. What does that look like to you?" I asked, pointing.

He stooped and examined my find with a slow smile. "Teeth? Maybe a jawbone?"

"It's mammalian," I said. "The teeth are differentiated."

"Yes, there's a molar. And an incisor. Or a canine."

"I wonder if they might be hominid teeth," I mused.

Frank lowered his face to within centimeters of the fossil, contemplating.

"You know, they could be. They look human to me. But what do I know?"

"Well, I know who we can ask," I said, cautious excitement in my smile.

"Let's make a cairn to mark the spot. We can show it to the experts tomorrow and have them confirm. Or deny," Frank said.

"True. I shouldn't get my hopes up. It could be a monkey. Or another kind of mammal," I said.

Still, my hands shook as we scrounged for the largest stones. Piling them one on top of another, we constructed a primitive pyramid, a talisman from the present to the past. Could I have possibly found a fossil of an early human? And what had led me to this spot? *Or who?*

CHAPTER 47

The next morning dawned, the rising gold orb seeming to portend a day of celebration. Mary Leakey peered through her glasses and grinned at me and Frank, an expectant expression on her face. We had finished breakfast, stacking dirty plates to be washed by the ever-patient Wawira.

"We're all very excited to look at your find. You think it might be a hominid?" she said.

"It was Henrietta who found the fossil," said Frank, to his credit.

"Good show," she said to me. "Always wonderful to hear when a fellow woman has made a discovery!"

My smile was almost too wide for my face.

"I don't know if it's a hominid. They're teeth of some kind. And maybe a jawbone. We built a cairn so we could find it again." I leaned over and spoke to her quietly. "It might not be much of anything. I'm not sure it warrants all of this attention."

She whispered back, conspiratorially. "Poppycock. It will give the muckety-mucks something to look at, if nothing else."

An animated party that morning, we trekked along, Frank and I, the Leakeys, the National Geographic VIPs, Maggie, and Kimaru. Ray brought his camera. A sense of pride surged through me. I may have discovered a human ancestor. And Mary Leakey praised me for it! I certainly hoped it did not end up like the 'stingray' at the Green River Quarry. A mess of nothing.

Excitement rippled through the crowd, all except for Maggie who stravaged behind. I noticed that Richard Leakey continued to ignore her, despite her efforts to engage him. Her eyes downcast, she scuffed along at the back. I slowed and fell into step with her.

"Are you alright?" I whispered to her. "You seem a bit down."

"Yes, just a bit gutted. Green with envy, to tell you the truth." She gave me a watery grin.

"I know you haven't been happy having to show me around all month. I know I've interrupted your work," I said.

"It's nothing personal," she said. "Every visitor delays my work. It's just the way it is. Without visitors, we don't have funding. Or scientists who care about our discoveries."

"Listen, I would never have found this fossil if you hadn't taught me what to look for," I said. "Besides, it might be an antelope or something. One like a million others."

"Oh, I hope not. Truly," she said.

We caught up with the group as the mid-day sun beat down on us. Adrenaline-stoked, I hardly noticed the heat. Rounding the bend where the camp vanished from view, Frank gave me a wink. I blushed under my hat, remembering the previous day. We walked on until the cairn became visible in the middle distance. I shivered and kept a lookout for snakes.

Hiking until the rock pyramid greeted us, I marched up to the jagged cliff and pointed out the teeth. The characteristically smooth shapes of dentin glistened in the light. Then I moved out of the way. Louis and Mary approached the cliff face almost reverently to examine the fossil. We were in their church. Mary carefully swept the teeth with a fine, soft brush, blowing gently to remove the debris. Her face glowed as she smiled.

"It's some kind of hominid. Look at the rounded shape of the premolar. It looks like it could be *Homo* and not *Zinj!*" she said to Louis.

"Yes, and the incisor is larger. We're pretty high up in the section here," he replied.

"Slightly older than Chellean Man though."

"Yes, OH 9 was a bit higher in the section."

"It looks like the teeth are set in a mandible. I think this one may be a female."

"You could be right—the jaw itself appears smaller."

Louis ushered the VIPs forward to examine the fossil. He recognized a public relations opportunity when he saw one, I thought. He spoke with his hands, elucidating about the potential significance of the find. The rest of us hovered in the background.

Finally, Mary turned toward me. "Congratulations! You have found the teeth of a Paleolithic woman. This is worth excavating. We'll start tomorrow."

The joy of discovery welled up in my chest. My eyes moistened with tears. All of my nervousness and self-doubt fell away, evaporating into the parched air.

"Would you and Dr. Bailey like to join the crew?" she added.

Words momentarily caught in the back of my throat.

"Yes, of course! Of course!" I blurted. "We would be honored."

Frank nodded and hugged my shoulders.

"You did it, Henrietta," he whispered in my ear.

Ray intervened. "I need some snapshots," he said. He positioned the Leakeys around the fossil. Then the VIPs were added to the mix. The rest of us waited behind him. Maggie inched up beside me.

"I am gobsmacked," she whispered. I turned to her and smiled.

"Thanks. I think," I said, not knowing what she meant.

"I mean I'm shocked. And surprised. In a good way," she said.

"Can I get a photograph of Henrietta and Mary examining the teeth?" Ray asked.

I grabbed Maggie's shirtsleeve. "Maggie too. Three fossil-women," I said.

"Four," said Mary, pointing at the teeth.

The three of us crouched around the fossil woman. I did not care whether the resulting snapshot would make it into the *National Geographic Magazine* or not. It was enough that my discovery was now documented, an invisible latent image on Ray's photographic film.

———◆———

Anticipation and Kenyan coffee fueled the following days. Under the skillful tutelage of the Leakey team, I dug, scraped, and brushed, gently removing the nearby sediment grain-by-grain. After shaking the surrounding rubble through wooden-framed sieves, I scoured the remaining bits for primitive tools or shards of precious bone. Motes of powdery clay drifted in the air at the sieving station. Rejected rock chips and cobbles assembled into piles. Of course, only Louis and Mary touched the skull itself. Through their capable hands and our steadfast labor, my hominid discovery slowly revealed herself. A fragmented skull, teeth, mandible, neck vertebrae, part of a clavicle. She emerged from the earth. A rebirth.

As I dug, I ruminated. *Had I had a mystical encounter? Or suffered from heatstroke? Who had saved me from the snake?* The experience left an imprint on me. Like undergoing metamorphism, I was now a changed form.

As we exposed the fossil of the Pleistocene woman, I studied her skeleton. *How had she lived? Who were her people? Who had she loved? How had she died?* A feeling of deep kinship bubbled up inside me. I felt connected to her. And to this place. I looked over at Frank. As if feeling my stare, he raised his eyes from the ground and smiled at me. And with that smile, I knew that we were bound together. Maybe not right away. I still had work to do. But our futures would be intertwined. Standing in the African dirt, covered in silt, sweat pooling on my face, hammer in my hands, I turned to stare across Olduvai Gorge.

My exploration had just begun.

CHAPTER 48

MIDDLE PLEISTOCENE, THE RIFT VALLEY, AFRICA

The ground rumbled beneath her. A lava dome, pushing up inside the nearby caldera, spewed ash across the savanna. The rejuvenated cone slowly entombed her valley in poison. Ancient after twenty-five dry seasons, her hair greyed, her teeth worn, many missing, Ifa walked painfully, leaning on a stick. She steadfastly refused to join Khoam and his family as the tribe departed. Astute after past treks, she knew in her heart that she could not survive another. Even as she hugged her grandson, she would not delay their departure.

The night eerie, the sound of the ashfall was punctuated only by silence. The hooting raptors flown, the humming veld crickets smothered, the snuffling pangolins ensconced in deep burrows. Ifa peered myopically out of anthracite eyes, focused above the horizon, as she watched for Kho to signal her from the night sky with his streaking lights. But the thickening cinders subdued any flashes.

Ifa could not comprehend that her contemporaries have undertaken a diaspora across Eurasia, to China and Java to the east, the Iberian Peninsula to the west. As they hunted the gigantic Ice Age mammals, they dropped their Paleolithic hand axes and scrapers alongside butchered and broken bones. They left behind the charcoal from their fires and imprints from the stone anchors of their temporary homes. As the people perished, their skeletons, with their massive, ridged skulls and modern, long limbs became buried under mud, ash, gravel, and silt.

Later in the Pleistocene, Ifa's distant progeny would undertake a more significant, more successful expansion. These descendants would populate the Old and New Worlds, migrating across rivers, continents, ice fields, land bridges, and oceans. They would build villages, plant crops, domesticate animals, create societies, wage wars, and maintain peace. Eventually, they would seek their roots, search for their ancestors, dig for their fossil remains, sequence their genome.

As Ifa settled down next to the diminishing fire, she pulled a hide around her and stared into the embers. She survived because of her people, her tribe. Ifa loved, fought, rejoiced, thrived; she birthed the next generation. Ifa succeeded.

She was Homo. She was us.

Palynological analysis of Pleistocene formations, Olduvai Gorge, Tanzania, Africa.

Dissertation by Henrietta Ballantine

Appendix B—Flora identified by pollen analysis from Bed II, middle Pleistocene.

Acacia sp. (Thorntree)
Cyperaceae (fam) (Sedges)
Juncaceae (fam) (Rushes)
Poaceae (fam) (Grasses)
Typha sp. (Cattails)
Phoenix sp. (Wild palm)
Phoenix dactylIsara (Date palm)
Cyanella (herb)
Satyrium (orchid)
Moraea (cape tulip)
Tritonia (flame flower)
Coffea arabica (Arabian Coffee)

AUTHOR'S NOTES

Scientific study has advanced significantly since Henrietta's time, especially in the field of physical anthropology and the study of early man. I tried to be true to the time period represented in the novel by reflecting what was known in 1961 when Henrietta made her trek to Olduvai Gorge. As far as I know, there is no evidence that Ifa's species, *Homo erectus*, buried their dead, wore clothes, or spoke a language during the middle Pleistocene. However, scientists believe that language may have begun as mimicry of sounds in nature, as I've depicted here. Evidence exists that these people built shelters anchored with circular patterns of rocks. Their Acheulean tools have been found across continents. Although *Homo erectus* used controlled fire, I have pushed its use to an earlier date than indicated by fossil evidence. An eagle-eyed geologist may also note the age of the Yorktown Formation and the scientific names of some of the fossils reflect the knowledge and nomenclature during Henrietta's time at The College of William and Mary in the 1950s.

Foremost I thank my husband, Bob, for his encouragement and support, especially during the writing of this book, and for his geologic insights. Many thanks to my editor, Melissa Jeglinski of The Writers Ally, and to my beta readers: Susan Bare, Melinda Crocker, James Lyon, Nancy Ochsenreiter. Thanks to Frank Jacobeen, neighbor, friend, and 'big picture geologist' who lent his first name for the book and provided feedback. Much love and thanks to my daughters, Marie and Anna, for their opinions and technology help.

This book is a work of fiction. Although the Leakeys were historical people, their portrayal in this novel is fictional and offered with the utmost respect. All other characters, businesses, and events portrayed in this book are fictional, and any resemblances to real people or incidents are purely coincidental.

SHORT BIBLIOGRAPHY

Barnet, Andrea, 2018, *Visionary Women: How Rachel Carson, Jane Jacobs, Jane Goodall and Alice Waters Changed Our World*, Harper Collins.

Bohme, Madelaine, R. Braun and F. Breier, 2020, *Ancient Bones, Unearthing the Astonishing New Story of How We Became Human*, Greystone Books, Vancouver/Berkley.

Bowman-Kruhm, Mary, 2010, *The Leakeys, A Biography*, Prometheus Books, New York.

Goodall, Jane, 1988, *My Life With the Chimpanzees*, Simon and Schuster.

Leakey, Mary, 1984, *Disclosing the Past, An Autobiography*, Doubleday & Company, New York.

Lieberman, Daniel E., 2013, *The Story of the Human Body, Evolution, Health and Disease*, Vintage Books, a division of Random House LLC, New York.

Tattersall, Ian, 1995, *The Fossil Trail, How We Know What We Think We Know about Human Evolution*, Oxford University Press, New York, Oxford.

Zim, Herbert S. and Clarence Cottam, 1951, *Insects: A Guide to Familiar American Insects. A Golden Nature Guide*, Golden Press, New York.

DISCUSSION QUESTIONS
FOR *FOSSIL WOMAN*

1. In the novel *Fossil Woman*, what parallels did you find between Henrietta and Ifa? How were they similar? How were they different?
2. As Henrietta grows up, she has difficulty fitting in with a peer group. How do women "find their tribe?" How did Henrietta and Ifa find their tribes?
3. As a child, Henrietta was characterized as "shy" and her mother as "overbearing". Would they be characterized in the same manner today?
4. What traditional roles are expected of Henrietta? Of Ifa? How do they each conform with these? How do they break out of these?
5. Discuss Henrietta's personal growth from her childhood, to her college years, and finally to her advocating for herself and traveling alone to Africa. What factors aided her in this growth?
6. Henrietta states that any future boyfriend of hers will be "smart, kind, courteous and a gentleman." Does Frank live up to these standards?
7. From an early age, Henrietta struggles with her sense of the spiritual. How do these struggles evolve?

8. The dichotomy between religious and scientific beliefs is seen in the book when Henrietta, and possibly her father, struggle with accepting church doctrine versus studying the scientific Theory of Evolution. Was this conflict more prevalent in the 1950s than today? What do you think?

9. Do you recognize any symbolism in the animals mentioned in the book?

10. Dr. Mary Leakey was a hero to Henrietta. What were the attributes that Dr. Leakey possessed that attracted Henrietta to her? What attributes does one look for in a role model?

11. Who could have been Henrietta's guardian angel? Do you think she was real or imaginary?